Unbridled

Double D Ranch
Book 2

Jeanne St. James

Sign up for my newsletter for insider information, author news, and new releases: https://www.authorjeannestjames.com/

Double D Ranch Series

Undone (Book 1)
Unbridled (Book 2)
Unrestrained (Book 3)
Undeniable (Book 4)
Unexpected (Book 5)
Uninhibited (Book 6)

Chapter One

Cara moved through the thick crowd, bumping into people like a pinball. Her multitude of apologies probably went unheard due to the deep bass thumping from the loud dance music.

She had never been to a nightclub—it had never been her scene—but she could imagine this would be a similar atmosphere.

The volume of *One More Time* by Daft Punk was deafening, to say nothing of the people trying to talk above the din, as well as others singing along with every tune the DJ was spinning onstage to rock down the house.

Or more like event hall.

Colorful lights ricocheted around the inside of the building named The Mane Event Hall. They tinted people different shades and occasionally blinded Cara as she worked her way around the large interior.

Drinks flowed freely. Resort guests danced without reserve: bumping and grinding, twirling and twisting. They laughed and shouted.

While everyone else was having a good time, Cara felt a little out of place.

Some attendees had dressed for tonight's fantasy theme. Glitter, fairy wings, gossamer skirts and body paint. Costumes in vibrant blues, greens, pinks, purples, and every other color a person could imagine.

Others ignored the party's theme by going naked or wearing risqué outfits. She spotted men and women alike wearing leather harnesses that exposed their breasts, as well as other parts.

When her elbow was knocked by two women making out along the wall, half of her lemon drop martini landed on the floor. The other half on her.

"Shit." She looked at the now-empty glass, the wet floor, then down at herself. That was a waste of a good martini.

She could head to the bathroom and try to clean up, or she could go back to her room and call it a night.

Only having checked in a few hours ago, she wasn't quite sure why she decided to attend tonight's special event. Her room looked more inviting by the second. As did the silence.

She had come to Double D Ranch to dip her toes into this unknown world, not to jump in feet first. It might be better to expose herself to this lifestyle in small doses in order to see if she was even interested. To see if it was for her.

She set her empty glass on a nearby tray meant for dirty glassware and continued on her way. If she kept moving, maybe no one would notice how out of place she looked. Or how awkward she felt.

This was not her scene.

She didn't belong here.

Someone would spot her, see she was out of her element, and call her out. She just knew it.

She glanced around to see if anyone was staring. Or pointing fingers.

Of course they weren't. She was being paranoid over nothing. Nobody cared she was here.

She decided to book this trip for that reason. The website stated the guests weren't pressured to do anything they weren't comfortable with. They could do whatever they wanted with anyone willing to do the same. Or guests could do absolutely nothing.

Once she ran across their website, it took her five days until she was brave enough to call. She unreasonably thought they would instantly know this world was not for her. Alarms would go off and red alerts would be sent out via text, phone, and email.

It was silly, she knew.

Eventually, she finally did call because, even after reading their FAQ page on their website—*three* times no less—she still had questions.

But then, she did tend to overthink things.

For some reason, she didn't expect a man with a toe-curling voice to answer. He was not only pleasant to listen to, but patient and helpful. Maybe he picked up on how intimidated and unsure Cara came across.

Her first question had her cheeks burning hot and she was glad it was a phone call instead of a video chat or in-person conversation. "Is this a...BDSM club?"

She had read plenty of erotica and erotic romance novels involving kinky sex clubs at the public library where she worked.

Funny enough, that unquenchable interest started when a regular library patron, to whom Cara normally recommended books, turned around and told her about a book by one of her favorite authors.

At the time, she had no idea a toe-curling, steamy romance about sex clubs would cause her to evaluate her own life. After the first one, she fell down a rabbit hole and couldn't read them fast enough.

Those stories hammered home the fact that her past sex life had been lacking.

Big time.

That simple book recommendation took her down a path she never expected. She began to search for a similar place to those she had read about in those books. But somewhere other than in her hometown. Where she might be recognized. Where she worked. Where she knew *so many* people.

"Not a club. A ranch resort. But it's really whatever you want to make of it. You can simply come for a getaway. Take a relaxing trail ride or a dip in the pool. Soak in the hot tub or get a massage. *Ooooor*...you can get spanked, choked, and fucked by a masked stranger." His tone came off as amused.

Fucked by a masked stranger?

What front desk employee talked like that? Was he messing with her?

He finished with, "The sky's the limit. The only limits will be of your own making."

"Is it a working ranch?" she asked next, then groaned silently and bounced her fist against her forehead.

"Well, it's not like you'll be chasing down and roping wayward cattle on horseback, but we do have livestock here. We have goats and cows for fresh milk and cheese, chickens for eggs, horses for trail rides..."

"Are there a lot of single guests?" She worried it would be painfully awkward if she went and no one interacted with her.

"If you can't find a willing single guest during your stay, plenty of couples are looking for a third. And if three aren't enough, sometimes random orgies break out. Nobody would notice or care if you joined in."

Random orgies? Really? Nobody would care if she just... joined...in?

"We have standalone lakefront cabins that have private hot tubs. We also have guest rooms in the lodge itself. Would you like to make a reservation?"

Her heart was pounding so loudly that she almost missed his question. *"Umm."*

"Hold on. Our reservationist just returned from break. I'll let her handle it. I look forward to you being our guest. I hope it's everything you're looking for."

She did, too, but she had doubts. "I'm sorry, but before you go...what did you say your name was?"

Something about his low chuckle gave her goosebumps. Not because he was creepy or anything, but because she could imagine herself blindfolded and his warm honeyed voice enveloping her while murmuring naughty suggestions into her ear.

Possibly reenacting a panty-wetting scene from one of her favorite books.

She shook herself mentally.

Even tonight, she still remembered his voice but regretted never getting his name to at least thank him. It was a shame, really, but as an employee, he probably wasn't allowed to fraternize with the guests, anyway. Not that it mattered. Simply trying to make her way through the crowded party proved plenty of actual guests were available to engage with. If they welcomed it, of course.

Another reason she picked this particular resort was how the website clearly stated multiple times that consent was not only important, but required. That alone made her feel more secure about booking since she'd be by herself.

The site also stated that anyone stepping out of line would be dealt with quickly since the management took their guests' safety seriously. All guests also had to electronically sign a legal agreement to that effect, as well as an NDA, when they made a reservation.

Now, here she was. All stemming from a crazy idea that got stuck in her head. She had never been this impulsive in all her thirty-one years.

To make this experience successful, she really needed to lean into the resort's motto: *Unpack, unwind and get uninhibited.* She already unpacked her bags, now she needed to follow through with the rest.

You can do this.

She might need another drink. Or two...

Or twelve.

As she fought her way to the restroom to attempt to dry her blouse, she stopped short when her path was cut off by a man walking on his hands and knees, wearing a tight leather collar around his neck with a chain leash attached.

He was one of the attendees not wearing a costume per se, but a leather harness around his torso. She blinked and as he kept going, Cara followed the line of the leash up to the woman holding the other end. She wore a black leather mini-skirt, a matching leather bra with holes exposing her pierced nipples, suede thigh-high, high-heeled boots, and a wicked smile. Every once in a while, she would give the leash a sharp jerk and make the man come to heel. In her other hand, she carried a long thin whip of some sort.

Cara leaned closer to the person standing next her; a woman wearing a red vinyl, form-fitting, one-piece outfit with a matching mask. "Is he supposed to be a dog?"

The dark-haired woman shook her head and shouted over the music, "Slave!"

Slave? Was that term even acceptable? It seemed wrong. But then, maybe it wasn't in this scenario?

"She walks him like a dog." Of course, she just pointed out the obvious like an idiot.

When the woman turned toward her, the eyes behind the mask slowly traveled from Cara's head all the way to her toes and back. "You must be new." Her bright red lips curled. "He has a humiliation kink."

She wasn't sure all the fiction she read had prepared her for this reality. Not even close. "What's that around his..."

"Cock?"

Cara nodded.

"It's a cage."

"It has a lock." She silently groaned. She kept mentioning the obvious!

"Of course."

Cara frowned. "There's not enough room for him to... grow."

"That's exactly the point. He needs to have enough discipline so he doesn't get hard. If he does, then..." She shrugged.

Not that she should be staring, but...the colorful lights were catching something sparkly tucked between his bare ass cheeks. She narrowed her eyes. "Is that a jewel?"

The woman's grin grew into a blinding smile and she laughed softly. "You are definitely new. That's an anal plug."

She knew what an anal plug was. She read about them, she'd just never seen one. In person, anyway.

She should've watched tons of porn before she came. For educational purposes, of course. At least she might have some basics under her belt instead of feeling like such a novice.

With a quick thank you to the very sexy lady in red, she continued toward the sign at the back, and above the crowd, that said *restrooms.*

No telling what she'd find in there.

Damn. She was so out of her element. Once again, her gut was telling her that this "vacation" might have been a mistake. Maybe she *should* check out and drive—

No. She would not wimp out. She spent a fortune on the reservation and the website clearly stated refunds wouldn't be given to guests ending their stay early.

She'd saved up for this and not taking advantage of what she already paid for would be a financial hit. Plus, after what she paid, she certainly couldn't afford to stay anywhere else. She would need to drive back home and take the loss.

You don't have to do anything with anyone, she reminded herself.

She could do what Mr. Sexy Voice said on the phone. Simply relax, take advantage of their spa—since the pampering was included—or lounge by the pool, enjoying a complimentary cocktail.

She could eat until she was as stuffed as a Thanksgiving turkey. Some of the online reviews—which she scoured before making her reservation—mentioned how delicious and fresh the food was since they tried to locally source as much as possible. A few stated that, unlike most resorts, the meals were far from cafeteria or diner quality.

She could also be active and head out on a trail ride. She could hike. Paddle around the serene lake. Sit around the bonfire. Take one of the ATVs out to explore. Feed the goats...

Damn it. None of those activities were the reason she came. *None.*

Once she entered the restroom, she breathed a sigh of relief when she found nothing kinky going on. Only two women chatting while they washed their hands.

After a quick nod in greeting, she stopped in front of the

large mirror to take in the damage. Snagging a few paper towels, she blotted the large wet spot. It wasn't helping.

"Looks like someone got wet," came from the woman remaining at the sink next to her.

"Yes, I..." *Wait.* She blushed. *Damn it*, she needed to stop that! "Someone knocked into my drink."

With a sly smile, her sink mate said, "I promise you, you can get messier than that here. Don't worry about the spot. Unless you're worried about it ruining your blouse?"

"No..." She only wore washable clothes. She leaned toward being more practical, and that included her wardrobe.

"Or you could simply take it off. Going topless is encouraged around here."

Fire licked at her cheeks at the idea of walking around with her breasts hanging out. She was certainly not ready for that, and she might never be. She gnawed on her bottom lip.

The woman squeezed her arm. "Look. Don't stress over it. You won't be judged for anything you do. You could walk completely naked around this ranch for a week and no one will blink an eye. They might give you an appreciative glance, maybe invite you to join them for a session or two, and then move on."

"A session?"

"Yes, in their room or cabin. Out along a riding trail. In one of the paddle boats. Or in one of the playrooms. If you keep yourself open-minded, the opportunities are endless. Do as much or as little as you'd like."

The voice over the phone whispered through her mind. *The only limits will be of your own making.*

"Enjoy your stay."

"Thank you. Same to you."

As the woman met Cara's eyes in the mirror, she purred, "I always do. This is already my third time here. I've visited a lot of clubs and resorts all over the world and I have to say, this place is now my favorite." With a last smile and a tip of her head, she walked out of the bathroom, leaving Cara alone.

Cara stared at the woman in the mirror.

Who are you?

What are you doing here?

Did you really think this was for you?

When have you ever done something so irresponsible?

She sighed. Then, with a last glance at the dark spot on her royal-blue blouse, she pulled in a bolstering breath, gave herself a nod, and headed back out to the party. One more lap around the room and another martini wouldn't hurt.

The second she stepped out of the restroom, the loud music and crazy lights bombarded her again. Was it possible that the crowd managed to swell even more? Where were all these people coming from?

Once her anxiety with the situation began to spike again, she realized it was time to go. It was all too much for her first night.

Like a quality wine, she needed to take small sips instead of guzzling down the whole bottle at once.

Not wanting to fight the crowd to escape, she searched for the closest exit.

Chapter Two

As soon as Cara spotted an exit, she worked her way toward it. Being at the rear of the event hall and near the ladies' room, it wasn't the same way she entered, but it was at least a way to get outside quickly to take a few breaths of fresh air.

Clear her head.

Maybe reevaluate the situation.

When she began to head back to the lodge, she noticed a group of people standing and chatting near the front corner of the hall. She changed course and decided to walk around the other side of the building, hoping not to run into anyone who would make her feel more out of place than she already did. Not on purpose, of course, but still...

At the very rear of the building, she was surprised to find an exterior stairway with a small lighted sign pointing up to the second floor that read, *Stairway to Heaven.*

With a frown, she glanced up and saw another sign over a second-level, windowless door that simply said *Heaven.*

Interesting.

She really should've sat down and read the guest binder

in her room that included all of the resort's details. In fact, she should've stayed in her room and read it from cover to cover instead of, again, jumping into this world feet first tonight. Normal people would've tested the water prior to diving head first.

She would start reading it as soon as she got back to her room and wouldn't leave again until she read every damn word. But what she wasn't doing tonight was climbing those stairs.

After quickly rounding the other back corner of the building to return to her room, she ran smack into a wall.

The impact caused all the oxygen to flee her lungs at the same time as long, strong fingers dug into her arms to keep her from falling backwards and onto her ass.

No, not an actual wall. A large, hard body that might as well be made of bricks.

"Whoa there! Are you okay?"

"Yes, I'm..." She shook her head. "No."

The brick wall released her and took a step back. "What's the problem? Is someone bothering you?"

Just myself.

Her gaze skimmed over him. Something about him felt familiar but she couldn't quite place him. Even so, the dark-blond man was sinfully handsome. She didn't need the sun to see it. The exterior of the event hall was very well lit. Most likely as a safety precaution. "No, I..."

"You..." he prompted.

She blew out a breath. "I'm just a little overwhelmed."

He smirked. "Some of the events *can* get a bit wild."

It wasn't that. "It's not my scene," she admitted.

One eyebrow shot up. "No? What is?"

She was a librarian. Her normal scene was a quiet library, surrounded by books. Her normal scene was getting lost in a good story and transported away to another world. Or helping others to do the same.

More recently, Cara's fantasy worlds included kink, lots of spicy sex, and BDSM. Tonight might be proof she shouldn't necessarily make it a reality. "I work in a library."

"I'd say that's quite the opposite of what's going on in there." He jerked his chin toward the building.

"Yes."

"A librarian, huh? Where are your glasses and messy bun held together with a number two pencil?"

She let herself relax a smidge and smile. "That's a stereotype."

He shrugged. "It's a sexy one."

"You think glasses and buns are sexy?"

"Sure. Why not? I think a lot of looks are sexy. That's why people role-play."

"You've been with someone pretending to be a librarian?"

"Sure, as well as school girl, maid, nurse...cheerleader..." His deep chuckle enveloped her. "Anyway, intelligence is sexy as fuck."

"You're assuming most librarians are intelligent," she countered.

"Aren't they?"

"Well...I do have my master's in library science." Like that was impressive. It wasn't like her career made her rich. Actually, it was the opposite. She'd wanted to be a librarian ever since she was able to read. Growing up, her family didn't have much, so losing herself in a good book transported her to places she never thought she'd be able to go. She could also pretend to be one of the characters for a little while.

"See? Super smart equals super sexy in my view."

Did he consider her sexy? Did she dare ask? If she did, would he answer truthfully? "We're usually nerds, too."

"Nerds can be fun."

"Are you a nerd?"

"I could be considered one. You work with words. I work with numbers."

"An accountant?"

"Not quite, but close enough. So...if what's going on inside isn't your scene, why did you come here?"

When he tucked a strand of her hair behind her ear, her heart fluttered. Normally she didn't like any stranger touching her without permission. So, why didn't his touch bother her? Was it because of where they were and what the resort was about?

"To the party or to the resort?"

He cocked his head. "I'll take an answer for both."

"I don't know." That wasn't a lie.

With his hands now on his hips, he studied her. "Have you ever done anything like this before?"

He couldn't tell she was out of her element? Or was he only being kind?

"No."

"Did you book your stay because you were curious?"

She released a dry laugh. "Pretty expensive curiosity." At the time, she was forcing herself to be brave. Once again, tonight proved she was anything but.

"Are you curious about this kind of life? Or are you here to discover your deepest, darkest desires?"

"I don't have any dark desires," she admitted. She had desires, but didn't consider any of them dark.

She frowned. Or were they? She had no idea what was considered taboo and what wasn't. At least in the real world and not in a fictional one.

"But you want to discover the real you who's been hiding deep inside."

She jerked up one shoulder. "Maybe I simply needed a change."

The corners of his very beautiful mouth curled up slightly. "Said the woman who broke off a long-term relationship full of shitty sex."

She stared at him, not sharing his amusement.

"C'mon. Admit it."

"I wasn't in a long-term relationship."

"You mean recently," he guessed. "Now you're here looking for what had been missing from your former... whatever."

She wasn't getting into her past relationship with a stranger.

She was in her thirties. She wasn't a virgin. She dated here and there. But it had taken her a while to scrape free from her former boyfriend. He had been determined to marry Cara. She had been determined not to.

But what this man guessed was true. The dry and uninspired sex had left something to be desired. She usually had to fake an orgasm to get Glenn to finish and get off her.

However, their problems weren't only about *their* sex life, but the fact Glenn had been having sex with someone else. Someone Cara was close to. She hoped her best friend found that the shitty sex with Glenn was worth destroying their ten-year-long friendship over.

The smartest decision she made was to keep her own place and not move in with him. It made breaking it off much easier.

For her, anyway.

His anger about her leaving him turned ugly and it took a while for him to finally face the fact she wasn't coming back to him. She'd rather stay single the rest of her life, read piles of books, and pull out her vibrator when needed.

While it kept life simple, sometimes loneliness crept in. It was that combination of loneliness and curiosity that made her search out a place like Double D Ranch.

"So, if it's not years of shitty sex with an asshole partner, what made you come here? I'll go back to my previous question about it being curiosity."

"More or less." Again, she wasn't discussing her former relationship with a stranger—she didn't even know his name—behind a building.

"And what did you see, do, or hear to bring that about?"

Oh crap. Should she admit it? Saying it out loud could make her sound like a naïve fool.

"You don't have to be ashamed of your answer. We don't shame people here. We encourage. Support. We even teach."

Teach. Maybe that was what she needed. Someone to hold her hand and explain the details. Details that could very well be wrong in many of the romances she'd read. At the time, she hadn't cared about accuracy since it was only fiction, but now...

Holy shit. Maybe *all* the books got it wrong and she was totally unprepared. She needed to know the truth. "I've...read things."

"Articles?"

She shook her head. "No, books."

"How-tos?"

"No..."

His brow dropped low.

"Fiction," she explained, wondering if she'd regret it. "Romance, erotica..."

"Wait..." He huffed out a breath. "You came here solely because you read sexy romance novels?"

Heat filled her cheeks. "That was stupid, wasn't it?"

"Did you do any of your own research?"

He thought librarians were smart. She just proved him wrong. "Isn't that what this is?"

He threw his head back and laughed.

She pulled in an irritated breath. "Have a good night."

He quickly sobered. "No, wait!"

When he grabbed her wrist to stop her from leaving, she glared at his hand. He released her immediately and threw up his palms in surrender. "Sorry. I wasn't laughing *at* you but because..."

"Because I'm a fool."

"No. If anything, you're brave. I've never read a romance novel but I can't imagine..." He shook his head. "It doesn't matter. What matters is they opened your mind to trying new things, right?"

"Yes."

He shrugged. "Then who cares about the reasoning used to come here? The fact is, you're here. Now you can safely see and experience all this place has to offer...in reality. The beauty of this resort is you can do as little or as much as you'd like. No pressure. You can spend your whole stay simply observing, if you wish."

His voice *really* sounded familiar, but she still couldn't place him. "Do you work here?"

He hesitated. "I'm not an employee."

"You're a guest."

"No."

"An interloper?"

One eyebrow shot up. "Interloper?"

"Do you need me to define it?"

He blinked, then threw his head back again and laughed without reserve. "I can figure it out. Listen, why don't you let me be your personal guide on this journey of self-discovery?"

"Does that pickup line normally work?"

His deep chuckle sent a bolt of lightning down her spine and it ended as a twinge in her pussy. *Damn it.*

"But would it be considered self-discovery if you're guiding me?"

"I'm willing to help. I know the ins and outs of this place and all that goes on here. I could be your mentor, guide, whatever you want to call me."

"What *should* I call you?"

"My name is Dayne. Yours?"

"Cara."

"Pleased to meet you, Cara." His eyebrows bunched together. "That name isn't very common but it sounds familiar. I might have talked to you on the phone."

That was why his voice sounded familiar! "The one who wouldn't give me his name," she mumbled.

"Well, now you have it."

"You said you weren't an employee."

"I'm not."

"Then, what are you?"

"My brother and I own this place."

She blinked. "It isn't some big corporation?"

"Apparently, I wasted my time writing the *About Us* page for our website if no one reads it," he said dryly. "Anyway, this place is family-owned. It was formerly my father's dairy farm, but once he passed, we turned it into this spectacular adult playground." He swept his arm out. "So, you can't find anyone better, at least to show you around, if you don't want to accept my offer of guidance."

"Right now I need to go back to my room and *unwind.*"

"That would be step two of the three suggested. Again, I can help with the third."

She tucked her bottom lip between her teeth as she considered him. He looked normal enough. And it *would* be bad for business if the owner of the resort was a serial killer... "I'll give it some thought."

"Just give me a shout if you'd like my help. With anything."

"And how would I get a hold of you?"

"I'm not hard to find since I'm always around."

She doubted he was *always* around. He had to go home at some point. "Thank you for the offer. That's very kind of you."

One side of his mouth hooked up. "I didn't make it out of kindness."

Of course he didn't. It was easy to see he had an ulterior motive. He probably hit on female guests all the time. With how he looked, she doubted he got shot down often.

However, she would not be an easy mark for him. She'd read through the guest binder tonight and tomorrow, explore on her own in the light of day. She gave him a single nod. "Goodnight."

Without waiting for him to respond, she turned and walked along the building toward the lodge.

"Welcome to Double D, Cara," she heard behind her. "Since I'm sure you've unpacked already, go unwind and prepare to get uninhibited."

If only it was that easy.

Chapter Three

WHAT FIRST CAUGHT Dayne's attention was a group of guests having what appeared to be an orgy. Right out in the open and in the light of day.

This was one of many reasons they secured the front entrance to the ranch with a gate and a guard. It helped their guests feel more free to do what they wanted, wherever they wanted, without the threat of strangers coming onto the property and causing problems.

To be on the property without a reservation, you needed to make an appointment and have an escort. They didn't want to deal with haters and blackmailers, paparazzi and lookie-loos.

Before opening the resort, they hired a security consultant to make suggestions on keeping their guests secure. Since he and his siblings didn't want to put them or their business at risk, it was worth the cost of that pricey consultation.

They also hired a retired State Trooper to be their Security Manager. Cameron Cook supervised all the security staff who sat at the gate, wandered the property, and monitored the cameras twenty-four-seven.

Dayne had just finished having a too long, very boring meeting with his two siblings, Dylan and Danica, along with their Guest Services Manager, Erin, and was now ready to stretch his legs by walking around the ranch and checking in with guests.

It turns out they loved the fact management was hands-on. In more ways than one. But according to the guest surveys, face-to face-interactions were one of the top five reasons for them to return.

If that was all it took, Dayne had no problem doing it. Plus, it also had him interacting with guests he might be interested in playing with during their stay.

Dayne was pretty much into anything, so it wasn't hard to find a partner or two. Or even four.

During the meeting, he'd been distracted by the short exchange between him and the guest named Cara last night. He kept checking his texts to see if she asked any resort employees to get a hold of him. Every staff member had his number, as well as Dylan's and Erin's, in case of an issue or question. They not only wanted to be accessible to their guests, but their employees, too.

As he now strode down the paved lane toward the lake in front of The Mane Lodge, the very sexy blonde woman was still on his mind. Before leaving the office area, he should've pulled up the reservation system on his computer to see if she checked out early and went home.

He sure hoped not.

Most of the guests he'd had naked encounters with were experienced, or at least knew the basics, and came to the resort to dig deeper into the lifestyle in a safe place.

Cara came off as completely green.

Normally, someone like that wouldn't end up on Dayne's radar. He considered the unsure and inexperienced too much work unless he was in the rare mood for vanilla sex.

Vanilla was okay on occasion, but wasn't his preferred flavor.

It turned out it wasn't his twin brother's either, since Dylan was now in a committed polyamorous relationship. Dayne had been shocked to find out that his straight-laced brother swung both ways and he'd been keeping this doozy of a secret from his own family.

His identical twin was now in love and shacked up with his former high school sweetheart, Erin, and their Facilities Manager, Ford.

Dayne grinned. All these years, he'd wondered how his identical twin's personality ended up so different from his own. It turned out Dylan and Dayne were more alike than he ever knew.

Dayne beelined toward the small group to check in on them. Make sure everyone was a willing participant. Maybe even watch for a bit. Possibly even join in, if no one was against the idea.

His plan last night at the fantasy party was to find a willing couple or throuple to join. Meeting Cara had derailed his quest. That part bugged him because it shouldn't have.

After their short encounter, instead of heading into the party or upstairs to Heaven, he regrettably watched her walk away. The whole time he stood there he had to fight the impulse to yell out for her to come back. He also fought the urge to chase after her.

Him being pushy might have spooked her and he didn't want anything to make her run fast and far away from Double D. Not before he had a chance to spend more time with her.

He remembered talking to her on the phone that day because, first off, he rarely answered the phone at the front desk and second, he'd been so surprised with how nervous she sounded. When he handed the phone over to Milly, one of the front desk staff, he really thought the woman would chicken out.

She hadn't.

Was it because of something he said during that conversation, or in spite of it?

He didn't know or really care. The fact was, Cara did book and show up, but apparently, last night proved once again that she was unsure of why she did.

Now he needed to convince her to stay and give everything the resort offered a chance. Maybe even give him a chance.

He had no idea why. The resort was currently full, with plenty of other guests more experienced, more confident in their sexuality and with their kinks, and not looking for anything other than a few orgasms.

Well, look at that. He'd actually described himself. He considered the resort his personal playground and, unlike his older-by-twenty-minutes twin, he was not in a rush to get tied down in any kind of relationship.

His feet stuttered to a stop once he got close enough to see the action, as well as everyone involved.

A large blanket had been thrown down on the grass by the lake. Beside it sat the basket supplied in every room and cabin, full of lubes, condoms, dental dams, and items like rope, small impact toys, and blindfolds. Even items like Wartenberg wheels. The basket only included toys capable of being sterilized after the guests left.

Not long after the grand opening, a guest suggested the resort open a little store so they could buy more personal use items, like vibrators, anal plugs and beads, and pocket pussies, in case a guest forgot to bring their own. Especially since Fisher Falls didn't have anything like it and most likely never would.

Dayne snorted. A sex toy shop in the center of Fisher Falls would have the residents' heads spinning even more than the Double D Ranch.

He was surprised at how much business the store did. So much so, they planned on expanding it to include leather-wear, naughty lingerie, and more. If they needed a larger area, they'd add it on to the resort's spa, Nirvana, where guests could book all kinds of spa treatments during their stay.

The business kept expanding, and along with that growth, their finances were quickly headed into the black after too many months of being deep in the red.

As a Certified Management Accountant—and now the resort's CFO—that made his number-crunching heart happy. Soon he might even be able to recoup the funds he had invested. On top of the equity from the house he sold in North Carolina, he also drained his savings and cashed out some of his long-term investments.

He had taken a leap of faith in his brother's idea and it seemed to be finally paying off.

As he approached the group, he noticed it wasn't only the six people involved—who might as well be playing naked Twister with how everyone was contorted—but a small crowd surrounded them. Some stood, some sat on the ground like they were enjoying a lawn concert, and another couple had pulled their canoe up onto the lake's shore close by.

None of the half-dozen people paid any attention to the observers since voyeurism at the resort was common, as well as expected, if sex was happening out in the open. If privacy was needed or required, plenty of places existed on the ranch to do it behind closed doors or blinds.

No, this group was obviously getting off on others watching them. Dayne agreed it could be a heady experience.

Dylan preferred that Dayne keep most of his sex life out of the public eye since he was a co-owner. Did he always stick to that? Of course not. His twin was not his keeper.

But again, it wasn't the guests getting it on out in the open that made him do a double-take, it was the fact that Cara, the woman who literally ran into him last night, was also standing nearby watching.

With her attention glued to the action, she didn't notice when Dayne stepped behind her. But now his attention was on her instead of the group on the blanket. He observed her reactions as she watched the group busy filling every orifice they had access to.

This morning, her long, blonde hair was pulled back into a simple ponytail—he loved that hairstyle since those and pigtails made great handles—and she was dressed more casually than last night.

She wore hip-hugging jeans, a cream-colored, off-the-shoulder, short-sleeved knit top with a black ribbed tank underneath it. She had worn heels last night, but today her feet were covered in some sort of soled slip-on shoes. More practical for the ranch's terrain.

Her dressy-casual outfit last night was on the classier side instead of over-the-top like most of the other partygoers. Today, the simpleness in what she wore was still sexy as hell.

Maybe it was simply her and she would look enticing no matter what she wore.

Or even wearing nothing at all.

"Good morning," he murmured. "Good to see you're still here."

She startled and, with a sharp intake of breath, turned to face him with her cheeks blazing.

He grinned at her expression of being caught red-handed. "Enjoying the show?"

After a quick backward glance at the active group, she returned her attention to him. "I feel guilty watching."

"Don't be. If they didn't want anyone to watch, they had other options."

Her brow wrinkled. "Is this normal?"

"Here? Yes. It happens often. Especially upstairs in Heaven." When all the rooms were in use, it was sometimes difficult to even get through the hallway with so many people standing in front of the windows watching what was going on behind them. The playrooms, along with the themed events, were very popular among the guests.

"I read about the playrooms last night. Whoever wrote the info in your guest binders should be commended. While it was very thorough, it was late last night when I read through it and I was tired. I want to make sure I read it right... they're all themed?"

"They are. If watching others gets you off, then I'd suggest spending time up there. Most people who book the rooms don't bother to close the blinds. If you like being watched, you could also reserve a room and put on your own show. I bet it would be a hit."

Her cheeks darkened even more.

Of course, Dayne would be up there watching if he wasn't invited to join her. But if she was blushing at simply watching an almost everyday occurrence here at the resort, he doubted she'd be down for giving strangers a show.

"I...this is the first time I've watched others..." She twisted slightly and flipped a hand toward the six people.

"Fuck?" he supplied.

She nodded.

"Are you enjoying yourself?"

She pressed a hand to her flushed cheek. "I..."

"You don't need to be embarrassed if you are. We don't judge here. And anyway, more people like to watch than you'd think. I'm sure you've heard of porn. It's a very lucrative industry."

He expected her to at least laugh at his dry humor but she was still too caught up in her own head.

"But this is live action."

"Even better. Unlike porn, there's no acting. Every reaction, moan, groan, sigh and grunt is real. So are the orgasms." His eyes flicked to the sight over her shoulder. "Turn around, Cara. You're missing it."

She pulled in a breath. "You remembered my name."

"Of course. You're hard to forget."

"Because I don't belong here?"

He grabbed her chin and dropped his head until he locked eyes with her. "Get that out of your head. Everyone is welcome here, but not everyone chooses to come and enjoy what we have to offer."

He followed the slide of her tongue over her lips. That simple action made his dick twitch in his jeans.

"Turn around, Cara," he encouraged again. "They want to give you a show. They might even be fine if you join them."

"I...can't."

"Maybe not yet, but you never know how you'll feel by the end of your stay."

She broke his eye contact. "*If* I stay."

"You'll stay." If he had anything to do with it.

"You sound so sure of that."

"I'm sure because I plan on giving you guidance."

"I didn't ask for that."

"Not with words, no. But you came for a reason and that's to explore your own sexuality. Maybe even discover things about yourself that might surprise you."

When she glanced up at him, her green eyes reminded him of two emeralds gleaming in the sun. "Do you normally *guide* guests?"

"No." He normally picked partners who needed no direction whatsoever.

"Then, why me?"

"Because you came alone and could use my help. I'm willing to provide it."

"And what do you get out of it?"

He reminded himself not to scare her. To treat her like a skittish rabbit and not act like a wolf about to rip her apart with his sharp teeth. With the right assistance, she could become more confident and comfortable with her sexual desires. "A repeat guest, maybe? One reason for our great reviews is that management is hands-on. Now, turn around."

When she stared at him for a few moments more, Dayne thought she would tell him to get lost, or worse, leave her alone. If she did, he would.

He was pleased when she turned and gave him her back. "I'm going to stand behind you. If I do anything that you don't like or aren't comfortable with, you only have to say the word. We take consent seriously here."

"What are you going to do?"

Was there a tremor to that question? "Only talk." Unless she ended up wanting more. "If you have questions, ask away."

"I know how sex works."

"I didn't say otherwise, but what's happening before you is more than simply putting a peg in a round hole."

When she slapped a hand over her mouth to smother a

giggle, he grinned. It gave him hope he could loosen her up a bit. If not a lot.

That was his goal, to free her from society's confines.

He stepped closer, until his chest was only a few inches away from her back. He waited a few moments before dropping his head so that his mouth was a hairsbreadth from her ear.

He didn't want to bother other guests with his words, but he did want to get her hot and bothered. He dropped his voice a little lower. "Keep your eyes on the group, but listen to my words. Pick one of the participants and picture yourself in their place. It doesn't matter who. Man or woman. Whoever you'd like to replace. Now imagine those hands, lips, and tongues being used all over your body, instead. You're sucking a hard cock. Eating a juicy pussy. Your nipples are being pulled and twisted. Your ass being teased, maybe even spanked. A thick cock fills your cunt, slamming into you hard and often, making you so wet. Can you imagine it?" he whispered. He sure could.

Her breathing hitched and she nodded.

"What do you want them to do to you, Cara?"

"Make me come."

Chapter Four

MAKE ME COME.

"That's expected. Tell me something you want that you wouldn't normally. Spank your pussy? Mark your flesh with teeth or a sharp pinwheel? Whip your ass until it's a pretty shade of red? Achieving an orgasm is the easy part. How you get to that point is the adventure."

"An orgasm was never easy."

His nostrils flared and his teeth clenched. "With the asshole who didn't know how to satisfy you?"

"Yes."

Just as he expected. She'd been disappointed in the past. That probably added to her sexual shyness. "Have you *ever* orgasmed?"

She nodded.

"With who?"

A ragged breath slipped from between her lips. "Myself."

"No man or woman has ever brought you to orgasm?" How could that be? She had to be in her early thirties and had never managed to have one damn decent partner? The anger flickering inside him burned hotter.

"I've never been with a woman."

No surprise. "Would you want to be?"

Her teeth sawed over her bottom lip as she considered his question. "I don't know. I've never thought about it. But no man has ever brought me to orgasm."

"What a crime," he murmured, fighting the annoyance so she wouldn't pick up on it. "I promise you, if you want to orgasm during sex, you've come to the right place."

Even the right man, if she was willing. To be the first one to bring her to orgasm...

That possibility was intoxicating and his cock agreed. Now he was even more determined to help her during her stay.

"I didn't see that guarantee on your website."

One side of his mouth pulled up. There it was. Her sense of humor. Dayne wouldn't be surprised if, once the nervousness wore off, her real personality shined through.

No true wallflower would book a stay at a resort built for sexual pleasure. She also could've left last night, or this morning, but she didn't. He took that as a sign she really wanted to be here, only she wasn't sure of what she wanted during the experience.

Again, he was willing to help her find what she needed.

His cock was, too.

"I'm going to remind you now that if I do anything you don't like or aren't comfortable with, tell me."

"Okay," she breathed.

She didn't ask what he was about to do. She wanted the surprise, the anticipation. Another good sign.

With a single finger, he drew her ponytail to the side,

giving himself access to the smooth skin on her shoulder exposed by her baggy top.

He brushed his lips across it before giving it a playful nip. When she shivered, goosebumps appeared. "Are your nipples hard?"

She nodded.

"Do they ache?"

She nodded again.

He snuck a peek over her shoulder to see just how hard they were. "For what?" When she didn't answer, he did it for her. "For someone to suck them, pinch them, even twist them?" He mentally raised his hand to volunteer to be that someone.

He could hardly hear her breathy, "Yes."

"Good. Are you wearing panties?"

"Yes."

"Are they soaked right now?" He was tempted to check for himself.

Patience.

This time it took her a moment to finally nod.

"Are you tempted to touch yourself right here, out in the open, while watching?"

"I don't know." The insecurity was back.

"If not yourself, who in that pile would you like to touch you?"

She took a moment to study each of the six people having sex before her gaze circled the growing audience. "Him."

Him? That was a tad disappointing. Dayne had hoped he'd be the one chosen to bring her to orgasm. Luckily, he had time to convince her that he was the perfect candidate. Plus, he was curious about her choice. What her type was. "Which him?"

"That one." She lifted her chin toward the blanket.

He followed her line of sight. "I see three men in that group. You need to be more specific."

"The one with the short dark hair and the scruff on his face. The abs."

Did she actually sigh out the word "abs?"

Dayne focused on the man she pointed out. It was the first time he'd noticed this particular guest. He might have only checked in this morning. If Dayne had to choose someone from the group—either man or woman—he most likely would've chosen him, too. He and Cara must have similar tastes. That might work in his favor.

However, Dayne might need to keep an eye on him. For his own selfish reasons, of course. Especially since the man had no problem being sexually involved with the other two men in the group.

Unlike his twin, he never kept it a secret that he'd have sex with anyone he was attracted to. It didn't matter to him if it was a man or woman. When the chemistry and experience were present, it made sex even better. More satisfying.

For him, anyway.

That chemistry seemed to exist with Cara from the moment she ran into him last night. However, he had no idea if she felt the same about him. Maybe not, if she was looking elsewhere. But then, he'd also told her to pick someone out from the group in front of her. Technically, he stood behind her. "Can I touch you?"

"You already did."

That was nothing. "Enough to make you come."

Her answer got caught in her throat. She cleared it and tried again. "Here?"

"Yes, here. While we watch them. If you want, I can give you that elusive orgasm."

"Are you cocky or simply confident?"

His lips curved up slightly. "Both."

"At least you're not afraid to admit it."

"I have my faults."

"Don't we all," she whispered.

"The fact is, I'm confident enough to know where not only your clit and G-spot are, but what to do with them. Best of all, I come with no strings attached. That means if I can't make you come, then you are free to find someone else who can. No messy breakup needed if you're not sexually satisfied."

"It sounds like you're trying to sell yourself."

"I'm simply spitting facts. So, I ask again, can I touch you?"

"I..."

"It's a simple yes or no."

"A touch can consist of a punch to the face or a tickle. I'm not sure it's so simple."

"I promise not to punch you. Any touch would simply be for pleasure. You can withdraw your consent at any time."

If she hesitated any longer, everyone on that blanket might soon be done.

"Okay."

Hot damn. Deep down he wasn't expecting her to agree, but was pleased to see she was open to trying new things as well as new people.

Hooking an arm around the front of her shoulders, he pulled her into him, pressing his chest to her back. It wasn't the only thing pressing into her. His cock was hard and he wouldn't bother to hide that fact. "Prepare to be impressed. And yes, that was cocky." Her body shaking against him with silent laughter made him smile.

Now he needed to get to work impressing her and make sure she agreed for him to be her personal guide. He was convinced the amount of work he was willing to put in would be worth it when it came to the resulting rewards.

With the tip of his tongue, he traced the delicate outer edge of her ear, then sucked her earlobe for a few seconds before whispering, "See your man there? We'll call him Jack for the moment. Jack's face isn't buried between her legs, it's buried between yours. The tip of his tongue is flicking *your* clit, his thick fingers are driving in and out of *your* sopping wet pussy. That scruff is scraping your inner thighs, turning them the slightest shade of pink. Him eating you out will bring about your first orgasm of the day, but it won't be your last. Lean back against me and put yourself in that redhead's place. Do you feel his mouth on you?"

She dropped her head back until it rested on his chest. With her leaning back against him, he could see the front of her a lot easier.

"*Yesss*," she breathed.

Her shirt also gaped enough so he could see her nipples punching through her tank top. He would get to them soon.

But first, Dayne needed to ignore the fact that another man had Jack's ass cheeks spread wide and was eating him out at the same time Jack ate the redheaded woman's cunt. He wasn't sure if eating ass would be a turn-on or turn-off for Cara, but it definitely was a turn-on for Dayne. If he didn't block it from his mind, he might just come hands-free in his jeans.

He needed to concentrate on the woman in front of him. Assure her that not all men were useless in bed. Or by a lake.

"Your shirt is long enough it'll hide what I'm about to do from everyone else, so don't worry."

After she nodded slightly, he slipped one hand under the bottom of her loose knit top and found the button to her jeans, thumbing it open and sliding the zipper down slowly. "You okay?"

Another barely visible nod. But she didn't tense up or tell him to stop. In fact, she melted back against him even more.

Once her jeans were open, he ran a finger along the elastic waistband of her panties before slipping his hand under them and down even further. Her smooth skin was soft and warm. He took a few moments to stroke the hair above her pussy, and while he did, he slipped his other hand under her tank top and up toward her breasts.

Her stomach quivered, but again, she didn't stop him.

The tips of his fingers brushed against the bottom of her bra. That bra was a nuisance and needed to go.

But he had to pick his battles and ripping off her clothes while they stood in the grass with a group of people nearby wouldn't be smart. It could very well spook her.

Instead, he pulled his hand free from the bottom of her shirt and decided to attack his problem from the top. Driving his left hand into her neckline and down into her bra, his fingers skimmed over a rock-hard nipple.

The little sound that slipped from her made him question if it was because she didn't like what he was doing or if she did. Nothing prevented her from using her words to stop him, so he proceeded.

He scooped one breast into his palm and gently snagged her nipple between his fingers to roll it. Of course, not as hard as he normally would and certainly not as rough as he wanted to.

Patience. It'll pay off.

Arching her back, she pushed her breast deeper into his hand. He stopped stroking her pubic hair and inched his fingers lower—giving her a chance to tell him to stop, if needed—until his long, middle digit found her clit. He was rewarded with a soft gasp.

He circled and flicked, then added his thumb so he could pluck and pinch gently. When her hips twitched, a quick glance proved her eyes had shut. "Open your eyes, Cara. Put yourself in the middle of that pleasure pile."

Her eyes opened but appeared unfocused as she once again watched the tangle of bodies on the blanket. But now "Jack" was kneeling over a woman's face while she was splayed on her back, getting rammed hard and fast by another participant. The woman's large breasts rocked with each slam.

"Look at how hard your man Jack is, look at how fast he's jerking his cock. All signs point to him about to come on your face. Will you stick out your tongue to catch that salty treat? Or do you want to make someone else lick your face clean?"

He didn't wait for her answers. He only asked the questions to make her think, to take her deeper into her imagination. To help put her in their place.

Thankfully, it was working.

The evidence was her ragged and rapid breathing and her fingernails digging painfully into his arm. He fought the urge to thrust against her since his erection was throbbing and his balls crying for relief. This moment in time was not about him.

It was all for her. If he had to suffer a little now, he might reap the benefits later.

He only hoped his plan didn't backfire.

With his thumb circling her swollen clit, he slipped his middle finger inside her, testing her wetness.

She was *soaked*.

After adding a second finger, he began to fuck her with them.

Her wispy moans and guttural groans filled his ears, drowning out the noisy group not far from where they stood.

He didn't care about them right now, he only cared about the woman he had promised an orgasm. He was determined not to fail.

With her hot, slick pussy pulsing around his fingers, he continued to pump them in and out. He then curled them to stimulate that little walnut-shaped button while his thumb continued to tease her swollen clit.

For being reserved, she sure was responsive.

Her hips began to rock in time with his rhythm, and by doing so, she pushed against his hard-on.

That was dangerous. His cock was like a stick of dynamite right now. One wrong move and it could explode.

"Cara," he groaned.

"Make me come," she whimpered. "*Please.*"

"That's my intention. I want to feel it, see it, hear it. Let yourself go, Cara. Allow yourself to have this pleasure. See what's possible."

He set his jaw, and despite being in a lot of discomfort, he ramped up his efforts. The little show before them was about to roll credits and he didn't want to still be standing there trying to coax her to a climax after the others finished. Because once they did, all the attention might turn to them.

That could end up backfiring.

It was one thing if she thought no one was noticing. It was another if she became the center of attention. She might get stage fright.

Even though this "Jack" already ejaculated all over the face of a female participant, he was still *very* erect. Either the man was a machine or he'd taken something to keep him that way.

For his own selfish reasons, Dayne hoped it was the first, despite it probably being the second.

"His rock hard cock is filling you. His balls are slapping your pussy. His lips are wrapped around your nipple and his teeth are nipping you there. He's adding a little pain to heighten your pleasure. You can't get enough. You want more, don't you?"

"Yes," she groaned. "I want more. I want to come."

"You're the one holding yourself back. I'm going to say it again, Cara, let yourself go. Let him feel the intensity of your orgasm. Soak his cock. Milk his balls dry."

Her head fell forward a moment before it slammed back against his chest at the same time her curvy ass slammed into his cock.

His grunt filled her ear. "Come, baby. Give him that sweet, sweet reward for all of his hard work."

"I... I... Ooooooh."

Her pussy clenched around his fingers and her body began to spasm against him. She ground her ass against his cock at the same time riding his fingers.

She might not be aware of how she was torturing him, but he sure as hell was.

Pushing his face into her neck, he held her tightly against him as she recovered, trying to avoid his own explosion. However, the slope became too slippery and he couldn't find a secure grip to keep himself from falling.

It had been a while since he teetered on losing this much control. Unfortunately, now wasn't the time for it, since he was fully clothed. And that would make a mess.

Shit. Shit. Shit. Don't do it. Don't...

Oh, for fuck's sake.

Chapter Five

Dayne needed to go back to the farmhouse to change. But first, he had to do two things.

"You okay?" he whispered into Cara's ear.

"Perfect," came out on a sigh and a shudder.

He grinned despite the damn mess in his boxer briefs. It had been worth it since he was the first man to ever bring her to orgasm. Hopefully, he wouldn't be her last.

He adjusted her bra and fastened her jeans, then pressed a light kiss to her bare shoulder. "I'm glad I could help."

"Me, too." She sounded a bit drowsy. "Are *you* okay?"

"Uh huh." If she couldn't tell he came, he wasn't about to volunteer that information. He should've had more control over his own reaction. "So, after that, are you ready for me to be your personal mentor?"

She turned to face him.

Jesus, she was beautiful. And sexy as hell. Add in the fact she currently had that afterglow about her...

"You did something no other man has ever done." His

grin grew but the lift of her palm made him keep his mouth shut. "That doesn't give you the right to be cocky."

Sure it did, but for his own benefit, he kept that to himself. "Got it. I need to remain humble."

She lifted an eyebrow. "Can you be?"

"Do I need to be for you to say yes?"

Instead of answering, she asked, "Why are you so determined to show me the ropes?"

If she only knew how literal the phrase "the ropes" was in this case. "Would you rather Jack do it?"

She glanced over her shoulder at the group, now cleaning up and getting dressed. "Is that really his name?"

"I don't know who he is." *Yet.* Finding out that info was the second thing he needed to do. Dayne only hoped the man stuck around long enough so he could talk to him once he was finished with Cara. "But if you're interested, I can find out."

Surprise filled her green eyes. "You wouldn't mind?"

"As the co-owner of this resort, I talk to guests daily. I wouldn't be doing anything I wouldn't normally do." He'd simply make that particular guest a priority.

"Then, yes."

"Yes? To me being your mentor or teacher or guide or whatever you want to consider me? Or yes, you're interested in our friend Jack?"

"Both."

"Wow. One orgasm and look at that confidence. Imagine how cocky *you* will be after a hundred."

She laughed softly ʲand reached up to pull her ponytail tighter. He would've preferred to do that for her, and while he had a hold of it, force her to her knees and have her suck his cock. Spent or not.

With a shrug, she said, "I think having more sexual freedom, and being confident about it, will be amazing."

"I can confirm it is."

"I'd like to experience some of the things I've read about."

Shit. He needed to warn her so she wasn't disappointed. "Just remember: what you read was fiction. It might not be the same in reality."

"I'm aware." She planted her hands on her hips and licked her full lips. Lips he wanted wrapped around his cock. "When do we start?"

"Eager, I see." He was, too, but he had things to do first. Like go clean up. "I have to head to my office to take care of some business. Can we exchange numbers so I can text you when I'm done? I'd love to start with a tour of the property."

She slipped a cell phone from the back pocket of her jeans, opened her contacts app, and handed it to him.

He plugged in his name and number, then sent himself a text so he'd have her number, too, before handing it back. "Done. You can text or call me at any time. Even with the simplest of questions or requests."

She tucked the cell phone away. "Thank you. I appreciate your... *dedication.*"

"I want all our guests to get the most out of their stay."

"But you'll be going above and beyond for me."

He tipped his head to the side and considered her. After what just happened, he had a feeling his efforts would be more than worth it. "Not a hardship. Why don't you head back to your room and rest? Or go hang by the pool and enjoy some cocktails. I'll let you know when I'm finished with work for the day so we can meet up."

"I look forward to it." With that, she headed up the grassy incline and back to the lodge.

As she did, he appreciated the glimpses of her luscious ass every time her knit top shifted while she walked.

Once she was out of sight, he turned his attention to the next item on his "to-do" list.

HEATH TRACKED the stunning blonde leaving. Despite being caught up in the activities on the blanket, he had noticed when she arrived. Not to mention how uncomfortable she appeared at first while watching a half dozen people—three women and three men, including himself—having a fun little orgy.

After checking into the resort a few hours ago, on his trek to his cabin to unpack his bags and get settled, he ran into a couple who invited him to join them and a few others.

Since relaxing, having fun, and having sex with like-minded people was why he came to Double D Ranch in the first place, he decided *why not?* He might as well start off his "vacation" with a bang.

He hadn't expected the group to have sex out in the open by the huge lake *right in front* of The Mane Lodge, but, for the most part, he was pretty much *a go with the flow* type of guy. No surprise their group activity drew a crowd of observers. Some even did more than only observe. Like the thirty-something hunk with the dark blond hair who joined the beautiful blonde bombshell.

He wondered if they were a "thing," or were open to playing with anyone. He planned to find out. He was interested in her, in him or, *hell*, both of them.

Now fully dressed, he gave nods and goodbyes to the rest of the group he recently got to know up close and personal and headed back to his cabin. He needed a hot shower and to decide what to do for the rest of the day. Maybe he could wander around and find a partner or two to join him up in a playroom tonight.

If he couldn't, he could always go up to observe and maybe he'd get lucky there.

When he left at the end of his week-long stay, he hoped all the sex he had here would tide him over for a while. Working long hours really didn't give him much time to cut through the bullshit of dating. Or all the unknowns and drama from hookup apps. Every time he gave them a shot, he ended up regretting it. Unfortunately, not everyone told the truth on their profile. Worse, not everyone was sane.

He preferred to keep his cock and balls attached to his body, thank you very much.

He wasn't sure why he booked a cabin since he was flying solo. He could have saved a nice chunk of change by staying in a room in the lodge, instead. Maybe next time.

If there was a next time.

The property was beautiful and the orgy was fun, but he still had plenty of time left to thoroughly check out everything this new all-adult, all-inclusive ranch resort had to offer.

Besides sex. And a lot of it, according to the reviews online.

"Hey!" a male voice called out behind him. Heath paused and glanced over his shoulder.

Well, look at that...

The dark blond hunk who'd been with the gorgeous woman with the ponytail was catching up to him. That would save him the time and effort of seeking him out.

Heath turned and waited, taking the opportunity to check him out from head to toe.

"I'm Dayne," the man introduced himself while he was still ten feet away.

"Heath," he greeted. His eyes zeroed in a small dark spot on the front of his khakis. Near his zipper. He lifted his gaze and met the man's hazel eyes. "Did you... have an accident?"

"She ground her ass against me, so..." His mouth twisted and he shrugged. "It was worth it."

Heath pressed his lips together. He got it. Shit happened. "Watching her come was worth it, too."

Dayne's eyebrows shot up his forehead. "You saw that?"

"Yes. Was I not supposed to?"

"I figured you were kind of busy."

"When it comes to sex, I'm good at multitasking." In more ways than one. He smiled.

"She caught your attention." It wasn't a question, but a conclusion. Interesting enough, zero jealousy colored his words.

"She did. Is she with you?"

Dayne shook his head. "A guest, the same as you."

Heath frowned. "And you aren't?"

Now close enough, Dayne jutted out his hand and Heath automatically shook it. "Dayne Lyons. Co-owner of this paradise."

Right now he'd hold back his opinion on whether it was paradise or not. "Oh. Do the owners normally fraternize with the guests?"

The man's lips twitched with amusement. "This co-owner does as much as possible."

Heath made a conclusion of his own. "So, you made this place your own personal playground."

"That wasn't the goal, but it ended up being the result."

To Heath, that sounded like predatory behavior. But he could be wrong since consent was emphasized several times on their website, also while checking in and even in the guest binder. However, this was an owner and not a guest. Did they hold themselves to the same standard?

The blonde Dayne had his fingers on—and in—certainly

looked like she was perfectly okay with everything he'd been doing.

He asked, "Is it the same for the rest of the co-owners?"

"The other co-owner would be my twin brother Dylan. And no, he's taken."

"*Ah.*"

"My sister also lives on the property. She's head chef."

A family affair, apparently. "'Also lives?' Does that mean you live here, too?"

"I do. I live on one side of the farmhouse located behind the lodge.

Well, that was convenient. "*Ah.*"

"When did you check in?"

"This morning." Heath paid extra to get an early check-in.

"Then, you haven't had a tour yet."

"As you saw, I was a little busy." Since Dayne and the woman weren't together... "What was the blonde's name?"

Dayne hesitated before answering. "Cara."

"Did she come solo?"

"I helped."

Heath blinked until it hit him what Dayne meant. "I meant..."

Dayne smirked. "I know what you meant. I was seeing if you had a sense of humor."

"I normally do but work's been stressful and overwhelming lately, so it might reappear once I decompress a little." That little orgy was a good start. The private hot tub behind his cabin would help, too. He might even book a massage.

"What do you do?"

"Nothing as exciting as owning a resort built around sex. I'm an investor."

A dark blond eyebrow rose. "Of?"

This man was awfully interested in Heath's life, but since he had already planned on seeking him out, Dayne only saved him the trouble.

"Stocks, bonds, real estate, whatever will make me money." Whatever made him *good* money. Especially since he lost most of it during his divorce. It took a while to rebuild his accounts and investments again. Unfortunately, he still owed the witch monthly alimony payments.

He never wanted to go through a divorce again.

"A day trader?"

"More like a pattern day trader."

"I'm an investor, too, in a way. As CFO of the resort, I handle the resort's funds and investments."

Sounded like they had more in common than only being interested in Cara. "What's your background?"

"Certified Management Accountant. However, I prefer my current job." He air-quoted the last word.

Heath was sure he did. Most likely for the perks.

"By the way, Cara showed some interest in you."

"It was mutual."

"She wasn't the only one." Dayne held Heath's eyes when he raised them. "If you'd like to join us on our afternoon tour, I'm sure she won't mind."

"Just the three of us?"

"Yes, unless there's someone else you'd like to invite?"

"I don't know anyone else," Heath answered.

"You were just in a fuckfest with five other people."

"Doesn't mean I know them. I couldn't tell you their names."

Dayne chuckled. "Well, if you'd like to join us, I'll be waiting in a UTV at the lodge's entrance." He glanced at his watch. "Maybe around three or so?"

"What's a UTV?"

"Utility vehicle. Like a four-wheeler."

"It fits three people?"

"This one fits four. So, if you do find someone you'd like to invite, there's room."

"Thank you for the offer. I'll think about it." With that, he continued on to his cabin. Both a hot shower and the hot tub were waiting for him.

Then, if he happened to be in the mood later, maybe a hot man and woman as well.

Chapter Six

The text stated Dayne would be waiting in front of the lodge at three.

The second Cara stepped outside, he was hard to miss. He stood out in the sun, with a hand raised to shade his eyes while he surveyed the lake.

Was there another orgy happening in the grass down there?

She stepped beside him and peered in the same direction. No orgy this afternoon. Just a couple having sex on one of the paddle boats in the middle of the water. She guessed people could find the most unique places to do it around here.

Dayne might be making sure the boat didn't tip and the guests ended up drowning. That would be bad for business.

She turned to him and announced, "I'm ready for my tour."

His head twisted toward her and his forehead creased. "Sorry?"

"My tour. Wasn't I supposed to be here at three?"

Before she could pull out her cell phone to double check

the text, clarity filled his face. Had he forgotten already? *Weird.*

"Ah, yes. You must have made plans with my twin."

"Twin," she repeated.

The man jutted out his hand. "Welcome to the Double D. I'm Dylan Lyons, one of the co-owners. You must've already met my twin, Dayne."

"He mentioned a brother but not that you're twins." Or maybe she missed that tidbit last night due to her nerves.

"Despite being identical, we're not exactly the same."

Dayne joined them and slapped Dylan on the chest. "Thankfully. Dylan is boring. Me? I'm a bundle of excitement."

She blinked as she took them both in. They certainly were identical.

Being constantly mistaken for each other had to be a pain. The only slight differences she could see between the two were the cut of their hair, which was still very similar, and the fact that Dayne was clean-shaven.

Dylan rolled his eyes. "Enjoy your stay..." He pointed to his brother. "Only, watch this one. I suggest carrying pepper spray."

"Pepper spray?"

Dayne cupped his hand around the side of his mouth, leaned in and stage-whispered, "His jokes are never funny."

"That was a joke?" she asked.

Dayne shrugged. "Exactly." He turned to her and tipped his head down. "Sorry for running a few minutes late. I got sucked into a virtual meeting against my will and I still need to go grab the UTV. Why don't you go back inside and hang out in the lounge or grab a drink by the pool. I can text you once I'm out front with it."

"That's fine. Take your time."

With a nod, his long legs ate up the ground as he headed around the exterior of the lodge and disappeared.

———

SHE HAD JUST FINISHED a glass of wine when she received another text. *Your chariot awaits out front.*

When she went back outside, she noticed that Dayne had parked a small utility-type four-wheeler only feet from the front doors. Perks of being an owner, she guessed.

The man himself was leaning back against the hood of the all-terrain vehicle with both his arms and ankles crossed. Despite him appearing bored, she couldn't deny the man was extremely handsome, as well as sexy. Even fully dressed, it was obvious he took good care of his physique.

So did his twin.

Dayne—she assumed this time it really *was* him due to the lack of facial hair—straightened and a genuine smile grew across his face when she approached. It was infectious and she didn't bother to control her own.

No point in being coy since the man had his fingers inside her earlier.

"I didn't get to ask this earlier because of my brother but... good day so far?" As soon as he shoved his dark sunglasses to the top of his dark blond head, she could see the gleam in his hazel eyes.

"Can't complain about it."

The lines at the corners of his eyes deepened. "We aim to please."

"Apparently," she teased, then jerked her chin towards the vehicle. It was open on the sides but had a roof and windshield as well as knobby tires made for off-road use. "Honestly, I thought we'd be walking."

"The property is three-hundred acres. Do you really want to walk?" One of his eyebrows cocked. "Unless you want to go on horseback?"

She'd never ridden a horse in her life. "Motorized transportation will work perfectly fine."

He flipped a hand toward the front seats. "Sit in the front with me."

Had he expected her to treat him like some sort of chauffeur and sit in the back? She climbed into the passenger seat expecting him to join her.

He didn't.

Instead, he went back to leaning against the hood of the UTV.

That was...odd. "Are we waiting on someone?"

Wearing a wicked smile, he glanced over his shoulder at her, then he tipped his head to his left. She looked in that direction, confused.

Then she saw him. Long legs ate up the distance between them. "Jack?" she whispered.

Was he serious? He invited the man she used in her imagination to...

Heat licked at her cheeks but also warmed her belly. Luckily, Jack had no idea she had objectified him. Her eyes flicked to the resort's co-owner. Unless Dayne told him?

She pressed hands to her hot cheeks. *Oh no.*

"His name isn't Jack," Dayne mentioned casually.

Of course it wasn't!

"It's Heath."

"You talked to him." She might as well climb out of the vehicle and go hide in her room. Or under a rock.

"I invited him along. He only arrived this morning and hadn't had a chance to check out the resort grounds."

"Do you always do private tours?"

"Absolutely not," was Dayne's answer as Jack—no, *Heath* —reached them.

His dark eyes flicked back and forth between Dayne and Cara.

"Heath. Cara. Cara. Heath," Dayne introduced.

"Hello, Cara."

Holy smokes! His voice wrapped around her like a warm hug. He could talk dirty to her—like Dayne did earlier—anytime.

The corners of his lips curled upward. "Hello, Cara," Heath repeated.

She shook herself mentally. "I...*uh*...hello."

She silently groaned. She sounded like an idiot. Did she lose all her brain cells this morning with that orgasm?

With a smothered, but still audible, chuckle, Dayne invited Heath to climb in the back, and as he did, Dayne slid into the driver's seat. He started the engine and called out, "Ready?"

Was she ever! Suddenly, she didn't have one regret coming to the ranch. She was about to spend time with two very scrumptious men.

She reined in her excitement since she really couldn't judge what kind of men they were based only on looks.

Panic washed over her. Maybe she shouldn't go alone with two strangers. Beside the fact that Dayne gave her her first male-induced orgasm, she didn't know him at all.

But before she could think twice about going, the UTV lurched forward and they were on their way.

"How long do you think we'll be gone?" she asked Dayne.

He glanced over at her with his brow furrowed. "Is there a problem?"

"No...I..." She squeezed her eyes shut. *Consent.* They emphasized consent here. And Dayne, as one of the owners, probably helped write the resort's policies. She opened her eyes and shook her head. "No. No problem. I was just curious if we'd be back in time for dinner."

"If we're not, I'll make sure you're fed when we return. I've got some pull around here." One side of his mouth hiked up. "Don't worry."

When he reached over to squeeze her knee gently, her skin prickled under her jeans. And, *goodness*, not in a bad way. But his hand quickly returned to the steering wheel and he concentrated on driving. Was it weird that she missed his touch?

She startled when Heath's voice came from directly behind her. "Did you enjoy the show this morning?"

Combined with his delicious voice, the memory of it caused her pussy to clench. She pinned her thighs tighter together.

"She enjoyed it much more than the party last night," Dayne answered for her, shooting her another quick, but concerned, glance.

"I missed it." Heath's disappointment was clear.

"They're usually Saturday or Sunday nights. Sometimes both. But believe me, there are plenty of other activities to take part in. Or make your own party. This morning proved only a blanket and some willing participants are needed."

"Last night's event was a little overwhelming," Cara finally admitted.

"Why's that?"

"This morning was her first ever orgasm not self-achieved."

"I'm sorry?" Heath asked.

She grimaced. *Shit.* Dayne's answer did not help relieve the heat in her cheeks. "It's true."

"You came to a resort built around sex to achieve your first orgasm?"

"It wasn't my—" She shook her head. "That wasn't why I came." Not for that specific reason, anyway.

"She's here to learn." Again, Dayne was speaking for her. She wasn't sure whether to be annoyed at his forwardness or be grateful he was answering for her.

"Learn what, exactly?"

Dayne once again answered. "Whether real life is as good as fiction."

Heath sat back in his seat and she waited for him to ask for an explanation. Surprisingly, he didn't. Instead, he asked, "How long are you here for, Cara?"

"Until Sunday morning."

"The same as me."

"But I'm still not sure if this place is for me."

Dayne glanced in the rearview mirror. Most likely to look at Heath, who answered, "That gives you a week to figure out if it is."

"Or for us to prove that it is," Dayne added.

She gnawed on her bottom lip. "I don't know..."

Heath asked, "What do you have to lose?"

"My dignity?"

Beside her, Dayne snorted. "No. You won't lose that at our resort. I know we discussed this already, but you're already here. And I'll say it again, you don't have to do anything you're not comfortable with. So, why not enjoy your stay? Here's the thing, how will you know what you're willing to try if you leave?"

"I agree with Dayne."

Of course he did.

Heath continued, "I'm curious about the lack of orgasms. Have you ever had a long-term partner?"

She nodded. "We were together for three years."

Dayne pulled the UTV up to the Mane Event Hall and shut off the engine. He turned toward her. "What happened?"

"You nailed it last night. This place is proof my sex life has been boring. Disappointing, really."

"This is the perfect place to change that," Dayne said as both men climbed out.

Heath came up to her and offered his hand to assist her in exiting the vehicle. "My sex life has been boring, too, lately. That's why I'm here. It's not because of my partners, but the lack of them," he explained.

He had a lack of partners? Impossible.

He was sinfully handsome and what she saw of his body earlier—which was everything—proved he stayed in good shape. If she had to guess, he was in his mid-forties. His clothes, now that he was wearing some, appeared to be quality. She had no idea what he did for a living but could guess that he was well-established and probably didn't have to scrimp and save to afford this week like she had.

Unless he had a questionable personality, he had to be a catch.

Once she had both feet on the ground, he said, "I've been a bit swamped lately with work, so I haven't had time to deal with dates or even hookups. I figured a vacation wouldn't hurt. So, here I am."

"How did you find out about the resort?" Dayne asked him as he hooked an arm through Cara's and began to guide her toward the event hall's front entrance.

"Believe it or not, I was searching online to find a place that would meet my requirements to unwind and this resort popped up as an ad."

"Well, it's good to know our advertising dollars are hard

at work." Keeping his arm linked with Cara's, Dayne pulled out a ring of keys and unlocked the hall's door. He stepped inside, unlocked a clear plastic box over the light switches, and with a flick of his wrist, the room lit up.

"Damn," Heath murmured, taking it all in.

It definitely looked different this afternoon compared to last night. No loud music, crazy lights, and even crazier costumes. It seemed super tame.

Dayne pointed out the stage, where the DJ had been set up last night, and the bar area, before directing them to the back of the hall. Where Cara had made her escape.

"You could do a lot with this space," Heath commented.

"That's the point. Weddings. Parties. Whatever. Even funerals, if someone wanted that." He grinned.

He led them out the back after shutting off the lights and locking up, then took them to the exterior stairway at the rear of the building; the one with the sign pointing up toward *Heaven*.

Dayne finally released Cara's arm and he motioned for her to climb the stairs.

Suddenly, her heartbeat was pounding in her neck. Upstairs was where the themed playrooms were.

You can do this. Take one step, then the next. The same as you're going to do this whole week.

As she climbed the stairway to Heaven, Dayne stayed on her heels.

Heath, following Dayne, asked, "So, what happened to that three-year relationship, Cara?"

"Sounds like shitty sex," Dayne answered, following her up the steps.

Unfortunately, that was only one part of it. "That, plus my best friend."

Dayne took the last step to reach the landing and used her shoulder to turn her toward him. "Sorry, what?"

Cara pulled in a breath, trying to cool the anger that wrapped around the memory. "My best friend happened." *So-called* best friend. A *real* best friend would never have stabbed her in the back like that.

Heath reached the landing and stood behind Dayne. She took note that their heights were very similar. Maybe Heath was slightly taller. Either way, they were both taller than her five-foot-five.

"And they didn't include you?" Heath asked.

What? Maybe that was normal thinking here on this ranch but it couldn't be in the real world. Could it? "Would that have made it any better?"

"It would for me," Dayne answered.

"Well, I'm not into women. Especially traitors." At least she didn't think she was attracted to the same sex, but she hadn't tested that theory. "Even if he had bothered to ask me first, I would've turned him down. Right before I packed my things."

"Sounds like you packed your things anyway."

She met Heath's eyes over Dayne's shoulder. "True. But I would've made that decision prior to him sleeping with her. That decision was taken away from me."

"I don't think they were actually sleeping." Dayne smirked.

The man was certainly turning out to be a smart ass.

"You've never had a threesome?" Heath asked.

"No."

He watched her carefully when he asked, "Are you against having sex with multiple people at the same time?"

She had read plenty of books where more than two characters were involved intimately. While reading, she tried to picture herself in their place. It had been both exciting and terrifying at the same time. "I'm not against them per se. I just never had the opportunity to try it, I guess." Though, she did watch the orgy this morning with great interest.

"Just not with other women."

"It's not my thing. This morning proved *you're* not against it, Heath."

He smiled. "No. But like sex between two people, it can be great or it can really suck. It depends on who you partner up with."

"Did this morning suck?" Dayne asked him.

"It did not. Nobody was selfish or jealous, or trying to be the center of attention."

She sliced her gaze back to Dayne. "How about you?"

Dayne shrugged. "Basically, I love sex. All kinds. With just about anyone."

Her eyes went wide. "Anyone?"

"Adults who consent, of course." He moved past her but paused before opening the door to Heaven. "Just be aware that the playrooms could be occupied and have the blinds open. Guests might also be in the hallway observing. Let's keep our conversation to a minimum."

She grabbed his arm to stop him from opening the door. "Wait. I still have questions."

Dayne turned and cocked an eyebrow. "Ask away."

"You said you're open to having sex with anyone. I assume that means not only women."

"Correct."

So, he was fine having sex with men. The same as Heath.

A thought popped into her head. "Trans?"

"I'm good with anyone."

Her eyebrows pinched together. "Anyone?"

"Anyone," he confirmed with a nod. "As long as they're into what I'm into, I'm good with them. I don't stick to one flavor. Plus, vanilla is boring."

If they're into what I'm into...

"What are you into?" she couldn't resist asking.

Dayne's lips twitched. "The list will be shorter if you ask what I'm not into."

"And that would be?" she prodded.

He met Heath's eyes for a second before swinging his back to Cara. "For another time."

"List one. I'm curious." This conversation was enlightening for sure. Being a librarian, she loved knowledge. She also loved to do deep dives into all kinds of subjects. Hence, why she was now at the resort. But this might be the first time she'd taken her "research" this far.

"Blood play."

She agreed with Heath when he murmured, "Understandable."

She didn't know everything involved with blood play and she wasn't sure if she wanted to find out. None of the books she'd read included that specific kink, but a lot of them did have power plays and Dom/sub relationships. "Are either of you a Dom?"

"I am not," Dayne answered.

When she glanced at Heath, he shook his head. "No."

"What about a sub?"

"No," both men answered at the same time.

Her brow wrinkled. "What are you?"

Dayne's smile was huge when he answered simply, "Horny."

She dropped her head to hide her giggle.

He went on to explain. "I don't need power over someone else, even during sex. I'm all about fluidity and pleasure. Giving and taking. I don't follow any rules. My brother is the rule follower. I'm the rule breaker."

"How about you?" she asked Heath next.

"It seems Dayne and I are on the same page."

Chapter Seven

"On the same page?" Cara asked Heath. "In which way? Horny or a rule breaker?"

He didn't bother to fight his grin. "Both."

"Are we done with questions for now?" Dayne interrupted. "Once we're done here and continue the tour, you'll have plenty of time to ask more."

"What if I have questions inside there?" Cara lifted her chin towards the closed, windowless door.

"If they're time sensitive, ask. If not, try to wait. Let's try to keep our voices down and not disturb anyone inside."

Cara nodded as Dayne pulled open the steel door.

Heath's heart sped up. He might not be into the Dom/sub dynamics, but he did have a few preferred kinks. Like Dayne, he loved sex and intimacy. He just didn't get enough of it.

Especially lately.

This break was sorely needed.

After Dayne guided Cara inside, Heath followed and shut the door behind him.

Glancing down the wide hallway lit by rose-colored lights, he was sure the playrooms were popular with guests. Since it was afternoon, only a few guests currently filled the hallway, gathered in front of windows with open blinds .

Dayne flipped a hand to their right and whispered, "Medical Room, if you're in the mood to play doctor, nurse, or patient. Blood play, golden showers and the like are allowed in this one. It's full of medical equipment and tools, of course, as well as an exam table with stirrups."

That could be fun. Unfortunately, the blinds were closed. He had to assume the room was not only occupied, but by guests wanting privacy.

Their hot-as-fuck tour guide flipped a hand to their left. "The Entertainment Room."

Since the room was empty and the blinds open, Heath could see it included things like a stripper pole in the center, a sex swing in one corner, and a Sybian saddle machine in another. The walls not facing the window were mirrored, as well as the ceiling.

This also looked like a fun room. He could picture Cara dancing around the pole and doing a striptease to some sexy music.

Dayne added, "The Sybian has a variety of attachments."

Keeping his voice down, Heath asked, "Are all the rooms usually equally busy?"

"No. We plan to reevaluate the less popular rooms in a few months and maybe change out the theme. Of course, some similar equipment and toys are in every room. Toys and tools commonly used, like whips, crops, paddles, dildos, and strap-ons. There are also supplies like lube, condoms, and dental dams; just like in your accommodations.

"We also didn't forget items needed for aftercare, like ice, ointments, bottled water, even sports drinks. We tried to think of everything, but if we missed anything important, we're always open to suggestions for toys, supplies, or even themes."

Being open to suggestions from their guests was a plus. It probably was a benefit to the resort, too. Keep a guest happy and they'll keep coming back.

Dayne continued down the hallway. "Room three is the puppy play room,"

Also unoccupied at the moment.

"Room four is all about bondage and restraints." Dayne paused in front of that window. Not only was it occupied, the blinds were wide open, a clear invitation for guests to watch. "Come, Cara. See if this is something you might like to explore." He reached for her and brought her forward to stand in front of him.

Heath stepped behind Dayne—not quite touching, but damn close—and studied the breadth of his shoulders and back. He had the urge to lick the nape of his corded neck, but managed to refrain.

Lifting his gaze, he pointed it at Cara while she focused on the action inside the playroom, then past her to see what she was watching.

A woman, wearing a skin-tight purple vinyl catsuit, showcasing a generous amount of cleavage, and three-inch spiked heels, circled a naked man suspended from the ceiling, bound by ropes.

Shibari. Japanese rope bondage.

A true art.

Dayne leaned forward and whispered, "The woman is the rigger or rope top. The man is the receiver or rope bottom. This form of rope play is called Shibari. Jute and hemp rope are used more often than not, instead of soft or silky rope. We've had experts come in and do demos for our guests and it's quite impressive, even breathtaking, when done right. I haven't done it myself, so I'm certainly no expert, but I do appreciate the skill involved. But as always, communication and trust are key."

Heath could hear Cara's breathing catch. He would love to see her bound like that. Those ropes would frame her curves perfectly.

"The rope can create sensations of pleasure or pain, depending on the technique used and what the receiver desires," Heath added softly. Like Dayne, he'd never had it done to him, but wasn't opposed to it with an experienced rigger.

The woman even had the man's cock and balls bound tightly, too. Heath wasn't sure he'd be down for that. Cock ring, sure. Cock cage, maybe. But the possibility of cutting off the circulation to his family jewels was pushing it a little too far for him.

Once the woman finished tying her last knot, she stepped back to appreciate her work.

"Let's keep going," Dayne encouraged after a few more seconds.

The blinds were closed on room five, and for whatever reason, Dayne skipped mentioning its theme, instead, stopping in front of room six next. "This room was set up specifically for impact play."

This room was where the most observers gathered in the hallway.

Once again, Dayne tucked Cara in front of him so she'd have an unobstructed view. And once again, Heath stepped close enough to sandwich the younger man between them. Heath flared his nostrils to fill his lungs with whatever subtle cologne Dayne wore.

He wondered if Dayne was a giver or receiver, or if he was fine with either, depending on the circumstances.

Heath himself was good with either, depending on the partner or partners he was with. Given a choice, he preferred to top other men but he'd bottom for someone he trusted.

The impact room was occupied by four individuals. A naked, dark-haired woman was strapped to a St. Andrews Cross. Since she faced it, they could see numerous raised welts all over her ass, back, and thighs. The tails on that flogger being wielded were not made of soft suede, but instead what looked like nylon paracord.

That was some serious shit.

For himself, he preferred a weighted flogger with soft tails. He found the heavy, rhythmic thumping relaxing. However, this woman looked relaxed, too, so he had no doubt she had dropped into her subspace.

In the center of the room was a custom-made spanking bench. On that bench was a man whose ass looked like it was on fire. Nearby was a wooden paddle with holes to give it more of a wallop. His arms and legs were secured to the legs of the custom piece with chains, a ball gag filled his mouth, and a black leather blindfold covered his eyes.

The man's fiery ass cheeks were kept spread open by some contraption he'd never seen before. Standing behind him at the end of the bench was a woman wearing a harness with a strap-on attached.

Heath sure hoped she had used a lot of lube because she was pegging the man with no mercy, especially considering the size of the dildo attached. It was far from average.

His own cheeks clenched at the size. He was up for almost anything, but he did have his limits.

A sound next to them had them glancing to their right.

A male guest instructed the woman he was with to plant her hands on the wall next to the window and tip her ass up and out. After quickly fumbling with his pants, he then flipped up her short skirt, ripped her thong to the side, licked three fingers and rubbed them against her plump, pink folds. Shuffling forward, he lined up his cock and jammed himself deep, causing the pretty brunette to throw back her head, mewing in pleasure. Gripping her hips tightly, her partner kept ramming hard and deep.

Heath was torn on whether to keep eyes on them, watch the action inside the room, or take in Cara's expressions.

Instead of simply watching, he decided to take a little action by pressing his lips to the exposed skin at the back of Dayne's neck, at the same time curling his hand around the front to collar it possessively.

He put his mouth to Dayne's ear and slightly squeezed his fingers tighter. Dayne's pulse raced against his palm. "Do you like that?"

"I don't hate it," came his rumble.

Cara turned her attention to them from the couple fucking only inches away.

Heath circled Dayne with his other arm, thumbing the hard tip of one nipple over the resort owner's polo shirt before running his hand down the man's abs and finally cupping the erection pressing against his zipper.

Heath pressed his own hard-on against Dayne's ass.

He figured Dayne invited them to a "hands-on" tour but didn't realize it would happen toward the beginning of the journey. "If I asked you to drop to your knees right here and suck my cock, would you?"

Dayne asked, "Would you like to see that, Cara?"

"I..." She cleared her throat, then lifted her chin and answered, "Yes."

"I can't do it here," Dayne whispered. "We can find a more secluded spot on our tour."

"Understood," Heath said. Most likely because he was a co-owner. Maybe he was limited to where and when he played with the guests.

Though, he did finger Cara out in the open this morning. But then, he had remained completely clothed and anyone from a distance might have only thought it was an intimate hug.

The man next to them planted himself deep one more time and his hips jerked as he obviously came. Not even seconds after he pulled out and tucked himself away, he glanced over at them and asked, "Anybody else?"

Dayne shook his head and Heath murmured a, "No."

Heath had no idea who the brunette was to the guy, but apparently he didn't mind sharing. While Heath would normally be up for that, he had his eye on another woman. Only, she was blonde with a hell of an ass he would love to wreck.

He doubted he would get that chance, but that didn't mean he couldn't fantasize about it. Luckily, he had almost a full week to see how far they could get.

Since her sexual experience seemed to be limited, he might not get very far at all in that department. This week needed to be all positive experiences for her. If they were, she might return and continue her education.

Too bad he wouldn't be here to help with that. However, the owner of the cock he was stroking would be.

"We need to keep going." Dayne's voice sounded a bit strained.

"Am I tempting you?"

"You are. And again, this isn't the best place to do anything about it."

"Understood," Heath repeated, reluctantly freeing him and stepping back.

Dayne blew out a relieved breath and pointed to the last two rooms. "Room eight at the end and on the right is for extreme play. Again, anyone into electro-stimulation, wax play, blood play and the like. We put it at the end on purpose. By the crowd down there, I'm taking an educated guess that the room is occupied with the blinds open. I'd say let's not shock Cara with that. Just yet."

Heath's eyes sliced to her. He agreed with not scaring her. "Baby steps," he murmured.

"I think it's for the best." Dayne turned toward her. "However, I don't want to take that decision away from you. If you want to head—"

"I'm good for now," she quickly answered, with her cheeks still flushed. She was also wringing her hands together.

Heath pulled her twisted fingers free from each other, lifting one hand to his mouth and brushing his lips over the back of it. "Like he said, you don't have to do anything you're not comfortable with. This place is set up for pleasure, not fear. Not everyone has the same tastes or kinks. Some desires are much darker than others."

"Apparently."

"No rush to figure out what you crave. It'll come naturally if you let it."

"C'mon," Dayne encouraged. "Let's finish the rest of the tour before dark."

As they headed to the exit, Heath wasn't sure which playroom was his favorite yet. He might have to try them all and see.

———

DAYNE SHOWED THEM THE SPA, the sheds, the barn, the paddocks, even the farthest fields in double time. Heath swore both he and Cara had to hang on to the jostling UTV so they wouldn't get launched out of it every time Dayne sped over a bump or hit a pothole along the dirt lanes.

On their way to the far end of the three-hundred-acre property, he only pointed at the new employee bunkhouse, explaining it was almost complete. He also did a quick drive-by of the half dozen employee cabins that were being built behind the bunkhouse.

The resort was set up similarly to a true ranch that housed their wranglers and ranch hands. The difference was, their business was merely enhanced by the livestock and animals they kept. They didn't rely on them to *be* the business.

On their return to the main resort area, Dayne hooked a sharp left at the cabins and parked behind the one farthest from the main dirt lane. He quickly shut down the engine and climbed out.

"Is this the more secluded spot you mentioned?"

Dayne's answer was, "It is."

Now, the only question was whether Dayne would actually get down on his knees or expect Heath to.

And what Cara would be doing during it.

Chapter Eight

THE CABIN'S exterior had been completed, except for installation of the doors and windows. Heath stepped through the framed-out doorway and glanced around to note, while the floor plan wasn't overly large, it could fit a couple of people comfortably. Despite the size, he could tell by the framed walls that it was set up nicely.

The open floor plan would make the space look bigger once it was finished.

Plus...

He headed toward the window openings facing the mountains to the north. It would have an awesome view.

One definitely different from his penthouse in Hoboken, New Jersey.

Hearing footsteps behind him, he turned to see Dayne approaching. Heath took his time checking out the man he guessed was in his mid-thirties, from the top of his dark-blond head all the way to his dusty boots. Dayne obviously changed clothes for the tour since he hadn't been dressed in jeans and boots earlier by the lake.

"You consider this secluded?"

"It's private enough," was Dayne's response.

That was all Heath needed to hear.

His hands automatically went for his belt. He didn't want to give Dayne time to change the scenario. Heath didn't mind sucking cock, not at all, but since that moment in Heaven, he'd been looking forward to having his in Dayne's mouth.

During the extensive tour, the anticipation of this moment had been killing him. He couldn't wait to look down and see the man on his knees, not look up while Dayne was on his feet. The heat in Dayne's eyes flared and he licked his lips when Heath shoved a hand into his boxer briefs.

He glanced around for Cara and found her still standing in what would eventually be the cabin's kitchen, staring in their direction with her lips parted slightly. Heath would love to see her on her knees at his feet, too.

But first...

Heath pulled out his cock and began to pump it. At the end of each stroke, he squeezed the tip until a glistening bead of precum formed.

He called out to Cara, "You could watch or you could join us. Up to you."

She skirted around the framed walls to join them in the cabin's back room. "Can I start by watching?"

"Of course," Dayne answered. "You don't have to do anything—"

"Right," she cut him off with a single nod. "I don't have to do anything I don't want to do. I can do as little or as much as I please."

Heath grinned. "Apparently, she got the memo. Do whatever feels natural for you. Watch. Participate. Whatever you desire."

"I'll watch for now." She headed over to a wood sawhorse

only feet from where Heath stood. Once she perched her ass against it, he turned back to Dayne at the same time the resort owner's hazel eyes sliced from Cara back to Heath in the midst of still fisting his hard-on.

Dayne locked eyes with Heath, lowering himself to his knees at the same time. His tongue slipped across his lips once more before using both hands to grab Heath's waistband and work his jeans lower until they were halfway down his thighs.

For unfettered access, Heath supposed.

Hell, if the man requested that he totally strip naked, Heath would do so without hesitation. He had no qualms about anyone seeing his body. At forty-five, he worked hard to stay fit and healthy. Between the long hours he spent working, along with the time spent working out, he hadn't had much time to jump into the dating pool lately. Plus, every time he risked dipping his toes in, he regretted it.

Anyway, being buck naked on the front lawn of the resort's lodge while involved in an orgy should prove he had no shame. At least when it came to nudity and sex. He was comfortable with it for himself as well as others.

He glanced once more at Cara before fully turning his attention to the man now settled at his feet. He pulled in a deep breath and released it slowly as Dayne's warm, wet mouth encircled his cock.

Damn.

Heath forced himself to keep his eyes open and watch the man work. And work, he did. Cupping Heath's sack, Dayne kneaded it gently and took the length even deeper.

No surprise the man knew what he was doing. This was not his first cock-sucking rodeo. *Oh, hell no.* In fact, Heath had to fight the urge to thrust into Dayne's mouth, possibly making him gag.

He forced himself to allow Dayne to control the blow job.

The depth, the speed, the suction.

Today, just like on the property tour, Heath was only along for the ride, knowing at some point they'd eventually get to the final destination.

But, *fuck*, it had been a while since his cock had been in a man's mouth. The last few times had been women.

Really, he didn't have a preference if it was a man or a woman, it only mattered on *who* that person was. And their level of expertise.

Dayne drew the flat of his tongue from Heath's balls up to the tip before taking the crown into his mouth and once again sucking him deep. He then fisted the root and squeezed, his mouth encircling the tip while pumping his length.

Heath groaned. *Holy shit.* If Dayne kept doing that, this would be over before Heath was ready for it to end.

Which, if anyone cared to ask, was never.

Dayne grinned around Heath's cock when he began to tremble, fighting the difficult battle to keep his shit together.

Despite Heath unclenching his hands and grabbing onto the longer hair at the top of Dayne's head, he still let the other man keep all the control.

With Dayne's gaze no longer locked with his, Heath blew out a ragged breath and risked another glance over his shoulder at the woman leaning against the sawhorse.

Color flooded Cara's cheeks as she focused on them. He doubted it was from embarrassment this time. Her rock-hard nipples and her ragged breathing were evidence of just the opposite.

No, this was turning her on.

Seeing her reaction made him even more determined to

make time for her this week. Whether Dayne was a part of it or not.

Dayne squeezing and tugging Heath's balls brought his attention back to him. But he was quickly distracted by a hand sliding along his exposed ass and slipping between his cheeks.

Was he...

He was.

Dayne began to tease and stroke his hole, encouraging him to relax. However, what his lips and tongue were doing made complete relaxation impossible. Not if he didn't want to shoot his load down the man's throat in the next thirty seconds.

One finger wedged its way inside. Then another.

Make that about ten seconds.

Without lube, two fingers were about his limit. Luckily, Dayne didn't try to push it any further. Instead, he used those long digits to find his prostate and stroke it.

"Oh, *fuuuuck*," escaped from Heath. "That's it. Like that. Damn."

Again, no surprise this man knew what he was doing. He owned a damn sex resort, *for fuck's sake*. He probably hooked up with all kinds of people and did all kinds of things.

But the triple threat of Dayne tugging on his balls, stimulating his prostate, and sucking him like a—

He didn't even get to finish his thought before bracing for his own orgasm. "I'm going to—"

Yep, he was toast. He couldn't even finish the warning.

With a groan and Heath's fingers gripping Dayne's hair hard enough to pull his scalp, he shoved his hips forward and came.

Since Dayne had to have recognized the signs, him not pulling free in time had to be done on purpose. Letting

Heath come down his throat was hot as hell. At least for him. He wondered about Cara's opinion on what she just witnessed. Hopefully, it turned her on.

As soon as Dayne released Heath's cock, he wiped the back of his wrist over his lips and sat back on his heels. A second later, his Cheshire cat smile was blinding.

Heath was starting to believe the resort's CFO had an arrogant streak.

With an offered hand, Heath helped haul Dayne back to his feet and mumbled, "Thanks," as he yanked up his jeans and secured them.

Dayne acknowledged him with a tip of his head, but looked past him to Cara. "Did that turn you on?"

Heath glanced over because he was also very interested in her answer.

With her bottom lip pressed between her teeth, she nodded. "I wasn't sure if it would, but..." She blew out a breath between pursed lips. "I was not expecting how it would affect me."

Heath asked, "Do you want us to help you with that?"

"You don't have to go out of your way to—"

"You're not the only one suffering right now," Heath told her.

Her green eyes flicked to Dayne, then down to the erection straining against his jeans.

"I don't want to be the selfish one here," Heath told her, then smiled. "I'm willing to give back."

"How?" she asked. "Are you going to give Dayne head next?"

"No. You are."

Her eyes widened for a split second.

"And while you're doing that, I'm going to take care of you."

She once again asked, "How?"

"We can always get creative," Dayne assured her. "I'm also not going to say no if you want to give me head, but I only want you to do it if *you* want to, Cara. You don't have to—"

"I know. I know. I don't have to do anything I don't want to do." She then whispered, "I want to."

"I have an idea." Dayne strode over to the sawhorse and dragged it to the center of the unfinished room.

Heath frowned. "What are we doing with that?"

Dayne moved around to the other side of the sawhorse and began to undo his jeans. "I'll stand on this side. She can use the sawhorse to support her hips. While she sucks me, you eat her."

Damn, that was a good idea, but... "We'll need something to cushion her hips."

"The easy solution for that would be to use her jeans," Dayne said. "She'll have to take them off, anyway, if you want to bury your face in her cunt."

While some people had strong feelings over the use of the word "cunt," Heath wasn't one of them. It didn't seem to faze Cara, either. However, Heath preferred to use it only in sexual situations and not as an insult.

"You want me to strip down right here?" Cara asked.

"If you want me to eat your pussy, yes," Heath confirmed. "If you're uncomfortable with doing so, then I can make you come by doing what Dayne did to you earlier this morning."

Her eyes went round. "You noticed?"

"Of course. I enjoyed watching you two more than some of the stuff happening on the blanket."

She glanced around. "What if someone comes? The construction crew..."

"They're done for the day, Cara," Dayne assured her.

"That's why I picked one of the cabins. Even if anyone does happen to wander in here, they probably wouldn't blink an eye. Sex and nudity are an everyday occurrence around here." He smirked. "More like an every hour occurrence."

"I wish I was more comfortable with my nudity."

"Maybe by the end of the week, you will be. Think of what we're about to do as a step toward that goal," Dayne told her.

She rolled her eyes. "You think it's that simple?"

Dayne answered, "It could be if you let it. Remember, *you* are the one holding yourself back. The more you keep your mind open and are willing to change, the more you will."

Heath could see the wheels turning in her mind. "If you're not comfortable—"

"Dayne's right. I am my biggest barrier and I need to kick it down."

"You only need to kick it down one block at a time. And at your own pace," Heath reminded her. "Don't let anyone push you to do something sooner than you're ready."

Dayne shot him an annoyed look. Heath returned it. He didn't want the guy pushing Cara past her comfort zone. If they—and Cara—moved slowly, that comfort zone would expand.

"If you're fine only watching and you don't want to do it, I can. I don't mind," Heath finally told her when she still hesitated.

"I want to," she whispered. "I do. This is why I came here. For the experiences."

She toed off her shoes and made quick work of shucking her jeans and panties. Most likely before she over-thought it and backed out.

As soon as she straightened, her hands covered her pussy.

Heath warned, "Sweetheart, I'm going to be up close and personal with that sweet pussy soon. No need to hide it."

When she slowly dropped her hands, Heath took in the darker blonde curly hair at the crux of her pale, slender thighs.

"I didn't shave..." She swallowed. "I don't shave."

"Good," Heath said. "Any man who insists a woman shave bare needs to go sit the fuck down. Most of us don't give a shit whether you're shaved or not."

"Let me guess...the former tool you were with insisted you shave?" Dayne asked, once again wearing an annoyed expression.

She nodded. "Yes, and I hated it."

"Was that the only way he'd eat you out?" Dayne asked next.

"Yes."

"And how often was that?" Heath asked. If that asshole *made* her shave, then he better have made the same sort of effort when it came to putting his mouth on her pussy.

"Not often," she admitted. "I began to think something was wrong...down there." She glanced over at Heath. "So, you don't have to..."

"I'm assuming nothing is wrong and he only used it as an excuse to be selfish."

"My doctor said I was fine. No issues at all."

Jesus fucking Christ. Heath wanted one minute in a dark alley with this dude. It sounded like he was the one with the issues, not her. Selfish lovers sucked. It was probably why she was so unsure about herself.

Heath would love to see her fully naked, but he needed to have patience. Getting naked in front of two men she knew less than a whole day would be a major step for her.

"If you're still worried about anyone seeing you partially

naked," Dayne started, "you really shouldn't be, Cara. You're absolutely beautiful and the rest of the world is missing out."

"Thank you for allowing us to be the privileged ones," Heath added and moved to stand on the opposite side of the sawhorse from Dayne.

Chapter Nine

Dayne wasn't lying when he said Cara was absolutely beautiful. Her body might be on the slender side but she still had plenty of feminine curves. Heath's preference might not be a shaved pussy, but Dayne didn't care either way. Shaved, trimmed, or the Amazon jungle...he was good with it all. It was the same when it came to men.

All he cared about was proper hygiene and great sex.

He and Heath now faced each other with only the sawhorse separating them. But it shouldn't be. Cara should be bent over between them.

His cock was so damn hard right now, he was anxious to get her lips wrapped around it as soon as possible. Only, he knew there would be a delay before that happened. As soon as he pulled out his cock, questions would be forthcoming.

He was used to it by now.

Heath tapped the top of the sawhorse. "C'mere, sweetheart. Bring your jeans with you." When she did, he plucked the denim from her fingers, folded them, and placed them on top of the sawhorse to help cushion her bare hips. He pointed to the floor in front of him. "Stand here facing Dayne."

She shifted into place.

She was only naked from the waist down and Dayne preferred she lose her blouse, too, but...baby steps. After this morning and now this, she was at least headed in the right direction and not sprinting to leave the resort in her rearview mirror.

Both Heath and Cara stared at Dayne, waiting for him to pull out his cock. He unfastened his jeans and warned, "Cara, just be cautious of your teeth."

She raised one eyebrow. "Do you plan to give me a reason to bite you?"

Dayne chuckled. "Biting has nothing to do with it." He shoved his jeans and underwear off his hips and down his thighs. Far enough to completely expose his cock and balls.

And waited for their reaction.

He had one of the more common penis piercings: a frenum piercing. He didn't regret getting it one bit. That was after he had canceled his appointment twice before finally getting the balls to do it.

At least he gave his piercing some serious thought before going through with it, unlike his tattoo. But neither Cara nor Heath had said a word about that yet. They were too focused on the silver barbell inserted through the loose skin on the underside of his cock, slightly back from the frenulum and where his circumcision scar was located.

"Think of it as an enhancer. Most women either love it or don't even know it's there. You know the condom ad: *ribbed for her pleasure?* Think of my piercing in the same way."

Curiosity filled Cara's expression. "Does it do anything for you?"

"Of course. It's the second most popular penis piercing

after a Prince Albert." He thumbed the barbell. This would be a good educational moment for her. "This type increases stimulation during masturbation, penetration, or even getting head. It also can enhance sex for my partners—whether anal or vaginal—since it helps stimulate the nerves." He pretty much had that speech memorized since he had to repeat it often enough. Actually, several times a week, depending on the number of partners he had and if they knew anything about genital piercings.

His gaze sliced to Heath to see whether the piercing bothered him.

Heath did look a little green, but what he said next explained why. "One night I hooked up with a guy with a Jacob's ladder. When he pulled out his dick, I almost dropped to my knees at the sight, and not because I was eager to give him head. I pictured myself in the piercing chair having a needle stuck into my cock *that...many...times.*" He followed that with a shudder.

Dayne grimaced. "Once was enough for me. The first one was worth it, but I was done after that. I'm assuming you didn't have sex with him?"

"Not after that emotional damage."

Dayne snorted.

Heath went on to say, "Look, I don't have anything against piercings but seeing that took me the fuck out."

"Because you put yourself in his place."

"Sure as hell did." A grin appeared when Heath asked, "So, you pointed out the piercing but you're just going to ignore the tattoo?"

Dayne wished he could ignore it since he was tired of explaining it. He really should get it removed.

Cara's eyes narrowed as she tried to read the words half

hidden by the neatly manscaped hair around his cock. "What does it say?"

At least she was squinting to see his tattoo and not because he had a tiny cock.

One side of his mouth hooked upward. "Take a seat."

Her chin jerked into her neck and she straightened.

Dayne should be embarrassed but after all these years, he was over it. Now it was strictly regret. "Look, I was young and dumb. I thought it was funny at the time." He'd been a freshman in college and drunk as shit. While most tattoo artists refused to ink anyone visibly intoxicated, that one must have been an exception. Or desperate for money.

Now he wished the artist had kicked him out the door instead of ignoring how intoxicated he and his friends were at the time.

Amusement crinkled the corners of Heath's brown eyes. "And now?"

"And now that I'm more mature, I don't find it as funny." He shrugged. "But it certainly is a conversation starter."

"Sure, if you're naked," Cara pointed out.

"Isn't that the best time to have a conversation?" Dayne winked at her.

She rolled her eyes. "Unless it's with your family."

"Or your urologist," Heath added.

He was done with this conversation. He was ready for the talking to stop and the action to begin. He was afraid if they waited too long, they risked Cara backing out.

Dayne slightly jerked up his chin at Heath, who answered with a single nod.

Heath squeezed her hips. "Bend over and show me that pretty pink pussy."

As soon as Cara moved closer to the sawhorse and bent over, using it to support her hips, Dayne stepped forward and held his cock a hair's breadth away from her lips. "Take it, Cara. Open your mouth and let me in."

When her lips parted, he moved close enough to feed her his cock. The second her wet, warm mouth encircled him, he closed his eyes for a few seconds to bask in the pure pleasure.

As inexperienced as Cara seemed to be, he had no idea how many times she'd done this before. Since she didn't balk at the idea of giving him head, he assumed that she had done it at least once before.

When she began to use her mouth and hand on him, he realized she either had a good amount of experience in this department or was a natural. However, he wasn't asking that right now because it was rude to talk with a full mouth. And he certainly was filling hers.

Heath urged, "Tip up that ass more."

The second she did, Heath dropped to his knees, spread her cheeks apart and buried his face, causing her groan to vibrate around Dayne's cock.

He didn't know who was getting the better end of the deal. Him with Cara sucking his cock? Or Heath with getting the first shot at eating out her pussy.

Dayne wanted that chance in the near future.

In the meantime, he was torn. Should he watch his cock sliding in and out of Cara's full lips or Heath while he ate her pussy?

Maybe divide his time between the two?

Seeing Cara's lips stretched around him and her cheeks hollowing out easily won out. Especially since Heath's face and Cara's pussy were both hidden from his view.

If he was in Heath's shoes right now, he'd be tempted to explore her ass. However, with Cara, they might need to have an in-depth discussion on her limits first. Not everyone enjoyed ass play. Some were uneasy about it for various reasons.

It would be smart to know where Cara stood before attempting it. Most likely, she might not even know that herself. It was a damn shame she didn't have any previous partners who weren't selfish sexually and cared enough to help her discover her wants and needs.

Maybe even her darkest desires.

He'd be happy to help her figure all that out and more. In fact, he'd make it his personal mission. This week would be dedicated to Cara...

Shit. He had no idea what her last name was.

Not important right now, dummy. Her lips wrapped around his cock was priority. He'd sweat the small stuff later.

After he came. After she came.

He'd invite her to join him for dinner and, if she accepted, he could dig deeper then.

Either way, he planned to keep tabs on her. He certainly didn't want to give any other guest the opportunity to take over her sexual education. Join them, maybe. Cut him out of the picture?

The thought of someone else's cock in her mouth or pussy, or even ass, made him grit his teeth.

What the hell? He'd known her for less than a day and he was already getting possessive? That wasn't like him. Not in the least.

What he loved about owning and living on the ranch resort was the variety. Of people. Of kinks. Of everything.

If you liked it, chances were, another guest did, too.

He had no reason to get tied down to a single partner. Or even two, like his brother Dylan. But this week he'd make that exception.

It *was* only a week. Both Heath, now his partner in crime,

and Cara would be gone come Sunday and his sexcapades would return to their regularly scheduled programming.

His dad used to say, *"Make hay while the sun is shining."* The sun was blinding right now so he needed to take advantage while he could.

Another groan drew his attention back to the woman bent over the sawhorse with her bare ass in the air. Heath's face was buried to the point where Dayne could only see the top of his head. But whatever he was doing to her made Cara suck Dayne more enthusiastically.

With zero indication of any sort of jealousy, Heath seemed to be the perfect partner to join forces with him to teach Cara the ins and outs this week. Not only was he clearly attracted to the woman they currently shared, but he also had an interest in Dayne.

The attraction was mutual. In fact, if it was up to him, he'd bend Heath over the sawhorse next. If Cara got worked up simply watching Dayne give Heath head, he wondered how much she'd enjoy Dayne fucking Heath.

Without a doubt, Dayne would.

Not even seconds later, he had to jerk his cock free from her mouth when she tensed. Dayne wouldn't risk being neutered if she was about to come.

"That's it," he whispered. "Come for us, baby. Squirt all over his face. Make a mess. Show us what you're capable of when it's done right."

Stroking his cock still slick from saliva, he watched her eyes slide close, her body twitch, and finally, her head drop forward as an orgasm rushed through her.

He waited for Heath to pop his head up, but he didn't. He remained face deep in Cara's pussy. Either he was lapping up Cara's resulting arousal or he was on a mission to give her another orgasm.

Either way, it was time for Dayne to come, too.

Curling his fingers deeper into her long, blonde hair, he lifted her lax face and whispered her name. When her eyes slowly opened, they appeared unfocused.

"Stick out your tongue," he ordered.

It took her a second for his words to sink in and when they did, she did what he ordered. He then slapped his cock against her tongue a few times before once again feeding her the length.

"I'm going to fuck your face," he warned. "But I'm only going to take it as far as you can handle. If I go too far, squeeze my thigh." He would restrain himself as best as he could, but giving her a way to tap out was necessary. In this scenario, he could get rough. Some people could take it. Some couldn't. He didn't want to push his luck and make it a bad experience for her. "Okay?"

"Yes," she whispered.

She was a good sport. "Breathe through your nose as much as possible and relax your throat," he instructed. "Whatever you do, don't panic. Remember, simply squeeze my thigh, if necessary, and I'll stop immediately."

"Okay."

Dayne glanced at Heath one more time. The man *still* hadn't come up for air.

Using her hair to grip both sides of her head, Dayne once again fed her his cock. The second she began to suck, he pushed his hips forward slowly until the head of his cock bumped the back of her mouth. He quickly pulled back and did it again. This would be a good test to see if she'd gag with how deep he was taking it, especially with his piercing.

So far, so good.

He continued to thrust his hips, going a little faster now, driving his cock deep but not enough to choke her.

Still, it was time to check in with her. He paused and tapped her cheek. When she opened her eyes, she lifted them to meet his. "You okay?"

With a full mouth, she couldn't answer.

"Blink twice, if yes."

He smiled when she flashed her eyes open and closed two times. Yes, she was definitely a good sport. Despite that, he needed to drill it into his head that she wasn't his typical partner during play.

If you're tempted to push it, don't. Not today. Maybe not even this week. Even though she's not a virgin, treat her like one. Don't make her regret this.

Give her only positive experiences and maybe she'll return in the future for more education and exploration.

If she did, for Dayne it could be a win-win situation.

Chapter Ten

Being buried face first in Cara's sweet pussy and savoring the results of her orgasm, Heath couldn't see Dayne at all. But he could hear the man's words, his ragged breathing and low moans.

He had hoped to give Cara one more orgasm before Dayne had his, but he wasn't sure if he'd have enough time. The man was about to lose it and Heath didn't want to miss it.

He threw in the towel and stood, but kept a tight grip on her hips. He was tempted to pull out his cock—once again hard and throbbing—so he could fuck her while she was still bent over the sawhorse, but he needed to remember that while Cara had some experience with at least one other lover, it was nothing similar to this.

He needed to be patient. While now might not be the optimal time to fuck her, the time would come soon.

Or so he hoped.

To get his mind off sinking himself deep inside her, he

concentrated on Dayne doing exactly that but with her mouth instead.

"*Fuck.* I bet your pussy is just like your mouth. So wet, so hot. Suck it harder. Take all of me. That's it. So damn good, baby."

With the urgency that Dayne thrusted between her lips, Heath was actually surprised she hadn't tapped out yet. However, she seemed to be a real trooper and now determined to get the most out of her stay at the resort.

Dayne's muffled grunt, tight expression, and uneven pacing were all signs he was about to blow. Unlike Heath earlier, Dayne managed to warn her before his impending orgasm. He even had enough working brain cells left to say, "Squeeze my thigh if you want me to pull out and come elsewhere."

Heath carefully watched the hand planted on his leg and was surprised when she didn't squeeze. She didn't bother to take the out Dayne offered.

Yep, a real trooper.

"Get ready," Dayne warned again. With one last groan, Dayne tightened his grip on her hair, shoved his hips forward, and stilled. His eyes squeezed shut and his chest pumped rapidly when his balls emptied down Cara's throat. "That's all for you, baby."

Damn, that was hot.

He knew the euphoria Dayne was currently experiencing since he'd experienced the same earlier.

After slipping from her mouth and refastening his jeans, Dayne tucked a thumb under Cara's chin to tip up her face before brushing his knuckles down her cheek. "Thank you. That was awesome."

Heath came around and she accepted the offered hand to

help her stand. As she shook out her folded jeans, he plucked her panties off the floor and held them out to her.

A soft smile pulled at her lips. "Thank you."

He was tempted to ask her if he could keep them for himself but he couldn't imagine she'd want to go commando under her jeans. "For handing you your panties or for the orgasm?"

She might even think him wanting to keep her used panties was a little creepy. But to him, it would be a little reminder of today.

Her smile grew. "Both."

"Was that your second male-induced orgasm ever?" Heath was ready to pat himself on the back.

"It sure was."

"Was it worth it?" Despite knowing the answer before even asking it, he still wanted to hear it.

Her green eyes lit up. "Absolutely. I've had more orgasms today than during my whole relationship with my ex."

"Your boyfriend was a dick," Dayne growled.

Heath agreed. "Don't ever settle for being treated like that again. In bed, or life in general. You deserve better."

"I won't. It only took being here a little over twenty-four hours, along with those two orgasms, to decide I'm done with selfish pricks for good."

"Shit," Dayne chuckled. "That leaves me out."

"You haven't been selfish at all," she countered.

"Like you said, you've only been here a little over twenty-four hours. Give it time."

Heath huffed and shook his head. "Most self-absorbed pricks don't realize that they're self-absorbed pricks."

Dayne smirked. "I have self-awareness."

Cara cocked one blonde eyebrow. "Are you saying I should spend the rest of the week with only Heath?"

"If I'm selfish, I would never agree to that," he answered on a chuckle. "All right. Right now you're stuck with me since I have the key to the UTV." He held it up and waved it.

"I also have two feet," Cara reminded him smartly.

Dayne glanced out of the empty window frame. "Of course you do, but the sun is going down."

"Are you saying your resort isn't safe after dark?"

"Oh, it's safe. But don't forget we back up to Moshannon State Forest as well as state game land. There are plenty of wild animals out there. And I'm not talking about the two legged variety." He clawed at the air and snarled.

"Like the Big Bad Wolf?"

"Try coyotes, bears, and elk."

Cara's brow furrowed. "Elk?"

Dayne's eyebrows rose. "Ever cross a pissed-off bull elk?"

"I can't say that I have," she admitted.

"Well, I have. I rate that experience a zero out of five stars. I also had to wash my underwear immediately afterward."

Cara slapped a hand over her mouth to smother her laugh, but Heath didn't bother to hide his.

"Okay," Dayne started, "if we have everything, let's get back to the tour. We have one more quick stop before dinner."

———

As soon as Dayne parked the UTV in front of the farmhouse located between The Mane Lodge and the barn, he explained to his passengers, "The resort was originally a dairy farm where me and my siblings were raised. After my father passed and he willed us the property, one of the updates we made to the original house was adding both wings

94

so we could all live here on the property." He jerked a thumb to his left. "My brother lives on the west side with his two partners. Our younger sister lives in the main house and"—he jerked his chin toward the west side—"I occupy the east wing."

"His *two* partners?" Cara asked.

"He's in a polyamorous relationship with our Facilities Manager, Ford, and our Guest Services Manager, Erin."

"Do they share her or each other?" Heath asked him.

"Each other."

"And it works?" Cara sounded dubious.

"So far. Enough so that they're building their own home away from the main resort area so they'll have more privacy."

"Do identical twins normally have the same sexual preferences?" Heath asked.

Dayne shrugged. "Good question. Maybe Google knows."

"Should we climb out?" Heath asked next.

Dayne shook his head. "Not right now. We're cutting it close for dinner. Are you two hungry?"

Cara pressed a hand to her stomach. "Starving."

"Must've been all that activity," Heath teased her.

"Breakfast seems like a week ago," she told him.

"Then, let's get you fed," Dayne said.

After dropping them off at the lodge, he returned the UTV to the equipment shed, then hoofed it back to the lodge to join them.

As they sat eating another delicious meal from the menu his sister was responsible for, they talked about everything, and a lot about nothing. But Dayne caught himself watching both Cara and Heath eat.

The slide of the fork between their lips, the way their throats worked as they swallowed, a sweep of a tongue to catch a crumb from the corner of their mouth. The way they moaned softly when they ate something extraordinarily delicious.

Thank you, Danica!

Of course, if anyone was capable of turning dinner into a turn-on, it was him. Actually, he was pretty damn good at turning most activities into something sexual.

As soon as the table was cleared, he invited them to join him in the lounge located off the lobby for an after-dinner drink. Both agreed, even though Cara kept smothering her yawns.

After grabbing a beer for both Heath and himself, as well as a glass of red wine supplied by a local winery for Cara, they settled in some over-stuffed chairs circling a low table.

The lounge and lobby were the only two sex-free, clothing-required guest areas on the whole resort. Anywhere else on the ranch? Anything went. However, it was highly suggested to dress appropriately for outdoor activities like horseback and ATV riding, as well as hikes.

The lounge was meant for simply that...lounging. Having intimate conversations. Relaxing. Reading. Playing billiards. Enjoying a nightcap. Even though it included a bar, it was more quiet and laid back.

Dayne turned to Cara. "So, Cara, tell me... Are you glad you stayed?"

She finished taking a sip of her Cabernet Sauvignon. "Yes, thanks to you two. I'm feeling more comfortable with both this place and my sexuality."

"You've only been here a little over a day, just wait until the end of the week," Dayne promised.

"You might be sad to leave."

It sounded like Heath wasn't looking forward to checking out, either, despite this only being his first day.

She ran a finger around the rim of her wine glass. "If I am, I'll have to save up for another stay."

Dayne's eyebrows pinched together. "Save up?"

Cara nodded. "I'm a librarian. Our salary doesn't quite correlate with the small fortune we have to spend on education to become one."

Heath frowned. "Then, why did you become one?"

She shrugged and sat back, balancing her wine glass on her thigh. "My love of books and knowledge. A library is a wealth of information and the programs we offer our patrons, whether in person or online, are priceless. Well, priceless to them. There's a cost to the library, of course, but they're worth every dime. I don't think people realize how many free resources are available through their local public library."

"No doubt, because I forget about the library," Dayne admitted, tipping the pint glass full of his favorite ale to his lips.

She tipped her head toward the bookcases in one corner of the lounge. "You have a small one in here."

"We do, but I had nothing to do with it."

"I noticed it's a mix of fiction and non-fiction. I'd be happy to go through what you have and make suggestions."

"A lot of guests leave books behind after they're done reading them. They usually take a book and leave a book in exchange."

"People have time to read while they're here?"

Dayne wasn't sure if Heath's surprise was real or if he was only teasing. "I often see guests reading by the pool, in the lounge, or in the lobby."

Cara nodded. "People who love to read will find a way to do so."

"Reading was what spurred you to book your stay here, right?" Heath asked her.

"Yes," she answered. "Some of the books I read opened the door to this whole new world for me."

Heath's brow dropped low. "But were they fiction or how-tos?"

"Very spicy romance novels." She rolled her lips under. "It turned into an addiction."

"Since you only read fiction, we'll be happy to guide you through this whole new *reality*," Heath offered.

"Well, the novels piqued my interest enough for me to read some articles online, too. By the way, you're already doing a bang-up job of *guiding* me."

Dayne grinned. "We haven't even begun to *bang* yet. Speaking of...do we want to meet up later?"

"All three of us?" Cara asked.

"Sure."

"I'm game," Heath announced,

"I may need to take a quick nap first," Cara warned on another yawn.

"Where?" Heath asked Dayne.

His gaze bounced from Heath to Cara before offering, "My place?"

"But you said you live with your family. Wouldn't that be awkward?" Cara asked.

"I do, but..." Maybe he shouldn't mention that his family was used to seeing random guests coming and going out of his wing like a revolving door.

"I couldn't imagine they'd want strangers staying in the same house." Heath said.

In truth, his siblings no longer blinked an eye over seeing someone they don't know joining them at the kitchen table for breakfast.

But...he wasn't sure if he wanted them to know about him taking Cara under his wing. They might think of her as some sort of "innocent" he was trying to corrupt and give him a bunch of grief about it. He'd like to avoid that headache. "The cabins do have some perks, like an oversized bed and private hot tubs."

Though, his bed was even bigger than the ones in the cabins. When Dylan ordered a custom-made bed for his wing, Dayne added one more to the order for himself. It was worth the extra money. It could fit four adults comfortably, the beds in the cabins only fit three.

"They certainly do," Heath agreed. "I was surprised how well-equipped my cabin actually is."

"We tried to think of everything. However, we're always open to suggestions." Dayne glanced at his watch. "How about we meet at nine?"

"We never decided where," Heath said.

"Let's meet at your cabin. We can take advantage of the hot tub."

"Why don't you swing by at eight-thirty, then?" He waved a finger between him and Dayne. "The two of us should have a little discussion first."

"To devise a game plan?" Dayne was up for just about anything. That comment might mean Heath wasn't. It would be best for them to hash out the details prior to doing anything more than oral sex.

"Yes, for us, but it also couldn't hurt to have one for her."

She raised an eyebrow. "You're going to come up with a game plan for me without including me?"

"It can't hurt for us to discuss how to handle this week if you're willing to let us help you."

"I'm willing," she said quickly.

"Good." Dayne didn't even bother to fight his smile.

"But Dayne, I can see you concentrating on me since you have variety at your fingertips every day. But you, Heath"—

she shook her head—"you're only here for the week. I'm sure you didn't expect to be with not only the same person, but one without the same or more experience than you. Won't you feel shortchanged?"

"Shortchanged? Hardly. I came here not knowing what to expect. Well, except for sex and a lot of it. Please don't think this is a burden to me. It's not. The glimpses we had so far today have shown me it would be worth scratching deeper below the surface. Plus, have you looked in the mirror lately? You're absolutely stunning."

She ignored the compliment and her brow creased in concern. "I don't want either of you to feel obligated. I also don't want you to regret spending all your time with me, Heath. This is your vacation, too."

"First of all, it wouldn't be just you, Cara." Heath circled his index finger in the air. "It would be Dayne, too. I'll tell you what, why don't we agree right now that if we end up not jiving, then we go our separate ways without any hard feelings."

"That sounds like a plan," Dayne agreed.

"Okay." Cara drained her wine glass and stood. "I'll go take a quick shower and a cat nap. I'll meet you boys at Heath's cabin at nine." She paused and came back to the table. "I guess I need to know which cabin's yours so I don't knock on the wrong door and end up with some new 'guides.'"

Dayne didn't want that, either. It was one thing to share her with Heath. It would be another to lose her to other guests. His heart was set on helping her discover her sexuality.

He was damn sure Heath's was, too.

Chapter Eleven

Heath originally came to the resort to experience a variety of partners, as well as try new things, since it was the perfect location for self-discovery. If he tried something and found it wasn't for him, he could easily move on with no regrets or hard feelings.

Nobody would be hurt in that decision.

However, between Dayne's expert blow job and eating Cara's pussy to the point of orgasm, he had to reevaluate his original plan. He liked the idea of helping someone with an open mind who was also eager to learn.

Of course, every guest here most likely started their sexual journey by losing their virginity. After that, how far they took it or the direction it went depended on the individual and their willingness to attempt new things.

Vanilla sex was perfectly fine for the average relationship. But to Heath—and obviously Dayne—that flavor could get boring after a while.

Similar to ice cream, some days he craved vanilla and

other days, chocolate or strawberry. It depended on his mood and his partner, or partners, at the time.

That train of thought brought him back to a conversation they had earlier at dinner.

Cara had asked, "On the tour, you two mentioned you'll have sex with anyone you're attracted to. Does that mean you're both considered bi?"

Dayne was the first to respond. "Truthfully, I'm considered more of a pansexual, but most people are more familiar with the term bisexual."

"How about you, Heath?"

"When asked, I simply use bi, too," Heath told her. "But really, I don't care how people label me as long as they're not using a slur." He'd heard plenty of those. Even from his ex-wife after she discovered he'd been with men before. It hadn't been a secret but he also didn't think it was important to bring up those encounters. The past was just that: the past.

Apparently, that info had been important to her.

Unfortunately, she never looked at him the same again. She also never let him touch her. She turned into an ice queen and froze him out. Of course, that led to the beginning of the end for their marriage.

If he'd known that the simple fact of him being attracted to men would be a dealbreaker for her, he would've told her a lot sooner and saved himself the heartbreak and financial hit.

"When did you realize you were bi?" Dayne asked him.

"Over twenty years ago, when I was in college." Heath chuckled. "Sometimes copious amounts of alcohol brings out most unexpected results. I was at a party over at a friend's apartment and a guy cornered me, daring me to kiss him. As someone who likes a challenge, I took him up on that dare and what started as a quick, dry kiss turned into a full-blown make-out session with tongues involved. He was shocked at my enthusiasm since he hadn't been expecting me to react the way I did. Honestly, I didn't either."

Dayne's eyebrows rose. "It didn't go any further than that?"

Heath scraped a hand down his beard as he relived the memory. "Not that night. I was pretty intoxicated and wanted to wait until I was sober enough to analyze what happened and how I felt about it. But when I wanted to seek him out the next morning and kiss him again, I figured that was a pretty good sign I wasn't one-hundred-percent straight. My eyes were definitely opened that day and I'm glad they were. I didn't realize until then that I had been repressing a major part of who I was."

"How about you, Dayne? When did you figure out you were pan? Or even bi?"

"I was like this ever since I can remember. But Fisher Falls, while close knit, isn't the most accepting community. Since it's rural, this area is also like living in a bubble. A lot of people never leave and aren't exposed to anyone different from them. A lot of residents here are automatically against anything they don't understand. Worse, they don't even want to make an effort to understand. So when I was younger, to be safe, I kept my thoughts about boys to myself. Now that I've returned and am older, I really don't care what anyone thinks of me. If they don't want to accept me, that's their problem, not mine."

"But when did you actually come out?"

Dayne shrugged. "After I left Fisher Falls. However, I kept it from my parents since I wasn't sure how they'd deal with it. Then recently I saw how my mother acted when she found out about my brother being the same way."

Again, that made Heath curious about the possibility of twins leaning the same direction with their sexuality.

"Your mother was okay with it?" Cara asked.

"She didn't even blink."

Heath couldn't miss the relief in his voice. "That's great," he murmured, wishing his parents had had the same reaction.

Cara's head tipped to the side. "But your father had passed already, right?"

"Yes. But my parents thought a lot alike so my hope is he would've reacted the same. I mean, it's possible since they were both 'live and let live' type of people. I think that's part of what made our childhood so great." Dayne turned his eyes back to Heath. "How about yours?"

"Mine..." Heath took a gulp of his wine and sighed. "They're pretty conservative and, to this day, believe a person's sexual attraction is a choice. Was kissing my first guy a choice? Sure. Was how I reacted to it one? No. Maybe that's why when I met my ex-wife, I proposed to her. To smooth things over between me and my family." Deep down, the "son" hoped that seeing him married to a woman would make his parents forget he was bi. In reality, as a mature man, he should've known better.

"Did it work?"

"Well, since the marriage turned into a complete failure after she found out I was bi, I'd say no."

"You didn't tell her before?"

"I didn't think I had to share my past relationships or sexual history as long as I was faithful to her."

Apparently, he'd been mistaken.

Dayne huffed, "If I had to divulge all of my past sexual history, I might as well write a book and just hand it over."

"It sounds like it would be a tome," Cara teased. "Or saga."

Dayne winked at her. "One that would make you blush more than those erotic romances you read."

That comment made Heath believe that Dayne was kinkier than what he'd seen so far. The resort owner was probably holding back, most likely due to Cara's inexperience.

Neither wanted to overwhelm her. They didn't want to abruptly shove her into this lifestyle, but instead, give her encouragement and gentle nudges. She would either enjoy it and continue on that path, or put on the brakes and find an alternate path she'd be more comfortable with.

They needed to consider her like a rose bud. With a little time and attention, she would eventually bloom into everything she was ever meant to be when it came to sex and intimacy. As long as Cara didn't wake up from her nap and decide she made a mistake by agreeing to come to his cabin tonight. For her, being with two men might be too much, too soon.

Heath had asked Dayne to arrive early so they could figure out how to handle each other without getting into any kind of push and pull in front of Cara. While Heath was open to being either the top or bottom, not all men were. He also had no idea what Dayne's limits were when it came to kinky play.

Once Dayne arrived, they discussed all that and more.

Luckily, it turned out that Dayne had no issues with catching or pitching. That alone alleviated any second thoughts about spending the week with only him and Cara.

He loved to give and receive. Sometimes even at the same time. Since Dayne admitted he was up for anything, Heath took him at his word.

They also addressed safe words, but when it came to Cara, Heath wondered if it would even be needed. At least when it came to all three of them together.

However, he left the idea open that if Dayne wanted to

play to the point where safe words were needed, they might have to exclude her. Or at least warn her first so she could excuse herself if it became overwhelming.

Dayne agreed that giving her options would give her more power.

Heath was relieved their outlook on kinky play aligned. The most important thing this week would be safety and communication.

He'd normally include trust in that list, but he'd only known both Cara and Dayne for less than a day. It would take time to build that trust. He wasn't even sure if that could be achieved in a week.

Heath swung his gaze over at the man looking sexy as shit as he leaned against the counter in the cabin's kitchenette.

What Heath found mind-blowing was the fact two of them existed on Earth. Even though he hadn't met Dylan yet, he reminded himself not to randomly touch anyone looking exactly like Dayne without confirming his identity first.

That would not only be awkward, but also a violation of the resort's consent policy.

Heath managed to stop staring at Dayne and glanced at the time. "She'll be here soon. Do we want to wait for her in the hot tub?"

Dayne pushed off the counter and slipped his phone from his jeans. "Sure. I can send her a text telling her to find us around back."

"Hopefully, she'll see it in time and not assume we ditched her."

"We can tack a note to the door, too," Dayne suggested. "Just in case."

They ended up doing both.

"I'm assuming you didn't bring a bathing suit."

Dayne smirked. "What fun would that be?"

Heath shrugged. "It could be fun to peel you out of it."

"If you're really looking forward to that, I can wear my boxer briefs."

"Then you'll have to go home commando."

"Nothing new. And it's not like it's a long trip." Dayne's warm chuckle made Heath smile and fanned the flames of his desire for the man.

"Do you want to use the bathroom or bedroom to get undressed?"

Dayne made a face. "Not necessary. I plan on seeing every inch of you and I figured you planned the same when it came to me. No point in putting off the inevitable."

Heath agreed. "Then, let's get to it." Did he sound too eager? Because he'd been impatiently waiting to see Dayne completely naked. He was sure the rest of him was as nice as the man's cock.

A glint appeared in Dayne's eyes. "We can help each other."

"If we do, we might never make it to the hot tub."

Dayne's grin turned wicked. "That's a very good possibility." He ripped off his polo shirt and tossed it over a chair at the two-person table situated between the kitchenette and the sitting area.

"We're doing this right here, huh?" Heath was unable to tear his eyes away from the man's chest. Dayne obviously took pride in his physique.

"Unless you're shy?"

Heath scoffed, "Hardly. Did I look shy by the lake this morning?" Was that orgy really only this morning?

Grabbing a fistful of cotton at the top of his back, he tugged his T-shirt over his head. When he could see again, he noticed Dayne had paused and was checking him out.

"I can't say you did." Dayne pulled the other chair away

from the table and sat to remove his shoes and socks. When he stood back up, his hands went to his waist. "Keep up."

Heath was already barefooted and had only pulled on sweatpants after his shower. "It'll take me two seconds to get these off."

"That's two seconds too long."

Someone was as anxious as him. "You already saw my cock. Up close and personal."

"Except I didn't see your ass."

"Not true," Heath replied and shoved his sweats down his thighs until they dropped to his ankles on their own. After he stepped out of them, he waited as hazel eyes inspected every visible inch.

"Yeah, at a distance. That doesn't count." Dayne circled his finger in the air.

"I can do that, but by the time I turn back around, you better be just as naked."

Dayne smirked. "You don't have to tell me twice."

Heath slowly turned in a circle, expecting Dayne to tell him to bend over next so he could do a much more thorough inspection.

Surprisingly, he didn't. When Heath finished his rotation, Dayne had shucked his jeans and briefs, but his gaze was still glued to Heath. Those eyes held a lot of promises Heath hoped the man would keep. "I pass inspection?"

"More like surpassed it. If we didn't have to wait for Cara..."

"But we do," Heath reminded him and circled his finger in the air. "Fair is fair."

"Just ignore the crazy tattoo on my ass," Dayne warned.

He had another one? How damn drunk had he been when he went to the tattoo shop?

When Dayne turned in place with excruciating slowness,

Heath saw nothing but a very attractive ass in which he wanted to bury himself to the hilt. Over and over.

He blew out a breath. "You lied."

A low rumble of laughter slipped from Double D's co-owner. "Being a broke college kid was the only thing that saved me from making more bad decisions that night. Otherwise, I'd be living with a few more regrets." He shook his head. "C'mon. Let's get out there before she sees the note and heads around back to find us AWOL."

Dayne's cock was already hard and his balls hung heavily.

Heath couldn't wait to explore every damn inch of him. Men turned him on, of course, but something about Dayne kicked that particular desire up a notch. If he didn't get the chance to fuck him tonight, he wanted—no, *needed*—to do it soon.

"I really want to bend you over and fuck you," Dayne murmured, stroking his erection.

"Funny, I was just thinking the same thing."

Dayne cocked an eyebrow. "That you want me to fuck you?"

"No, that I want to fuck *you*."

"I don't think we have time to do either before Cara gets here."

"*If* she shows up."

"Don't jinx—" Just then, Dayne's phone dinged and he dug through his discarded clothes to find it. "She confirmed she's on her way. Let's head out." He tipped his head toward the rear of the cabin.

To access the hot tub, they had to walk through the cabin's only bedroom. On their way through it, Heath grabbed the three thick towels he had stacked on the bed earlier. He offered Dayne one to wrap around his waist, but he declined.

"Have you explored the toy closet yet?"

Heath certainly had. It was impressive. "I assume every cabin has one?"

Damn, that big bed was calling to him right now. And definitely not for sleep.

"Of course. We aim to please."

Heath yanked his gaze from the man's muscular, drool-worthy ass. "Do the rooms at the lodge have the same?"

Dayne shook his head. "Not as extensive as the ones in the cabins since the rooms are much smaller." He slapped his bare ass cheek. "Are you staring at my ass?"

"I was going to say, with some of the toys and equipment supplied, if Cara opened her closet, she might be shocked. And yes, I am."

Dayne paused with his hand on the knob to the door leading out back. "Maybe, maybe not. She read a lot of erotic fiction, remember? However, she might not be able to identify some of the stuff."

"She's a librarian. She's probably a pro at researching."

Dayne grinned. "True." He flipped a switch by the back door and headed outside.

Heath followed and saw the small white lights strung around the back deck all lit up. It gave off the perfect amount of glow to make sure they could see but not enough to prevent an intimate setting.

After they removed the tub's cover, Dayne turned on the jets and underwater lights. It made the hot tub look as inviting as his ass.

"Let's get in. If you want, we can learn more about each other until she gets here."

Heath wasn't turning that down. Especially if it included hands-on learning.

Since the deck had been built around the hot tub, no steps were needed to get in. The back deck also had a gas fire pit and quality furniture for hanging out. The set up was inviting. This trip was really turning out to be worth every penny and it was only the first day.

Heath lowered himself into chest-deep, bubbling water with a sigh. *Oh, yes.* it might have been worth the extra money to have a private hot tub. Dayne climbed in next but instead of settling across from him, he immediately climbed onto Heath's lap and straddled it.

By doing so, Dayne was playing with fire.

Heath's hands went automatically to the man's hips while Dayne's went to Heath's face, gripping it and smashing their mouths together. As Dayne's tongue explored every nook and cranny, a groan shimmied up Heath's throat. Dayne stole it and exchanged it with one of his own.

Heath's erection ended up being crushed by Dayne's weight while his poked Heath in the gut. He was tempted to wrap his hand around it but if he did, he was afraid shit would get out of hand long before Cara showed up.

They needed to keep control of both their heads and hands. At least for a few more minutes.

But, *damn*, it was hard. Of course, so were they.

Fortunately, he had thought ahead and tucked a few condoms and packets of lube between the folded towels, just in case things went far enough in the hot tub to need them. Unfortunately, knowing they were that close, his fingers were itching to reach for them.

With a tilt of his head, Dayne deepened the kiss, their tongues fighting a battle that was playful and not for control. For Heath, that was refreshing since the few men he'd been with in the past few years tended to want to dominate him, to hold all the control and leave him without any.

It was a nice change to have an equal playing field with neither having anything to prove and both only seeking or giving pleasure.

Releasing Dayne's hips, Heath curled one hand around the nape of Dayne's neck and used the other to thumb a very taut nipple as mouths and tongues playfully battled.

A loud clearing of a throat made them come up for air. "Am I interrupting?"

Heath reluctantly pulled his head back even farther because he couldn't get enough of Dayne's lips. Now that Cara had arrived, things were about to get even more heated than the hot tub water, which was pretty damn hot. "No. Perfect timing."

Dayne floated away and settled that fuckable ass in a seat. "We were only waiting on you. Get in here."

She was wearing what looked like a loose dress. Heath suggested, "You can ditch the clothes here or, if that makes you uncomfortable, take one of those towels and go inside to undress. It's up to you."

With her bottom lip caught between her teeth, she surveyed the situation for a few seconds before asking, "You're both naked, aren't you?"

"Are you saying our cocks are too small for you to see them?" Dayne teased.

She laughed softly. "I can't see much with the way the water is churning."

Heath held his breath as she began to pull the dress over her head.

Damn. He'd been wrong. She wasn't wearing a dress, but a swimsuit cover-up. As much as Heath had been looking forward to seeing her completely naked, that swimsuit...

Was totally unexpected.

Not because she wore one, but because of how damn drool-worthy it was.

Heath whistled softly. "Wow."

"Goddamn," Dayne groaned.

The bright-red one-piece with the deep plunging neckline barely kept her cleavage in check and the stretchy fabric certainly did nothing to hide her hard nipples poking through. Round cut-outs on both sides emphasized her trim waist, and the cut at the legs was high enough to expose her curvy hips.

Heath swore it was sexier than a thong bikini. Maybe because it showcased her figure. Or maybe it was simply because Cara wore it.

"Ditch the suit," Dayne told her. "You won't need that. Though, I have to say it looks damn good on you."

She tugged at one of the shoulder straps. "I bought it for this trip. I'm certainly not wearing something like this to swim laps at the Y."

"Are you comfortable in it?" Heath asked.

She pressed a hand to her stomach. "Not really. It's not a style I'd normally buy."

"Well, you should be," Heath assured her. "It's perfect for you."

"But not for us," Dayne said. "The only suit you need in this hot tub is your birthday suit."

Cara giggled softly. "Got it."

Chapter Twelve

DAYNE DROPPED his hand under the water to tug on his balls while Cara took her time peeling off her suit. He'd been looking forward to this moment since making the arrangements to meet tonight.

He felt like a voyeur as she turned away and slipped one strap and then the other off her shoulders.

"Sweetheart, do you want us to avert our eyes until you're in the water?" Heath asked.

What the hell? Dayne glared across the tub at him. Heath only gave him a shrug back.

Cara glanced over her shoulder and shook her head. "No." She pulled in a breath. "I..."

"Right. She's fine. Continue, Cara," Dayne urged.

She faced the cabin again and pushed the bathing suit down farther, over her hips and down her thighs. The red fabric dropped softly to her feet.

Her ass was close to perfection. What would make it even better was if he sank his teeth in and left his mark behind.

When she turned, she had one arm across her chest, crushing her breasts, and the other hand covered her pussy. Doing so was only putting off the inevitable.

She wouldn't have come tonight if she didn't want to be with them. Clearly, she did. She only needed a little more confidence.

They all started somewhere and with each experience, with each partner, they built on their knowledge and skills. Of course, he and Heath were here to help her do so. This week would give her a good base on which to grow.

"Sweetheart..." Heath held out a wet hand, offering to help her into the tub. She would have to choose which hand to give him if she wanted his assistance. "If you're not feeling sure about this..."

"I am. I'm just"—she shook her head—"being stupid."

"There's no reason to rush. We have all night," Heath assured her.

Dayne countered, "If we sit in this tub all night, we'll boil our future children. But I guess that's one way of preventing unwanted pregnancies."

"I'd rather rely on birth control," Heath muttered.

Dayne realized that was info they hadn't discussed yet. "Are you on birth control?"

"Yes, but I figured we'd still use..."

"Don't worry, we will," Heath assured her. "Not only for you, but for us, too."

Her eyes widened slightly. "Do you two plan on—"

"Screwing each other tonight?" Dayne finished for her. He sure as hell hoped he'd get an opportunity to fuck Heath tonight. "It depends on how the night goes. But the night's getting shorter the longer you stand there."

Heath sighed. "Don't listen to him."

"No, he's right. I came here to embrace and explore my

sexuality. I can't do that if I'm constantly worried about whether I deserve to be here."

Dayne's eyebrows shot up. "You're still worried about that?"

"Yes. It's ridiculous, I know."

"You came to a place where no one will judge you. Where no one cares how experienced you are. Where no one will force you to do anything," he reiterated.

"Then, I lucked out when I found this place."

"Well, you lucked out when you found us." *Or when I happened to run into you your first night. And again the next morning.*

"I won't argue that." She pulled in a breath and when Heath offered his hand again, she finally dropped both arms and took it.

Dayne's gaze raked down her body from head to toe. "You certainly don't look like any librarian I've ever known."

She raised one eyebrow. "Do you know many?"

One side of his mouth hiked up. "Of course not. But it sounded good." As she began to step into the tub, he yelled out, "Wait!"

She froze and so did Heath.

"I have an idea." Dayne moved closer and tapped the edge of the tub. "Sit here."

Heath shot him a glance before returning his attention to Cara and helping her sit on the tub's edge with her feet dangling in the water.

"Perfect," he whispered before nudging Heath. "Now, move out of the way." Heath put his hands up in surrender and made room for Dayne, who asked, "Are you ready for everything about to happen tonight?"

"What all is going to happen?"

"Besides what I'm about to do with you right now, we

actually didn't make a detailed plan. We'll let things develop organically. You can count on having an orgasm or two—or even a dozen—but other than that, simply assume *anything* can happen."

"Anything?"

"Does that scare you?" Dayne asked cautiously.

"No. I wouldn't have agreed to join you two tonight if I was scared. I'm only a little anxious about the unknown."

"At any time, you can tell—"

"Yes, I know. I will."

"I only ask that whatever we do, you give it a chance before you stop. If you're not comfortable, we can move on to something else. If you think of something you want to try, don't hesitate to let us know." Dayne shot a quick glance at Heath. "I think we're both willing to do whatever you ask." Hopefully that made her feel more empowered.

"What are we doing first?"

He might as well get to the point. "I'm eating your pussy until you squirt all over my face."

She sucked in a breath.

"Spread your legs."

She parted her knees but not wide enough to accommodate him, so he pushed her legs farther apart. "That's it. Keep them open like that. Give me some room to work my magic."

He glanced up at what sounded like a little snort. He made a mental note that making her laugh seemed to help her relax more.

Sex didn't have to be serious, or even hot and heavy. It could be fun and playful.

Keeping a grip on her knees, he ignored Heath hovering behind him and fully committed to the naked woman sitting in front of him. He kissed a path from her left knee to the top of her inner thigh, skipped over the temptation in front of his nose, then started again at her right knee, kissing his way back to the top again.

He put his mouth in front of her plump pussy lips and when his warm breath touched her there, she jerked.

"Do you want my mouth on you?" He touched the very tip of his tongue to the dark blonde hair above her cunt.

"*Yessss*," she breathed.

"Tell me what you want."

"You."

He tipped his eyes up to hers. "No."

"Your mouth on me."

"More."

"I want you to eat me out until I come." Her words had turned husky.

"Just once?"

"Once will be enough because I know it won't be the only time tonight."

"And you'd be correct," he said before parting her lips to expose the little pink pearl hidden there.

Her breath shuddered and she scraped her nails through his hair before curling her fingers around the back of his head. For a second, he thought she was about to shove his face between her legs.

He wouldn't have a problem with her taking the initiative. "I want to hear you tonight. Again, if you want something, tell us. If you'd like us to change the way we're doing something, tell us. Don't be shy. Let the world hear every damn cry, moan, groan, and whimper. Let yourself enjoy tonight and don't hold back."

"I won't," she whispered.

"I'll hold you to that." With that said, he dragged his tongue from her already surprisingly slick pussy up to her clit. He began by sucking gently and flicking it with his tongue. "Don't hold back," he murmured against her.

Solid heat pressed against his back.

Heath.

With his erection sandwiched between Dayne's ass cheeks, Heath alternated kissing, licking, and nipping along his damp skin. His lips traveled across his shoulder, the nape of his neck, the top of his back.

Dayne couldn't let that distract him, as much as he wanted it to. He reminded himself that he was on a mission to get Cara to come.

He made her hips jump when he scraped his teeth over her sensitive nub, but it was when he plunged his tongue in and out of her that her thighs began to tremble. Her nails dug into his scalp, encouraging him to continue.

Still pressed tightly against Dayne's back, Heath kept thrusting his cock between Dayne's ass cheeks and reached around to snag his nipples, pinching and twisting.

Ignore it. Focus.

But when Heath fisted his cock and began to stroke, Dayne could only tolerate it for so long. If Heath kept it up, he would be tempted to bend him over the edge of the tub and fuck him hard and fast.

He ripped his mouth away from Cara and forced out, "You're playing with fire."

"That's the point." The vibration of Heath's murmured words against his neck shot straight to his cock.

"The point is to make Cara come, not me. I can wait." Did he want to? No. But he was trying not to be selfish.

An idea came to him that might redirect the other man's focus. He pulled Heath's hand free from his cock, interlocking their fingers and guiding their index fingers to Cara's pussy. He pushed them inside to fuck her.

She groaned and her breathing hitched.

"Do you like that?" Heath asked.

Dayne was glad he was taking over, since right now his mouth was busy.

"*Oooh* yes."

"Cup your breasts, sweetheart," Heath encouraged. "That's it. Now twist your nipples."

Dayne plucked her clit with his lips and continued to plunge their fingers in and out of her. With her hips rocking against his mouth and their hands, she threw her head back. A loud gasp filled his ears and her thighs crushed his head. A second later, he was free again.

She was *finally* losing some of her inhibitions. Even if it was only for this moment, it was a step.

She'd better be close because he couldn't take much more. He was so damn hard, it was painful. Add in the fact that Heath was once again sucking on Dayne's neck, his moans vibrating against his skin, and Dayne's control was quickly slipping.

He desperately wanted to fuck Cara. He wanted to fuck Heath. *Hell*, if it was possible, he'd fuck both at the same time.

When her hips surged upward, Cara slammed her pussy into his face and an orgasm ripped through her. Her whimpering became a full-blown wail, filling the air around them.

Thank fuck. He couldn't be more pleased she was letting herself enjoy this. Losing herself in the moment, in her orgasm. Not worried about her reactions or anyone hearing her.

Tonight was already a win in Dayne's book when normally he never considered any night a success until he himself came. Preferably more than once.

He really appreciated the fact that, despite being a bit

reserved and feeling out of place, she was willing to join two men she only met within the last twenty-four hours. While that normally wouldn't be considered a big deal at this resort, Cara was different.

Being different was perfectly fine in Dayne's book. It kept things interesting.

When her body went limp, Dayne sat up with a grin. "I'll have to assume by your reaction that I did an okay job."

Her eyelids slowly lifted at the same time a smile crossed her face. "You did."

"Are you ready for your next one?"

"Yes." Her gaze landed on Heath.

Was she expecting tonight to be a repeat of this afternoon? Where they only ate her out and didn't get to share her in any other way?

Because that wasn't the plan. Not that they had made an official one.

"Then, let's get that done." Grabbing her hips, Dayne encouraged her to slip into the steaming water. He pressed a kiss to her lips before handing her off to Heath.

Dayne didn't want to be selfish. Well, in truth, he did. But group sex—whether a threesome or more—tended to suck when someone wasn't good at sharing.

He didn't want to be that "someone" tonight.

"Hold on." Heath moved through the water to the stack of towels he had placed on the deck next to the tub and pulled a strip of condoms from between them. "I have lube, too."

"She doesn't need lube. She's plenty wet already."

"It was meant for us."

Dayne shook his head. "Later." But he could definitely get onboard with that idea. The anticipation of fucking Heath for the first time made his cock even harder.

Heath ripped open a condom wrapper and held the latex disc out to him.

Dayne took it but shook his head. "It's for you." It went against his grain to allow Heath first shot at fucking Cara, but he wanted to be a team player.

Letting Heath have her first might give Dayne a shot at the man later.

Their gazes locked as Dayne's hand dipped under the water and he found Heath's erection. He didn't miss the flare of brown eyes as he fisted Heath's hard length a couple of times before rolling the condom down to the root.

Heath grabbed his face and kissed him long and hard. When they finally broke the kiss, Dayne pointed to one of the seats. "Now, sit."

That heat in Heath's eyes turned into a roaring fire. With a nod, he sat and offered Cara a hand.

Dayne stepped back and asked her, "Are you ready for this?"

"Yes."

"We're both going to fuck you tonight. I need to be sure that you want that."

She nodded. "I do."

Good. It would've been extremely disappointing if she didn't.

"How do you want me?"

In every way possible. "Sit on Heath's lap." When she moved to straddle his lap, Dayne added, "Facing me, so I can play with you, too."

Chapter Thirteen

Cara's blood hummed and her body vibrated. Not only from that intense orgasm, but from the anticipation of what was about to come. Or *who* was about to come.

So far, these men knew how to satisfy her and her reactions came strictly from what pleasure she received. Nothing was forced. Nothing was faked.

Even more impressive was how patient they both were. Not only with each other, but with her.

With Heath still gripping her hips and Dayne holding her hands, they helped her sit backward on Heath's lap. The way Dayne wanted.

Heath pressed his mouth to her ear. "Line me up, sweetheart. I'm about to give you your next orgasm."

The confidence oozing from these two men was certainly rubbing off on her. Of course she wasn't ready to streak naked across the three-hundred-acre property or use one of the playrooms up in Heaven with the blinds open, but they were proving to her that she *did* belong at the resort.

The guests didn't only include experts in Shibari. Or

those well-versed in BDSM. Or people seeking out certain kinks or fetishes. This resort was welcoming to everyone, whether this world was new or familiar to them.

If she had left last night, or even this morning, after being overwhelmed at the themed party, she would've missed all this. She would've missed this time with Heath and Dayne. She would've missed this eye-opening experience.

Now she was thankful she ran smack into Dayne last night.

"Cara?" Heath's voice invaded her thoughts. When she glanced back at him, he looked to be in pain.

She faced Dayne again when he asked, "Are you having second thoughts?"

Instead of answering, she reached down, found Heath's condom-covered cock, held it where it needed to be and sank down.

A groan rumbled against the back of her neck, where his face was pressed, and his fingers dug deeper into her hips. He filled her completely and his warm breath now beat heavily against her skin.

Planting her feet on the bottom of the hot tub, she used that leverage to help her rise and fall, riding his cock from root to tip.

It had been a while since she had sex with a man. Her last relationship didn't want to make her rush into another one. However, today proved one thing: her mindset had been off all along. She didn't *need* to be in a relationship to enjoy sex and intimacy. She also didn't need to care what *anyone* thought about her.

Sex wasn't dirty; it was natural. Craving time, attention, and physical touch was part of being human.

Since Dayne was on his knees before her in chest-deep swirling water, she curled her fingers around his head, then reached back to do the same with Heath. She pulled them closer together. "Kiss."

Neither hesitated to do so. Cara remained still when their lips fused together.

She didn't expect a simple kiss to be so hot. No one on the blanket this morning by the lake had kissed each other. Maybe it was because kissing seemed more intimate and personal than intercourse?

She didn't know.

But the passion these two men put into their shared kiss was palpable. This was not an act or a show for her benefit. They truly *wanted* each other. That was what made it such a turn-on. Not only for her, but for each other.

She not only got to witness their mutual unbridled desire but, even better, she was lucky enough to take part in it.

After a few more heart-pounding moments, they pulled apart, both breathing hard and staring intently into each other's eyes. She had no doubt they would do more than kiss tonight and she looked forward to it.

"Now me," she urged. Cupping Dayne's face, she pulled him to her until their mouths meshed and their tongues tangled.

No surprise he was such a good kisser. *This* was how a real kiss between lovers should be. Not dry and passionless like done with family or friends. Or asshole boyfriends.

Would these men be capable of giving her orgasms during intercourse? Would that prove she hadn't been the issue with her previous relationship, despite her ex leading her to believe it was?

He had been the one lacking in the bedroom, not her, but he didn't want to hear it.

A warm tongue drew a line down the center of her neck, reminding her that Heath had been more than patient and she needed to stop making him wait. When she began to ride his cock again, her and Dayne struggled to maintain the kiss.

She made a mental note to revisit kissing later. With both men.

"So beautiful, baby." Dayne whispered, thumbing her nipple. *Lord*, his voice was like an aphrodisiac. Between that and him playing with her breasts, he was making her melt. "*So* damn beautiful." The tip of his tongue traced the outer shell of her ear, before he sucked on her earlobe. "I can't wait to be in his place. You riding my cock. Filling you. Fucking you. Those gorgeous tits filling my palms. Your nipples hard and aching. Your pussy squeezing my cock, soaking it. Your little gasps filling my ears. I cannot fucking wait."

Holy crap. With a groan, she ground down against Heath's lap, driving him even deeper.

Dayne continued his onslaught of dirty talk, filling her head with ideas of what they *could* do and what they *would* eventually do. All she had to do was say yes.

She mourned the loss of his mouth at her ear, whispering all those dirty suggestions, but she quickly got over it when he pulled her nipple into his mouth and his hand dove down into the water and found where her and Heath were connected.

The more he played with her clit, the harder she ground down on Heath's cock. Both circling her hips and rocking back and forth.

Heath's soft groans turn into deep grunts and what sounded like whispered curses. Was her pleasure his suffering? If so, she wanted to relieve it.

Before she could do so, Dayne grabbed a handful of her hair and yanked her head back. Her gasp was caught by his kiss, but he quickly moved on, sliding his lips down her arched neck before returning to her aching nipples. He scraped his teeth over one, then the other.

Only, he did not release her hair. In fact, his grip tightened. Lightning shot through her and landed deep in her core. Her pussy pulsed around Heath's cock as he made the small thrusts upward.

"If I didn't think I'd drown, I'd suck on your clit as you ride him."

Heath's "Another time," sounded a bit strained.

"We've got all night," Dayne reminded him.

"We've got all week," Heath countered.

"True, and we should take advantage of it."

"Isn't that what we're doing?"

They're having this debate *now*?

"I have responsibilities—"

Cara cut off Dayne with, "You two only have one responsibility right now. Can we take care of that first?"

Dayne grinned and a puff of warm breath from Heath's huff hit her neck, making her shiver. She rose up on her toes and dropped her weight down on him once more.

Heath grunted from the impact. "I'm waiting on you, sweetheart."

She wanted to come. She *needed* to come. She wanted to prove to herself she *could* come with a partner. She was sure Heath would hold back his own orgasm until she obtained hers. But that didn't mean she wanted to drag it out and make him suffer needlessly. Though...was he truly suffering by waiting on her?

Dayne pinched her clit hard enough to make her jerk against Heath. "Grab her hair."

The second Dayne released it, Heath wrapped strands of her hair around his hand and pulled until her scalp stung.

It was a hurt like no other. One she didn't want to avoid but wanted more of.

Is this why people loved to be spanked or whipped? Or even bitten? Where the discomfort wasn't quite painful but more pleasurable? She might have to test that theory. Without a doubt, she could do that with the two men she already trusted, despite only knowing them for a day.

How crazy was that?

She would never be in a situation like this if she wasn't on the ranch. Wasn't in a safe place like this. Back in her hometown of Carlisle, Pennsylvania, she wouldn't be climbing naked into a hot tub with even one naked man she hardly knew, forget two.

Never before in her life did she think she'd be involved in a threesome. Even after reading the books that led to her booking this trip.

Her fantasy had always been someone else's reality.

No. Her fantasy was now *her* reality. She had the opportunity to do *everything* she ever read about. Every sexual situation she mentally plugged herself into while reading.

Dayne's thumb circled her clit and she stopped moving the second one of his long fingers once again touched where Heath and she were connected. He didn't stop there. He wedged his finger inside her, alongside Heath's cock, and stretched her even further. "There you go, baby, fuck us both at the same time. We both want to feel you come."

For a second, the extra digit was uncomfortable, but she adapted quickly and moved again, riding Heath and Dayne both at once.

"Come all over his cock, baby, let yourself go."

She did exactly as Dayne suggested. Keeping her eyes locked with his, she moved frantically, chasing after her second orgasm of the night. The only thing holding her back was herself.

Like Dayne said, she needed to let herself go. Open the floodgates. Allow herself to enjoy this moment and the ones that followed.

Dayne twisting her nipple sent her careening off the edge. Her breath caught when what felt like electrical sparks exploded through every inch of her, from her scalp to the soles of her feet. Her toes curled and her fingernails dug into Heath's thighs.

Heath muttered, "Thank fuck."

When the final wave faded away, she melted against Heath. Dayne withdrew his finger and sat back on his heels with a wicked smile curving his lips and a fire burning in his eyes.

Heath then warned, "Hang on, sweetheart." Controlling her hips, he lifted her while raising his ass off the seat, then met her on her way back down, slamming his cock home.

"He's about to come inside you."

Another mini-orgasm surprised her, especially when it was caused simply by the combination of Dayne's words and Heath's actions.

She continued to cling to Heath's thighs as he drove up and into her over and over, his teeth now planted in her shoulder. Not actually biting, but more like keeping a hold on her.

Unfortunately, his rapid thrusts were creating a tsunami. The waves of water splashed over the side and hit the deck. Dayne quickly pushed the stack of towels to safety before taking a seat across the tub with his attention back on them.

Within another minute, Heath's movements became choppy and his teeth dug deeper into her flesh. He released her hair and grabbed both of her breasts, squeezing so hard she cried out.

But as with the hair-pulling, it was more pleasure than pain and woke up every one of her nerve-endings.

She was about to beg him to do it again when he dropped back to the seat and tensed right before she heard a garbled, "I'm...coming."

A deep grunt filled the air when his throbbing cock caused her to whimper and grind against him once more.

Holy crap, she wanted to come again already.

With Heath's forehead now pressed to her shoulder, he blew out a long breath.

"My turn," Dayne announced and quickly pulled another foil pack from between the towels, ripped it open, and rolled on the condom. He wasn't waiting for Heath to do it for him because he had zero patience right now. Not after watching Cara come while riding the other man's cock. Not after watching Heath come as intensely as he did.

He'd had a lot of sex in his life. In fact, he'd lost count on how many times and with whom. If he had to guess, more than the average man. He had tried so many different things, with so many different people. None, not a damn one, had affected him as much as watching these two together.

The sex hadn't even been extreme or kinky, proving it wasn't the actual sex itself. It was the people involved.

It was the surprising, instant connection all three of them had. Normally, none was needed for Dayne to invite someone up to the playroom, or to his wing in the farmhouse, only physical attraction and the willingness to play.

Basically, all he was after was the final result. Sure, he had fun along the way and met some interesting people, but as soon as it was over, he had no problem watching whoever he'd been with walk away.

Maybe it was Cara's "innocence" that called to him. Or Heath's spectacular physique. Or the fact that he was willing to partner with Dayne this week to help Cara, despite the fact so many more women—and men—were currently on the property where he could easily "get in, get out, and get going."

But one thing was for sure: Dayne did not want Cara going anywhere else.

When Heath lifted her from his lap, Dayne guided her to the opposite side of the tub, where he once again sat in one of the molded seats.

He waited until Heath was done removing the full condom, tying it shut and setting it aside before asking. "Do you want her facing me or you?"

With a lopsided grin, Heath answered, "I can work with either."

"Do I have a say?" Cara asked.

"Of course," both men said at the same time.

"Then, I want to face Heath this time."

"Climb on board," Dayne urged, squeezing her hips gently. "I'm more than ready for you."

He didn't even wait. Once she turned away from him, he speared her with his cock. He held her down on his lap for a few moments and pulled in a breath, then met Heath's knowing eyes over Cara's shoulder.

It was at that moment he knew: if he wanted her to orgasm before he emptied his balls deep inside her, he would have to control her movements. Her bouncing enthusiastically on his lap would take him out way too quickly.

Since her past male partners never made her orgasm, he couldn't fail her. Especially after Heath succeeded.

But, *damn*, the way she squeezed his cock and mewed softly as he filled her completely...

She was flirting with disappointment without even being aware of it.

Once she began to ride his cock, Heath asked, "Can you feel his piercing?"

"No," she answered on a groan.

"Most likely due to the condom," Dayne forced out, not really in the mood for conversation. He was already clinging to the edge of sanity by a quickly fraying thread and they had only just begun.

He collared her throat with one hand and fisted her hair into a ponytail with the other since she seemed to be into the hair pulling. That also exposed the delicate nape of her neck. It was too damn tempting.

When he sank his teeth in gently, she twitched against him. That might have just backfired on him.

He shot a pleading look to Heath, who instantly recognized it and sprang into action. "What do you need to come, sweetheart? Tell us what you want."

"Keep doing what you're doing and..."

"And?" Heath prodded.

"Talk dirty to me."

Talking dirty was one of Dayne's favorite hobbies. It might distract him enough to hang on longer, or...it might sabotage him.

You cannot disappoint her.

He again caught Heath's attention and jerked up his chin in a silent plea. With a quick answering nod, Heath began to tell her everything he wanted to do to her this week, whether it was over the top or not. Dayne had to block out his gravelly voice and his words. Instead, he concentrated on controlling every move Cara made. Slowing her down or making her pause when necessary.

He had no choice but to guide her because he was having trouble controlling himself. This hadn't happened to him in a very long time. What was it about her, and maybe even Heath, that made him revert back to when he was less experienced? When he was practically in the same place Cara was experience-wise?

Ignore the way Heath's making her squirm with his touches and words. Ignore the fact her pussy's pulsing around you and her whimpers and gasps are trying to permeate your brain. Trying to wreck you.

Ignore it all.

He blew out a breath. *Damn it*, he couldn't. She was going to break him. Since running into her last night escaping the party, all he wanted was this chance.

Don't fucking blow it.

"Baby, you have to come soon." Did that sound like a whimper? He hoped not.

"I want to..."

Just do it!

"I...Oh...Just..." She wiggled as if she was trying to free herself from his tight grip.

He released her so she could do her thing and immediately clenched his teeth when she began to bounce wildly on his lap.

A muscle jumped in his cheek as he fought his own release as long as he could and began to count backwards in his head. *Ten... Nine... Eight... Seven...*

Six. Five. Four. Three. Two...

Oh, thank fuck.

Her body bowed against him as an orgasm ripped through her.

It didn't even take a fraction of a second before he gave up and gave in.

With a lift of his hips, he came.

It took him a minute for the euphoria to pass, for the world around him to return to his consciousness. Once it did, he brushed his lips over the soft skin at her nape and finally released her hair.

Heath helped her off his lap. "I don't think I've seen anything more beautiful than when you come, sweetheart."

"I have to agree," Dayne said. "But you run a close second. I can't wait to see you come when I fuck you."

Chapter Fourteen

Last night, Heath had scooped Cara up into his arms and carefully climbed out of the hot tub. He toweled her off while Dayne shut off the jets and covered the still-steaming tub.

While having sex in a hot tub wasn't new to him, having it with Cara, then watching Dayne do the same with her, quickly moved the experience up toward the top of his list as a favorite. It might be replaced quickly since they still had the rest of the week together.

As long as no issues popped up between them.

After he carried her into his cabin, Dayne followed and none of them rushed to get dressed. Instead, they all collapsed on his bed, still naked. Heath took that as a sign they weren't finished for the night. As long as Cara was willing, that was.

If she decided to leave, whether due to being too tired or because she'd had enough of them for the night, then Dayne was always welcome to stay behind, if he was interested in further action.

Because Heath sure was.

Cara's eyelids quickly turned heavy as they sprawled out over the oversized mattress. But before they had sex again—*if* they had that chance—he was curious about what she might consider her limits.

He had started with the obvious. "You like your hair being pulled."

"Apparently." She appeared surprised at that discovery herself.

"What else do you like?" He'd rather ask than assume, even though she might not know those answers yet. "Do you want us to spank you?"

She chewed on her bottom lip for a moment before answering, "I don't know."

"Did you enjoy it when you were bitten?"

"Yes."

"Would you want it done harder? Hard enough to leave an impression in your skin?"

She considered his question. "Maybe. It depends."

At least it wasn't an outright no. That might be one area they could explore further. "Tie you up?"

She hesitated.

Dayne impatiently picked up from there. "Gag you? Blindfold you? The sky's the limit, Cara. Your limits are yours and yours alone. We will respect whatever they are, so always feel free to make suggestions."

"I'm simply trying to see what you think your hard limits are at this point. That doesn't mean you can't try new things, whether you're unsure or not, and you can always change your mind." He met Dayne's eyes since the resort owner was now lying on his side with his dark blond head propped in his hand. "No matter what, we're both willing to help you figure out what you enjoy or don't. We don't expect you to like everything or even the same things we do. You have your own desires and needs. So will we. And like Dayne said, make suggestions. I can't speak for Dayne, but I'm up for almost anything."

She cupped his cheek. "I do appreciate your willingness to assist me this week." The sincerity of her words made his heart skip a beat. She glanced over at Dayne. "Both of you."

"Well, we also don't want to be selfish. We're both willing to be available to you, to help in any way, but don't take that as if you can't find others to do the same." Heath didn't want her to feel obligated to spend time with either him or Dayne. This was not an exclusive arrangement.

"Hey, speak for yourself." Dayne yawned loudly. "I think it's time to take a little nap."

A nap wasn't the only thing that happened after that. But later, when they had sex again, both he and Dayne focused on Cara once more and not each other, other than some kissing, touching, and teasing.

Heath was so ready to do more with Dayne, whether Cara was present or not.

But now that the sun had risen, he blinked up at the ceiling, realizing they had all fallen asleep in his bed. Since his limbs were entangled with a sleeping Cara's, he carefully extracted himself, doing his best not to wake her. At least until he figured out where Dayne was.

Once he was clear and on his feet, movement just outside the bedroom door caught his attention. He quickly, but quietly, yanked on a nearby pair of shorts and headed out of the bedroom.

Dayne was finishing up pulling on his clothes.

Heath closed the door behind him so they wouldn't disturb Cara. "Ditching us already?"

Wearing a crooked grin Heath found very damn sexy,

Dayne shook his head. "Not a chance. I want to go for a run before I put on my CFO hat for the day."

No wonder the man was so lean and muscular. Though, he probably did more than running. "How far do you run?"

"I try to do five at least three times a week."

"I'm the same but I do it on a treadmill in my building's gym."

"I'll be stuck using a treadmill once the weather turns to shit, but right now it's perfect running weather and the view can't be beat." Dayne's head tipped to the side. "Want to join me?"

The offer was tempting despite the fact he was still tired from the long day yesterday—between traveling and everything else—as well as last night's events.

He glanced back at the closed bedroom door. Cara could use some uninterrupted sleep. The shadows under her eyes were proof they had kept her up too late last night.

He returned his attention to the man waiting for an answer. "I'll join you."

Dayne nodded. "I need to head back to the house to change. Want to meet me by the barn?"

"Sure. I'll leave her a note so she doesn't think we've abandoned her."

———

Dayne usually didn't spend more time with a guest other than what it took to say hello or check in with them to make sure they were enjoying their stay. One exception was the time it took to eat breakfast after having sex with them all night. Dani's delicious breakfasts were the least he could do to thank any participants ending up in his bed.

He certainly didn't go for a run with any of them. Besides

providing exercise, breathing in the fresh air and taking in the mountain views, running normally helped clear his head. It was a good start to a workday before numbers filled his gray matter.

After stretching, both he and Heath took off at an easy jog to warm up. They headed down the dirt road toward his favorite trail in the state game lands butting up against the resort. Now was the time to take that trail before hunting season was in full swing.

"Have you ever run on a trail before?" Dayne asked him.

"No. I live in Hoboken where there's not a dirt trail to be seen. I've run outside a few times, but like I said, I usually use my building's gym. It's pretty badass."

"Do you live in a condo?"

"Penthouse."

Damn. "That had to set you back."

"It did. Of course, I'm still paying for it and will be for a long time, but it was worth it since it's close to the city, top restaurants, and entertainment. The beach is within driving distance. So are airports. Another positive is, it's only about a four-hour drive here. Have you always lived in this area?"

"No. Once I left for college, for obvious reasons I stayed gone until my father died and left the farm to me and my brother."

"Are you glad to be back?"

"Now I am," Dayne answered honestly. "I wouldn't have stayed if we had sold off the dairy farm instead of building the resort."

"That's right. You told us this used to be a dairy farm on our tour yesterday."

"My brother and I couldn't wait to escape. It turns out, we both prefer milking cocks over milking cows."

Heath barked out a laugh.

"Watch your step and don't roll your ankles. Keep an eye out for loose rocks and downed branches on our path," Dayne warned as they veered off into the woods onto a narrow dirt trail.

"Do you normally wear a hydration vest?" Heath asked next.

"Yep. Besides water, it's smart to carry bear spray." Dayne patted one of the pockets. "Plus, it holds my cell phone and some other stuff."

Heath's head began to swivel. "There are bears around here?"

"You haven't noticed them?"

Heath slowed down for a second and fell back. When he caught up, he was chuckling and shaking his head. "I meant the kind that walks on four legs, not two. And I've never been into bears, the two-legged kind."

Dayne shrugged as he picked up the pace a little. So far, Heath had no problem keeping up, even on uneven terrain. "Black bears will try to avoid humans, but you just never know. They also aren't the only wild animals around here, so it can't hurt to be both aware and prepared. Especially when I'm running alone."

"Good to know." A second later, Heath said, "I'm assuming you're not married. And if you are, I hope you have an open relationship with your spouse."

The subject change gave him whiplash. "No, I never married." He never had the desire to tie himself down to one person.

"Any kids?"

Was this only small talk or was Heath attempting to get to know him better? "No. I was never in a rush to settle down and become domesticated." He actually valued his freedom to do whatever he wanted, whenever he wanted. As long as it was legal, of course. "You?"

Heath shook his head as he ran by his side. The path was narrow enough that they kept bumping shoulders. They *could* run single file. In fact, if he told Heath to run in front of him, he could watch his ass bounce in those black silky running shorts he wore, or the muscles flex in his long legs.

Dayne couldn't wait for the chance to throw those legs up in the air and plunge—

"Divorced, remember?"

Dayne shook himself mentally. He needed to pay attention to obstacles on the trail. "Ah yes. You did mention an ex last night at dinner. Sorry to hear that."

"It was for the best."

"She left you?"

"Yes, and unfortunately, I'm still financially recovering. When she left, so did most of my money, including savings and investments."

"Really? And you own a penthouse in Hoboken?" How rich had he been before his divorce? Or had he been living above his means?

"Right now, the bank and I own it. The bright spot was, she quickly found her next man—who she told me is a *real* man, by the way—and the alimony payments will stop once she remarries. Hopefully soon."

"See? This is why it's easier to find someone, or some-ones, for the night, get your rocks off and then say goodbye. No heartbreak. No financial damage."

"Easy enough to do until you fall in love."

Dayne grimaced.

"You don't believe in love?"

"I do. My parents were the epitome of love. They were two halves of a whole. But that doesn't mean it's for me."

With that, Dayne sprinted up the next slight incline, leaving Heath in the dust.

He was done talking about the topic of love.

Once the terrain leveled out, Dayne kicked his pace into another gear, pushing himself. Either Heath would keep up or he wouldn't. The path was easy to follow so he knew Heath wouldn't get lost.

But after five minutes, he slowed enough to glance over his shoulder without planting himself face first in the dirt.

Heath was nowhere to be seen. *Shit.*

He reversed course and ran back down the trail. He wouldn't be a good resort host if he didn't check on Heath to make sure he didn't twist an ankle, break a leg, or have a damn heart attack.

As he rounded the second bend, he found Heath at a dead stop with one hand on his hip, leaning forward slightly and breathing hard.

Once Dayne reached him, he jogged in place so his muscles wouldn't lock up. "You okay?"

Heath nodded and his words were dispersed between pants. "I didn't realize this would be a race."

"It's not. But you're in damn good shape. I figured you could keep up."

Apparently not with the way the man was trying to catch his breath.

"Not on this terrain. Plus, I'm quickly learning that trail running is a whole other animal versus running on a treadmill. I'm using muscles I didn't even realize I had."

"That it is." Dayne glanced at the runner's watch he wore. "You want to keep going or head back?"

"Is there somewhere along this path that will give us a view of the valley?"

"Not unless you want to run up one of the mountains. We can head back and go at a slower pace."

Heath peeled off his sweat-ringed T-shirt and used it to wipe his face. "I'll pass on running up any mountains."

Dayne grinned. "I thought so."

His gaze slid over Dayne. "I guess I'll have to settle with the view I'm currently seeing."

Dayne stopped jogging in place, pulled out his water bottle and offered it to Heath. When he took it, he squirted some water into his mouth before handing it back. Dayne did the same before squeezing some over his head and shaking it like a wet dog. Water droplets flew, barely missing Heath. "Need to cool off a little?"

Before he could answer, Dayne squirted water on Heath's chest. With a mumbled curse, goosebumps appeared all over the man's damp skin.

Dayne bit one corner of his bottom lip. They were out in the woods with no one around. However, they were no longer on the ranch and instead, on state-owned land. Where anyone could come along.

But right now, the risk might be worth the reward. Last night they had concentrated on Cara. They were now in a spot where they could concentrate on each other.

He only needed Heath to be willing.

It was time to find out if he was.

Dayne closed in on Heath until the tips of their running shoes touched. The brown eyes meeting his most likely reflected what could be seen in his own: heat and anticipation.

The man sure looked willing and he did not move away.

Curling his hand around the back of Heath's neck, Dayne pulled him closer. He murmured, "I'm still thirsty," before dragging his tongue over Heath's very firm pectoral muscle to lick away a remaining bead of water.

"I'm sweaty."

What he just tasted was most likely perspiration and not water, but if Heath thought that would deter him... "A little sweat never stopped me before. I consider that a little seasoning."

Hell, he once spent a night with a guy who loved to lick armpits. The riper they were, the better.

He quickly pushed that out of his head. Despite the exercise, Heath didn't smell ripe, he smelled edible. He looked edible, too.

"So, since we're alone now...out here with no one around..." Dayne started.

"Except squirrels and chipmunks and possibly bears."

"Are you interested in working up a sweat caused by something other than running?"

Heath glanced around. "Out here?"

Dayne didn't bother to answer the obvious, but instead, captured Heath's mouth. Being "out here" must not be a problem, because the man returned the kiss with a lot more enthusiasm than Dayne expected.

That was a good sign.

Since Heath was only about an inch taller than Dayne's six-foot, they were well matched in size. Neither had to accommodate the other by bending their knees or rising up on their toes.

When Dayne swept his tongue through Heath's mouth, the other man sucked on it before digging his fingers into the back of Dayne's head and deepening kiss even more.

Heath's rock-hard cock was another good sign that he was willing to make the most of them being out in the woods. Alone. It didn't take long for them both to be out of breath, no longer from exercise, but the fact they both wanted each other and had been waiting for that opportunity.

If all went well, the wait would soon be over.

Heath released his head so he could grasp Dayne's ass and grind their erections together.

Damn.

Driving his hand between their sandwiched bodies, Dayne stroked Heath's erection over his running shorts.

It wasn't enough. He needed so much more.

He went for it by plunging his hand beneath the silky fabric and encircling his hot cock.

As soon as Dayne began to pump his fist, Heath groaned and jerked his hips away, freeing himself. "*Ah*, for fuck's sake. It'll suck if I come in my shorts."

Dayne was worried about that, too. "I second that." One accident this week was more than enough. He grabbed Heath's arm and tugged. "Let's go find a more private spot."

Chapter Fifteen

"WE DON'T HAVE A CONDOM. Or lube."

"One thing I quickly learned from running the resort and being *actively* involved is, sex can happen at any time, anywhere. Always be prepared." Dayne patted his vest. "Like the bear spray."

"Well, thank fuck you're a Boy Scout," Heath teased.

Dayne dodged branches and skirted ankle-breaking obstacles as they ducked through the woods. "More like a horny man with plenty of guests at his fingertips every week."

"Lucky you."

He sure was. "I have a personal playground that also pays my bills. I consider it a win-win situation."

"I take it that you're like a rolling stone who likes to fuck anyone catching your eye, but your interest in Cara isn't quite the same as it's been with other guests." That was a clear deduction and certainly not a question.

The man wasn't dumb. Dayne preferred a little intelligence along with his partner, or partners, of the moment.

"No." Heath was right. For him, Cara certainly wasn't all the rest.

If he was being honest with himself, he wasn't sure why. He tucked that tidbit away and would investigate it at a later time. He'd only known her for a little over a day. Heath even less.

"I bet a guest never ends up in your sights more than once," Heath continued.

"Not usually. But it's not only Cara who's caught my interest."

"Apparently, since you're dragging me through the woods."

Dayne immediately released Heath's arm. "If you don't—"

With a crooked grin, Heath snagged Dayne's arm and began to pull him in the direction Dayne had been heading. "I didn't say all that. Where are we going?"

"Luckily, this area was a playground for me and my brother growing up, so I know it like the back of my hand."

"Lead the way." When Heath released him, his fingers trailed slowly over Dayne's skin. Now *he* was the one with goosebumps.

Damn. He'd been thinking about fucking Heath ever since yesterday when he came across the man on the blanket by the lake.

Was it finally going to happen? Or would they disagree on who was doing who, despite them both saying last night that they were flexible?

Another few hundred yards brought them to a small clearing surrounded by tall pine trees and several huge, gray stones jutting up from the ground.

"Dylan and I used to play king of the hill here."

Heath's lips flattened out. "I'd prefer not to picture you as a young boy right now, thank you very much."

Dayne laughed. "Sorry. I just find it ironic that I'm back here as an adult ready to cross swords again." He unhooked his vest and set it aside on a nearby boulder.

When he turned, he took in the man he wanted so badly that he could taste it. The intensity of that need threw him off kilter. What the hell was going on with him?

Was it because Dayne would've normally hooked up with Heath and moved on already? Was the wait for what he wanted screwing with his head?

It had to be.

He grabbed the sweaty T-shirt hanging around Heath's neck and tossed it on top of his discarded vest. But as soon as he reached for his own shirt, Heath stopped him and gave him a sharp yank. Their bodies crashed together at the same time as their mouths.

The man was a great kisser and that alone was a turn-on. Kissing wasn't something he did on a regular basis, but for some reason, Dayne couldn't get enough of Heath.

The taste. The feel. How he looked. His easy-going nature.

Dayne was afraid that if he was into relationships, he'd want to explore this unexpected connection a lot deeper.

But he wasn't. And he had no plan on being tied to anyone.

As they continued to kiss, lick, and nip each other, fingers skimmed and brushed the same way their mouths did.

A scramble to shove down each other's shorts proved that both of them were getting impatient. When Dayne shifted his hips, his shorts finished falling to his feet. Seconds later, Heath's shorts did the same.

His hard cock was aching and Heath had to be suffering

from the same ailment, evident by his frantic touches and kisses, moans and grunts.

They needed to move this along before they jerked each other off in a rush for a release. While that end result might be okay, it wasn't how Dayne wanted to spend his time in this hidden spot alone with Heath. This was an opportunity he didn't want to pass up.

Heath tugged on Dayne's bottom lip with his teeth before slowly releasing it. "No head today."

Brown eyes met his. Since it wasn't a question, Dayne assumed Heath wanted the same as he did and that wasn't a blow job. Not right now. "No. I've been wanting to do this since I saw your performance on the blanket yesterday."

"You said that."

"Worth repeating."

"When I watched you and Cara," Heath began, "I honestly never thought I'd get this chance. At the time, I had no way of knowing you were bi. Or that we'd end up naked in the woods together."

"When you say 'this chance,' what do you mean exactly? I really want to fuck you." Dayne was stating the obvious, but they needed to figure out logistics before they went any further.

"And I want to fuck you," Heath countered with a furrowed brow.

Shit. Would this end up being a problem? "Is this going to be a fight over which one of us does the other first?"

"Not from me. I'm willing to take my turn as long as you are."

That was a relief.

Heath's eyebrows pinched together. "Do you have more than one condom?"

Dayne went over to his discarded vest and pulled out

two, along with four small packets of lube. He tossed one foil package at Heath, who caught it.

Heath flipped it over and over within his fingers. "I should get the first shot since I'm a guest, right?"

"I don't remember that being one of the resort's policies," Dayne answered dryly. "We could play rock-paper-scissors to figure it out."

Heath snorted. "I'm game if you are."

Jesus. Here they were, two grown men naked in the middle of the woods playing rock, paper, scissors to see who got the first shot at fucking the other.

After three rounds, they finally had a winner.

"You won fair and square." Luckily, Heath didn't sound at all disappointed.

"I'm wondering if we should add this game to the resort's events..."

Another snort exploded from Heath and he set aside the condom he was holding. "You could have a weekly game night. Add in strip poker and naked Twister."

"Now that's an idea!"

Heath shook his head. "I was kidding."

"I know, but offering a game night for the guests might be fun. Okay, do we really want to have a conversation right now? We're both naked. We're both hard." Obviously.

Heath raked his gaze over Dayne, making his cock twitch. "You look great in clothes, but I have to say, I prefer you naked and hard. Despite that piercing and ridiculous tattoo."

"Ditto. On the naked and hard part, anyway." Dayne pointed toward a large rock that came up to about their waists. "Plant your hands on that and bend over."

With his teeth, he ripped open one of the lube packets and approached, taking in every inch of Heath he could see in the bent over position. "Has it been a while?"

Heath glanced over his shoulder, his eyes flicking from Dayne's face to the open pack of lube in his hand. "Depends what you consider a while. For you, it might be a few days."

That was true. "How long has it been since you've caught instead of batted?"

"Since I haven't had a chance to date much lately, that answer is, unfortunately, a while."

"That means I might be busting your ass, too. We'll go slow."

"And you?"

"You don't need to go slow with me," Dayne flat out told him.

"Why am I not surprised?" Amusement colored Heath's tone.

Dayne shrugged and gave him his most innocent look.

Heath snort-laughed and, with a shake of his head, turned back to face the rock and adjusted his stance and hand placement.

Dayne ripped open the condom, rolled it on, generously covered himself with lube, then stepped up behind Heath. He spread the man's cheeks apart, dripped more lube on Heath's exposed hole and squeezed the rest on two of his own fingers.

"Ready?" Dayne whispered. He sure as hell was.

"I think you'll need more lube."

"I plan on it, but I want to work some inside first. I know what I'm doing, so let me do it. I want this to be good for both of us." If it was, he hoped for a repeat performance. With Cara involved next time.

He inserted his slick middle finger into Heath and plunged it in and out a few times before adding his index finger. He then scissored them to see how tight Heath might be.

Heath didn't tense at all, but instead rocked his hips back and forth while releasing a groaned, "Fuck me."

Dayne would be happy to oblige. He slipped his fingers free and pressed the blunt end of his latex-covered cock to Heath's opening. He should ask him again if he was ready, but Heath clearly knew what came next in this scenario.

He managed to unlock his jaws enough to say, "Tell me if I need to stop or slow down."

"I will. Now fuck me."

"Ask and you shall receive." Dayne did just that.

Within a few strokes, his heart was pumping right out of his chest. His breathing became uneven and Heath was pulsing around his cock.

"More," Heath moaned.

Dayne had been trying to avoid grabbing Heath's hips due to his hand being covered with lube, but...

Screw it.

It was time to give the man what he was asking for.

Holding onto Heath's hips, Dayne thrust harder and as deep as he could, but also tried to keep his wits about him.

Since he loved fucking both women and men and never would want to choose, he now understood why his brother was so happy with having both Ford and Erin as his life partners. He had the best of both worlds.

That would also be the only way Dayne would ever settle down. Not that he was contemplating that at all. No way. He had years ahead of him to take advantage of what the resort had to offer. He wanted to make the most of it.

His hips began to piston, plunging his cock into Heath before pulling out far enough that he could almost see the crown.

He was doing his best to keep himself together, but he was slowly losing the battle.

No. Not slowly. He was barreling down the track and ready to fly off the rails.

He blew out a breath. He figured Heath wouldn't care how quickly he came, but Dayne did.

This was too damn good to cut it short.

When Heath began to slam back into him, Dayne teetered to the point he might not be able to recover.

He counted to ten in his head. He crushed his own lip between his teeth. He thought about the boring paperwork waiting for him on his desk.

Fuck. None of that helped.

He finally had no choice but to let go. He pushed forward and stilled, his balls emptying deep inside Heath.

He couldn't hear anything over the ringing in his ears or his own breath pumping in and out of his lungs, so he sure hoped Heath wasn't saying anything important.

As soon as he was back on solid ground, he opened his eyes and stared at the muscular back of the man he just fucked. He dropped his forehead against it and took a minute to compose himself.

Heath patiently waited for Dayne to pull out before straightening. Dayne yanked off the condom, tied it off, and put it aside. He was raised to carry out anything carried into the woods. Like a condom full of cum.

"You okay?" Dayne asked.

Heath turned to face him. "Yeah. I can pretty much figure out you are, too."

One side of Dayne's mouth pulled up. "Damn right I am. Thank you."

"Don't thank me. I get my turn next."

That he did.

"By the way, I couldn't tell you're pierced."

"Pity. I guess we'd have to go bareback for that experience."

Heath made a sound, then grabbed the condom that had been set aside, along with the last two lube packets.

As Dayne began to move into position, Heath stopped him with a shake of his head. "No. Not like that."

Dayne raised his eyebrows and watched Heath quickly encase his cock in latex before leaning his bare ass back against the rock.

One thing was for certain, Dayne would never look at that boulder the same again.

A lube packet appeared in front of his face. "Do you want to lube yourself up?"

"No, you do it."

Heath ripped open the first packet and did exactly what Dayne had done: spread the lube all over his cock before taking care of Dayne.

At the angle Heath perched against the rock, Dayne couldn't quite sit on his lap, but he could easily back into him. "You don't need to ask if I'm—"

Ready.

Instead of finishing, he grunted as Heath rammed his cock into him, emptying Dayne's lungs of the breath he'd been holding.

Damn, the man filled him up completely. Heath wasn't huge but he was thicker than most girth-wise. Luckily, Dayne had no problem handling it. He actually welcomed the fullness.

Heath made short, quick thrusts, spearing his cock inside him while pushing and pulling Dayne's hips into him.

This man was in no way holding back. He had probably been waiting for this moment as much as Dayne had been waiting to fuck him.

He closed his eyes and listened to Heath's heavy breathing and the rhythmic slap of their bare, heated skin, as well as the occasional grunt.

If he hadn't just emptied his balls, he'd be rock hard right now. Even so, every stroke that dragged Heath's cock over Dayne's prostate still managed to milk the little fluid that remained.

Every once in a while, Dayne could climax without ejaculating. And today, Heath somehow managed to pull that off. He had to lock his knees to stay on his feet.

Without a pause in the action, Heath asked, "Did you just come again?"

"*Mmm hmm,*" was all Dayne could manage.

"Holy shit," he whispered.

Dayne gathered his brain cells so he could form actual words and not sound like a blubbering idiot. "It happens sometimes if I'm drained dry but I'm not done playing."

The first time, he had no idea it was possible. After that, he did some research to see if it was normal.

"I'm..."

Heath didn't have to say anymore. Dayne could finish that sentence. Heath had reached his tipping point.

Seconds later, with a low roar, his hips slammed into Dayne's ass one last time before he collapsed backward against the rock, taking Dayne with him.

They both stayed like that for a few moments.

He wasn't sure if Heath was contemplating life right now, but Dayne could honestly say: *life was good.*

———

HEATH GLANCED over at Dayne to see that he had paused

while getting dressed to close his eyes and turn his face up to the warm morning sun breaking through the trees.

The sweat from their cardio workout—the run and the sex—had now dried on their skins and both were in desperate need of a shower.

Hot water on his overworked muscles would feel good.

Heath pulled his still-damp running shorts up his legs. "We should get back soon. Cara might be wondering if we've been eaten by those bears."

As much as he wanted to get back to her, he also hated the idea of ending this quiet moment out in the woods.

Dayne's eyes slowly opened and his chest expanded as he pulled in a deep breath. "I can't even begin to tell you how many hours I spent on this mountain as a kid. Back when summer seemed endless and my biggest worry was how to get out of doing farm chores."

Dayne laughed softly at some distant memory and the softness in his features stirred something in Heath that was better left alone.

"Once those chores were done, my brother and I would hike through these woods like we were out to discover a new world. Even in our teens, we'd come up here to talk about our dreams, what we'd do when we finally escaped Fisher Falls. Not once, in all those years, did we ever think of this place as our forever home. We always knew we were destined for something bigger than this little town could provide."

Heath couldn't help but laugh at the irony of the *something bigger* they ended up bringing to the very town they had been determined to escape, which seemed to drag Dayne back to the present with a longing smile.

"But you're right, we should get back to Cara, and I need to get my work done so I can spend time with you two later."

"Is this weird for you?" Heath asked, wondering if what

they'd shared had prompted the man's walk down memory lane.

Dayne's hazel eyes met Heath's, but his expression was suspiciously blank. "What?"

Heath perched his ass against the boulder to pull on his socks and sneakers. "Spending a few days with the same people."

Dayne finished pulling on his own socks and running sneakers, tugged his T-shirt over his head, then shrugged on his hydration vest.

That vest had come in handy this morning for sure.

After Dayne was done, he finally answered, "Yes."

"But you plan to do it anyway," Heath concluded.

"It's less than a week. I'll survive."

Dayne's tone said otherwise.

Heath chuckled softly. "You don't sound so sure."

"Honestly, my brain is screaming that this is a trap."

Heath's laughter quickly dissipated. "What do you mean?" He certainly wasn't out to trap anyone and didn't want to be trapped himself.

"What we did up here took me back to my childhood." Dayne shook his head. "Not the sex, of course, but spending time out here in these woods. For a little while this morning, it lifted the weight of my responsibilities off my shoulders and I felt...carefree. Even content. I don't know how to explain why that feels...dangerous."

Or he simply didn't want to.

Heath's brain might not be screaming the same, but he understood where the man was coming from. "Is it because this feels like more than simply sex?"

"What do you mean?" Did the blood drain from Dayne's face?

Heath explained. "I came here not expecting to make any

connections. Have fun? Yes. Relax? Yes. Spend my stay with the same two people? No."

Dayne's brow furrowed. "You're not obligated."

"Of course I'm not. And neither are you. But I'd regret not exploring whatever drew the three of us together."

"Attraction and sex. Simple."

"If only it was," Heath countered.

"You think it's more?"

"I don't know. I mean, I saw you two yesterday, and despite being very occupied, I had a difficult time keeping my focus on what was happening on the blanket and off of you two. There was something about Cara's reaction to what you were doing to her..." Heath shook his head. "It was real and pure. Maybe it's because she's not jaded and is looking at what goes on here with fresh eyes."

"Funny, that's what drew me to her, too. And that's usually not the type of person I seek out."

"Me, neither."

"C'mon let's go check on Cara. I can take her to breakfast while you fulfill your obligations." Heath hooked an arm around Dayne's neck as if they'd known each other for more than a day.

"Adulting. I give it zero out of ten stars," Dayne muttered as they headed back to the trail.

"But look what you have achieved because of all of that adulting. A successful business that caters to people like us."

"People like us," Dayne repeated in a murmur. "What some might consider degenerates."

"I can't imagine you care about what people think."

Dayne shook his head. "I gave up on that a long time ago. Twisting myself into a pretzel in an attempt fit into societal norms got old quickly. How about you?"

"I decided after I married to appease my parents, that I

needed to be true to myself if I was ever going to be happy again."

Dayne playfully knocked his shoulder into Heath's. "And look at you now, having sex with strangers on a blanket in front of an audience one day and the next, sex in the woods with a man you've only known for a short time."

That was the kicker. It felt like he'd known both Cara and Dayne for so much longer than that. They had slipped into a fast and easy companionship.

Would that continue? Heath wasn't sure, but he sure was willing to find out.

Chapter Sixteen

"God, he's beautiful." Cara's whispered words escaped her lips before she could stop them.

Was it rude to point that out while standing between two other men? Especially two she'd been intimate with many, many times?

"He is."

She glanced up to see Dayne's attention also glued to the man on the other side of the glass and not on either of the two women inside the playroom who she expected him to be appreciating.

"I agree," Heath murmured with his hand splayed along the small of her back, right below Dayne's arm, where it was curled around her waist and holding her close.

Both men seemed to be staking their claim. She wasn't sure if it was for her benefit or to make the other guests gathered in front of the window aware she wasn't available to them.

The idea of being "claimed" was quickly growing on her.

"If he turns you on, it's perfectly acceptable to participate from this side of the glass," Dayne whispered.

"How?"

"You could masturbate. Just like others are doing."

Her mouth gaped open as she glanced up and down the hallway. Not only were they not the only people standing in front of room two, but Heaven was packed and some guests were playing with each other or themselves right in the hallway. All of the playrooms were currently booked and almost half had the blinds open, inviting others to watch.

This wasn't the first time the three of them had visited Heaven as a trio this week. In fact, they used room number one, the medical-themed room, only two nights ago. With the blinds closed, of course. They had checked with her first to see if she'd be comfortable with keeping them open, and since she didn't know what either of them had planned, she decided to go for privacy.

That night, they had used various equipment, but they kept the play tame when it came to her. On the other hand, the men had pulled out all the stops with each other.

She had received quite an eye-opening education. They did stuff she never read about in any of the addicting erotic stories or what she'd researched to appease her curiosity. Mostly because she hadn't known they existed.

Before this week, anyway.

At first, some of the "medical" equipment they used on each other made her cringe. Then she saw how much they both got off on it, whether they were playing "patient" or "doctor."

The craziest "toy" Dayne pulled out of the room's cabinet was a thin medical-grade, stainless-steel rod. Dayne assured them he had experience with it from not only using it on others, but also having it used on him.

Heath was a little unsure about having a metal object inserted into his urethra, especially after Dayne warned it could cause damage if not done properly. However, once he agreed, he didn't regret it one bit.

Dayne explained that the goal during *sounding* was to stimulate the sensitive nerves in the urethra that could bring about pleasurable, intense sensations.

While Heath did enjoy it, he admitted he wasn't sure if he ever wanted to risk using that toy again. Cara didn't blame him. Watching Dayne insert it made her almost drop to her knees.

But for the rest of the time, she mostly watched the men play with each other until they cried out for mercy and relief.

Honestly, she had never been more turned on. The best part was when they put her on the exam table, placed her feet in the stirrups, and Heath sat on a rolling stool between her legs to eat her out. She was afraid she'd now have to blank out that experience every time she went for her annual gynecological exam in the future.

Afterward, they both took turns fucking her, leaving her boneless, well satisfied, and ready for a long nap.

Tonight, they stood in front of room number two, in which the theme was "entertainment." Of course, she recognized a lot of what that mirrored playroom included, like the stripper pole in the center and the sex swing in one corner, but what caught her interest during Dayne's tour last Monday was the Sybian saddle machine. Once Dayne took the time to explain the potential of it, along with what attachments were available, she decided she wanted to give it a shot. Unfortunately, the room was booked solid all night and both she and Heath were checking out in the morning.

This was their last night to be together.

She'd be sad for them to go their separate ways. She

would love to return in the future, but she'd have to save up first. Of course, Dayne would remain here, Heath would drive east to Hoboken, and she would return home to Carlisle and her quiet life as a librarian. After spending a week at the resort, she might find her normal everyday life boring.

Heath and Dayne had given her their time and attention, and went out of their way to make her feel comfortable, no matter what was going on, when neither had to do so. Plenty of other guests on the property—both women and men—could've taken her place. Veterans of all kinds of kinky and sexy play.

Unlike her.

She really appreciated their selfless dedication to her this week. In turn, she had taken their "education" seriously and absorbed as much as possible.

While she'd be sad to check out come morning, the only bright spot would be being back home with her Boston Terrier. She had definitely missed her beloved Buttons.

Hearing, "No one will care if you do," pulled her out of her thoughts and back to the action inside the room.

What? Oh, that was right. Dayne suggested she masturbate right there in the hallway, amongst a crowd of people.

Her pulsed raced at the thought. Since tonight was her last night, she *should* push her limits, which wasn't anywhere near the men's.

"Or we could assist you, like I did that first morning," Dayne reminded her, his voice low and husky.

"Or you could let what you're watching make you soaked and we can help you with that little problem later," Heath suggested, this thumb brushing back and forth across the small of her back.

She glanced over her shoulder at the room behind them with the Sybian. She should've tried that earlier in the week when the resort wasn't so busy. Dayne mentioned the guest numbers had swelled on Friday night and the resort was booked solid for the weekend.

That was great for Dayne and his siblings, but not for her in this moment.

Next time, she told herself. If there was a next time. Only, if there was, would Dayne still be interested in spending time with her? Plus, Heath wouldn't be here.

If she returned, she might be on her own.

What a depressing thought.

Especially since she now trusted them both completely. They did everything in their power to make her feel comfortable as well as special and neither had pressured her to push herself beyond her limits. Even so, her boundaries had expanded every day and night she spent with them.

But still, she had so much more to figure out, more to explore. Despite that, she wasn't sure she wanted to do any of these things with anyone else.

It was a dilemma. One she'd think about later. Right now, she needed to take advantage of what little time she had left. Their last night needed to be memorable.

"If you don't want to do that, I have another idea," Dayne said. "I have a stash of items at my place for sensation play. Are you interested?"

Sensation play?

"I'm game," Heath answered quickly.

Dayne chuckled. "I was asking Cara."

Heath tipped his face down to hers, his brown eyes holding a glint. "Say yes to this, sweetheart. I promise you'll enjoy it."

She glanced at Dayne again. "Will your family care?"

His mouth hung open for a few seconds before snapping shut. "Not at all."

"They're probably used to it, right?" Heath asked.

Dayne simply shrugged.

Did he not want to admit that his wing in the family residence saw a lot of action? It wouldn't surprise Cara because, over the last week, he mentioned several times that the resort was his personal playground. That meant he took advantage of everything it had to offer.

"I don't want to masturbate here. I can do that at home when I'm by myself. I want to make our last night together memorable. I have no idea what sensation play involves but I'm game, too."

Heath dropped his hand and took a step back. "I like the sound of that."

Dayne slid his arm from her waist up to her shoulders, giving them a squeeze. "Me, too. And I agree that we should make the most of our last night together. Let's go."

———

Dayne made her wait outside of his bedroom while he and Heath prepared a few things first.

While they did that, she heard Heath say, "The fridge in my cabin is bigger. Is that all you have? No kitchenette or anything?"

Cara was also surprised to see only a microwave and mini-fridge tucked in a corner of the large, open living space.

"My siblings and I share a common kitchen in the main house."

His wing of the house was really nice and spacious, but she could definitely tell a bachelor lived in it. The furniture was quality, but basic, and the decor sparse. However, the sepia-colored framed photos decorating the walls were stunning. She assumed most, if not all, were taken in the area or on the property since they included artistic shots of the surrounding mountains as well as livestock.

One photo depicting a cow acting spunky and playfully kicking up her hoofs caught her attention. During their tour, Dayne had explained that this property used to be a dairy farm, so she could only imagine this was one from his father's former herd.

Whoever the photographer had been, they had a very good eye.

When the bedroom door opened, Dayne peeked his head out and crooked a finger at her.

Once she stepped into his bedroom, Cara took it all in. Soft music filled her ears, the vanilla scent from a burning candle filled her nostrils, and the lights were dimmed low. "This almost feels like a spa."

One wall in his expansive bedroom was lined with what appeared to be built-in cabinets or closets. His oversized bed frame had heavy-duty posts in each corner. Screwed into those wood posts, and in plain view, were eyebolts that appeared utilitarian and not decorative. In the center of the large room, where the ceiling was reinforced, several more eyebolts could be seen.

She'd been wrong. His bedroom was nothing like a spa and more like a torture chamber. Or more like a pleasure chamber, since Dayne didn't seem to be a sadist.

Dayne stopped in front of an open cabinet and swept his arm toward it. "These are only some of my toys." The pride for his extensive collection was palpable. He pulled out a black, silky blindfold and held it up. "We'll blindfold you. Not knowing what comes next will enhance your sensory experience. However, depending on what we use, we might warn you about some items first."

She hoped so, because the thought of being blindfolded

made her already pounding heart tumble in her chest. The unknown was both exciting and terrifying at the same time. But then, most of the new things she tried this week had been that way. Both Dayne and Heath seemed to have a knack for knowing what her limits might be, even when she didn't, and made her feel at ease.

"By losing your sense of sight, your other senses—taste, touch, smell, and hearing—will be enhanced," Dayne explained, like she didn't know those facts already.

Even so, it was nice that both Heath and Dayne made sure she always knew what was going on. For the most part, anyway.

Heath gave her a wink and a sexy grin. "All senses except your sight will be in play."

"If anything we do gets to be too much, don't hesitate to use the safe word we gave you. Say it and we'll stop immediately."

A couple days in, they discussed safe words and why they were necessary for more extreme play. Not once had she had to use it so far.

Her breath rushed from her. Did they think they might push her to the point she'd need it tonight? Of possibly having to tell them to stop what they were doing with a ridiculous, random word like *cabbage?*

At first, she couldn't even repeat it without giggling.

Dayne handed the blindfold to Heath, then pulled out two brown leather cuffs with some sort of wool lining.

Holy crap, they planned to restrain her. She had wanted tonight to be memorable, but...

Was she ready for this?

She *did* trust them to not do anything she couldn't handle, and they hadn't broken that trust yet.

Next, Dayne pulled a step stool out of another closet and

placed it under the area with the reinforced ceiling. He hooked a vinyl-coated wire cable to one of the eyebolts in the ceiling before setting the step stool out of the way.

When the men then turned toward her, a shiver skittered down her spine at what she saw in their eyes.

They appeared starved.

"Time to get you naked." Heath's husky voice made her nipples agree with him.

They weren't the only hard body parts in that room. She could see the bulge in Heath's jeans and a glance at Dayne proved he was raring to go, too.

Not only did her nipples ache, her pussy twinged and her blood rushed through her veins.

Every inch of her body hummed in anticipation as the men circled her, working together to rid her of her shirt, remove her shoes, slide her pants down, unhook her bra, and dispose of her panties. Until, finally, she stood completely bare in front of them.

Her confidence with being naked in front of others had also grown exponentially this week.

"Hands," was all Dayne had to say.

With her pulse pounding in her throat, she held out her hands. Dayne and Heath buckled a lined cuff on each of her wrists. This was the first time in her life she'd ever been restrained. She'd soon find out if she'd love it or hate it.

But if it wasn't for Dayne and Heath, she'd never know. Without them, she'd never have had any kind of experience like this. And at this point, she couldn't imagine doing this with anyone else.

Dayne attached the carabiner dangling from the cable to the cuffs, then drew her arms up until they were stretched over her head, but left her feet firmly planted on the floor.

That was reassuring. She wasn't sure if she wanted to be hung from the ceiling like a side of beef.

Once she was secured, Dayne whispered, "Damn, that's a sight. Beautiful, Cara. I think we're the luckiest men on this resort right now." His hand stroked her back, then squeezed her ass cheek.

At the same time Heath lightly kissed the tip of each nipple, murmuring, "Agreed." He grasped her mound roughly while pressing a quick kiss to her lips before pulling away.

After Dayne finished circling her, the two men faced each other. Her pussy clenched simply from seeing the unbridled desire in their eyes as they took each other in. Their uneven breathing and the unmistakable erections pressed against their zippers left no doubt about how turned on they made each other.

What a shame she'd miss seeing those reactions once they blindfolded her.

Taking turns, Dayne and Heath removed the other's clothing piece by piece. Not a single inch of slowly exposed flesh was left untouched, kissed, or licked.

If she was the jealous type, this would be the time for that with the way they were fully appreciating one another. Their attention solely focused on the other man and not her.

Luckily, she wasn't jealous. Not even a little. Instead, she was happy they shared that same passion with her.

After they finally parted, while stroking his cock, Dayne told her, "That's only a preview of what's to come."

Grabbing the blindfold from the bed, he stepped behind her and slipped it over her head.

Her world went black.

Holy crap. She'd read plenty of spicy scenes involving women tied up and blindfolded. The well-written ones had always titillated her. Now it was no longer a fantasy and actually happening to her!

She managed to control her breathing so she wouldn't hyperventilate.

It'll be fine. Simply enjoy this new experience. It's fine. It's fine...

She had to trust that they knew what they were doing, so she forced herself to relax and go with the flow. She reminded herself that whatever they did was usually more for her benefit than their own.

She startled when Heath's voice came from only inches away at the same time sharp metal points rolled across her upper back, pricking her. "This is a Wartenburg wheel. It has sharp teeth that could easily draw blood if misused. I don't want to cause you pain, but I want you to be hyper aware of everywhere I roll it. If it becomes too much, say your safe word."

She nodded and breathlessly whispered, "I will."

But once he gently rolled it across her back a few times, something else touched her. Light sweeps of what she assumed was a large feather followed the same path.

Every roll of the wheel was followed by a brush of the plume. The two items were polar opposites: the feather more of a caress, the pinwheel more like being poked with tiny ice picks.

She didn't know whether to groan or laugh.

She did neither when a hand grabbed her ankle and lifted her leg. When the metal spikes rolled over the sole of her foot, she squealed. When the feather swept over the bottom of her foot next, she jerked with how much it tickled.

"Do you like that?" Dayne murmured.

"I'm not sure. Do it again," she encouraged before sinking her teeth into her bottom lip and holding her breath as the same actions were repeated on her other foot. This time, her leg jerked involuntarily and she hissed out a breath. "No. No... Cabbage!"

Immediately, her foot was released. "Stop everything or only that?" Heath asked.

"Doing that on my feet. It's too much." It made her want to jump out of her skin.

"Can we proceed with the wheel?" Dayne asked next.

"Yes."

Out of the two, Dayne *loved* to talk dirty. Tonight was no different. As both men worked, he released a constant stream of naughty words, filthy promises, and knee-wobbling guarantees while they continued to forge new paths all over her. The wheel's sharp points were even rolled back and forth over her nipples. Funny how that turned her on, unlike with her feet.

She lost track of how long they continued to use the wheel and feather because she had fallen into some sort of trance. Or a state of euphoria.

Was this feeling of floating in the clouds similar to slipping into a subspace?

One night she had asked a barrage of questions about the Dom/sub relationship, a dynamic she ran across in the more erotic books she read. Despite the fact neither man took either of those roles, they answered her questions as thoroughly as they could.

While their answers piqued her interest, she wasn't sure it was something she'd want to try.

Because of her current state of bliss, it took her a few seconds to realize they had stopped using the Wartenburg wheel and feather. A sharp tug on her hair quickly cleared away that foggy feeling and one of them—she didn't know which—began pulling a brush through her hair using long, sensual strokes.

She groaned at the pure Heaven of it.

It had to be Dayne wielding the hairbrush, because his pussy-twinging words began to wash over her all over again.

Of course, he didn't stop there. The stiff brush bristles made contact with her skin, making her aware of every nerve ending in her body. Long strokes continued down her back, her arms, her legs. Across her butt cheeks, her belly, her breasts.

Her skin had to be turning pink by now.

But they weren't done yet. Oh no. Not according to Dayne's non-stop stream of wicked words. They wanted her climbing out of her own skin and begging them for release.

As if he could read her mind, he said, "You'll come on our time, not yours."

She shuddered.

Chapter Seventeen

"THIS IS another item I need to warn you about first," Heath whispered close to her ear.

Oh shit.

Though, the Wartenburg wheel really hadn't been that bad. At least not enough that she'd add it to her short "never again" list.

"This will be very...stimulating," Dayne warned. "Maybe even shocking."

What? Did they plan to hook a car battery charger to her nipples like a torture scene in a spy movie?

"It's called a Neon Wand," Heath explained. "It'll feel similar to static electricity. Since the setting's adjustable, we'll start on the lowest and increase the intensity as we go. Again, if it becomes too much, don't hesitate to speak up."

Her insides now twisted at what was about to come. She could simply tell them no, to not do it, and they would respect that decision. But again, when had they done anything to her that she couldn't handle? Other than tickling her feet, of course, which to her was more like torture than pleasure.

A crackling sound made her brace. She had to at least give it a shot. She owed it to herself to try as much as possible during this week. Tonight was no different.

As fingers separated her folds, she opened her mouth to say "cabbage" but she couldn't get it out fast enough. Her clit was zapped, causing her to gasp and her body to bow. The intensity of it sent a bolt of lightning crackling from her clit to her center.

Holy crap. It was shockingly and unexpectedly...pleasurable. It didn't seem to be a lot of voltage, only enough to stimulate every place it touched.

The fine hairs on her arms stood as Heath ran the wand over her from head to toe. At some spots, he increased the power. In others, it was more mild.

It was definitely a type of sensation play she wouldn't mind exploring again in the future.

Then, without warning, the wand was gone.

What was next? Did they plan on using every toy in his closet on her?

She listened carefully as the two moved away, most likely grabbing something new.

It wasn't long before she knew she was right.

When hot liquid dripped on her breasts, she jerked against her bindings and gasped. Were they pouring the hot wax from the candle on her? In a panic, she shouted, "Is that wax?"

Dayne's answer was short and to the point. "No." He also didn't bother to explain.

A tongue chased a rivulet of the thick substance as it slowly dripped off her nipples.

Definitely not wax since it was edible. "What is it?"

Heath *mmm*'d in a way that sounded like he was having the best meal of his life. "Honey. So sweet. Like you."

More drips of very warm honey followed, as well as more licks to clean up the sticky rivers. A mix of deep moans ensued. Some from the men. Some from her.

This was something else she'd add to her *do again in the future* list, even though she had no idea with whom she'd do any of this stuff. Maybe she'd eventually find the right partner, someone she could trust and be vulnerable with.

She ignored the voice in her head telling her she'd already found them.

The truth was, neither man belonged to her. This had only been a week of fun and discovery. Nothing more. They owed each other nothing.

No lie, she'd miss both of them. More than she really wanted to admit.

Could she really get attached to not only one man, but two, in only a week's time? Apparently. But now was not the time to get melancholy. She was naked, restrained and had two hot hunks giving her their undivided attention.

Enjoy the moment. Don't worry about tomorrow.

Once all the honey had been licked from her skin, she wondered what they'd try next. Whatever it was, she was sure it would be unexpected.

Besides Dayne's constant stream of erotic talk, they didn't warn her about the next items first.

However, she had educated herself about them. Not only did she read about nipple suction sets in the romance novels and during her online research, she had wanted to try them and almost ordered a set for herself.

Tonight, she was getting her wish. Even better, she didn't have to use them on herself.

The more they twisted the "screws," the stronger a

vacuum it created and the further her nipples were sucked up into the plastic chambers. She learned that the increased blood flow to the nipples would make them more sensitive as well as cause them to become larger due to swelling. It was a tantalizing mix of pleasure and pain.

An interesting fact she had also gleaned from her research was that some women could orgasm from nipple stimulation alone. She was curious if she was one of them.

When it was on the verge of becoming too much for her to bear, they stopped twisting the screws but left the suction cups in place.

How much more would they do to her? They had to be running out of sensory play items soon, right?

Apparently not.

Something plastic—shaped like an oxygen mask—cupped her mound. A pumping sound could be heard next, reminding her of when a nurse used a manual blood pressure cuff.

What the—

With each pump, the flesh of her folds was pulled tighter into the cup.

"Like the suction cups on your nipples, this pussy pump will bring more blood to this area, making that pretty cunt swell and your clit more sensitive."

It was a weird sensation at first, but after a few moments, she got used to it. And surprisingly, she liked it.

It remained in place while she listened to the men move around the room, gathering items that might be used on her or each other...

Until she heard the creak of the bed. They weren't taking a break, were they? She was still suspended from the ceiling with suction toys on her nipples and pussy. "Are you going to leave me like this?"

"We can't leave those on her too long," Heath warned.

Should she be worried?

"We won't be long," Dayne assured him.

Heath responded dryly, "I wouldn't say that's a positive."

Cara picked up the humor in Dayne's voice. "It depends."

"What's going on?" she asked. "Tell me what's happening."

"If we tell you, that will defeat the purpose of using your imagination," Heath explained.

It didn't take long for her to figure it out despite the fact they kept talking so low that she couldn't hear everything they said. But soon, they couldn't stay quiet enough. And it didn't have anything to do with them talking.

The slide of skin across the sheet. The tearing of a foil package. The wet burp-like sound of lube being squirted from a tube. The slap of a hand against skin.

A soft grunt.

A long sigh.

A deep groan.

Then a rhythmic thumping.

They were fucking each other and she was being forced to listen.

She had no idea who was doing who. At least until they began whispering encouragement and louder demands.

"Give me your cock." *Dayne.*

Heath growled, "Take it. All of it."

"Harder," Dayne demanded.

"Fuck," Heath groaned.

Ragged breathing now filled any gaps between the words. "*Fuck.*"

"So...damn...hot. So...fucking...tight." Heath again.

Their words washed over and through her, heating her

insides. The picture in her mind's eye of what they were doing with each other fueled the heat into a roaring bonfire.

They were well aware that she loved to watch the two of them together and to be denied that...

Did they *want* her to self-combust? Reduce her to a puddle on the floor? Beg for them to remove the blindfold?

She was wondering what their end game could be.

Or maybe they didn't have one.

Cara began to shake from the built-up sexual frustration. Her pussy was throbbing in the pump. Her clit and her nipples had their own heartbeats.

She needed a release and needed it soon because she was losing her damn mind. "Please... *Please...*"

She was on fire. Burning up. No longer from the warm honey that had been drizzled all over her, but from the two men and their willingness to spend a week opening her eyes and mind to their erotic world and all its possibilities.

But this week had only been the beginning and not the end. She had so much more to learn, see, and do. Her stay at the resort and the time she spent with both Heath and Dayne had only whetted her appetite and made her even hungrier for more.

Her imagination was running wild and she didn't think she could take any more. With no use of her hands, she only had one way to stop the ravenous ache between her thighs.

Despite the pussy pump still being attached, she tensed and released the muscles in her thighs while squeezing them together until the friction brought about an orgasm. Once it ripped through her and her current pent-up frustration was gone, she could hear again.

But they were both silent and only the soft music filled the room.

Were they done?

A moment later, she discovered they weren't finished with each other or with her.

The night had only begun.

179

Chapter Eighteen

For once, saying goodbye hadn't been easy. Of course, that alone was messing with Dayne's head.

In the past, he normally preferred sexual encounters that only skimmed the surface. What happened between him, Cara, and Heath during that week together had been real and had gone much deeper than ever before.

Somehow, both Cara and Heath managed to dive below the surface and hold him below the crashing waves. Only, he wasn't sure how to navigate those dangerous waters. Or even if he'd need to learn.

Now that they were gone, would he simply drown? Or would he fight his way back to the shore, drag himself out of the water and go about his life like their week together never happened?

Was that even possible?

So many thoughts had swamped him ever since Heath and Cara got into their respective vehicles and drove away.

Despite the hollow feeling left behind, he had no regrets about being with them, and *only* them, for an entire week.

Well, maybe one, but it was more of a selfish regret. He wished Cara had been experienced enough that he and Heath could have fucked her at the same time.

Realistically, that would have been rushing things and it probably would not have gone well, anyway. Cara would have needed a lot of prep to take two hard cocks at once since she had never done anal before.

Since their time had been limited, neither he nor Heath wanted it to end up being an unpleasant experience for her. Not if Dayne wanted her to return to the resort.

He hoped she would.

The same with Heath.

However, if she *did* return, would she want to spend more time with him, or would she prefer a different experience with someone new?

For some reason, that last part twisted Dayne's gut.

He'd never been possessive of anyone before and didn't like this feeling at all.

The resort is your playground. Don't limit yourself.

He tried to convince himself that he hadn't had sex with anyone else for the last two weeks because he had too much sex the week they were guests.

But deep down, even he didn't believe that.

Yes, they'd had a lot of sex, but it wasn't any more or less than what he normally would have had.

The fact that he had zero interest in anyone else right now scared the shit out of him since it never happened to him before. He also never had such a deep attraction to anyone the same as this. Where he couldn't get enough.

It wasn't only for one or the other. It had been *both* of them. How could he fall this deeply for two people at the same damn time? And in only one week?

Was he sick? Did he snap?

Or was he simply tired of the revolving door in his wing? Finding new sex partners every night could be exhausting. Not only would he have to find the right ones, they had to figure out boundaries.

He now knew most of what turned on Heath and Cara as well as what turned them off. What their limits were. How to get them to orgasm more quickly or how to selfishly delay it.

Quite simply, the three of them had fallen into an easy sexual relationship. They gelled.

Finding partners to take their place, even for a night, would take more work right now than he was willing to do.

He couldn't wrap his head around it all. The hollowness in his chest. The crazy feeling of loss. The even crazier realization he currently had no interest in others.

This was not Dayne Lyons. He had to have been a victim of body snatchers. No other plausible explanation existed.

While he hated to have to go to his brother for advice, he needed to talk to someone about it. If anyone would understand what he was experiencing, it would be his twin, since Dylan had gone through the same thing.

Only, look where Dylan was now. In a committed relationship. With both a man *and* a woman. Is that what Dayne wanted?

Shit.

The three of them only spent a week together. A damn week! Less than seven days wasn't enough to determine whether he wanted a committed—or even semi-committed—relationship with them.

Heath lived in New Jersey. Cara in Carlisle. A long-distance commitment meant he'd hardly ever have sex again. Especially since their visits would most likely be few and far between since both had busy lives elsewhere.

He couldn't survive that.

A bit dramatic? Sure. One thing Dayne was serious about was sex.

Unfortunately, when he went to find Dylan, his twin wasn't alone. Their sister Danica was hanging out in their brother's office, too.

Of course, a day couldn't end without him giving one or both of his siblings shit. Being a shit-stirrer was in his blood. "Are you two discussing our crazy food bills and how to keep it within the budget I gave you?"

Dani barked out a laugh. "Budget? What's a budget? Quality ingredients are priceless."

Dayne rolled his eyes and, with a huff, threw himself into the seat next to her.

"What's up?" Dylan asked with his brow pulled low.

"I need to talk to you about something."

"So, talk. Nothing has ever stopped you from running your trap before."

Dayne glanced over at Dani, waiting for her to excuse herself.

Of course, she didn't. "If it has to do with the business, I want to hear it, too, since I'm a silent partner."

Dayne snorted. "You are *far* from silent."

Dylan shook his head. "Okay, spill. I have important things to do."

"Are you saying I'm not important?"

"If that's what you heard..."

"I think I'm broken," Dayne reluctantly confessed.

"You're only figuring this out *now*?" Dani snort-laughed. "We've known it since you were two."

"You weren't even born yet when Dyl Weed and I were two."

Dani grinned and shrugged. "Mom said you are the way you are due to a lack of oxygen to your brain."

"Then it's Dylan's fault. He hogged the womb."

Dylan clicked his tongue. "I should've choked you with the umbilical cord. What a wasted opportunity."

"I'm telling Mom."

One side of Dylan's mouth pulled up. "She'd agree with me."

"Boy, Ford and Erin have really changed you. Though, despite the effort, you're still not funny."

"What do you want, Dayne? Is it important? Or are you in here to waste my time?"

"And mine," Dani added.

"You could leave at any time, sis," Dayne suggested. "No one's making you stay."

She tapped a finger against her bottom lip. "I don't know. You look a little green around the gills. Is it an STD? Did you knock up one of the guests and need to take a paternity test?"

Dylan's expression turned from amused to serious in a flash. "You better not be spreading shit around this resort. And if you—"

"I didn't!" exploded from Dayne. "Don't listen to her. She's only jealous she's not getting laid."

Dani's expression twisted. "How do you know?"

"We all live in the same house."

"Who says I can only have sex in the house? Why would I want to bring anyone home and risk them meeting you two boneheads?"

"*Are* you banging someone?" Dayne asked.

Dani rolled her hazel eyes. "Like I would tell you."

Dylan leaned back in his office chair and sighed. "Good. I don't need to hear whether our baby sister is or isn't having sex." His gaze landed back on Dayne. "Why are you broken?"

Dayne's eyes flicked from Dylan to Dani and back to

Dylan. Did he really want to reveal what he was about to reveal with his sister in the same room?

Would it matter? She'd probably find out eventually, anyway. It was difficult to hide anything from his siblings when they all lived in the same residence.

For now, anyway. Once Ford finished building their house along the back of the three-hundred acres, his brother, Ford, and Erin would be moving out of the farmhouse.

Dayne shook his thoughts free when Dylan shouted his name.

"I'm not sure if you noticed that I've been alone at the breakfast table for the last couple of weeks."

Dylan glanced at Dani for a second before turning his attention back to Dayne. "Hard to miss."

"So, it *is* an STD?" Dani fought the amusement on her face but failed. "Is it chlamydia?"

"Jesus, Danica! No."

Her eyes bugged out. "Herpes?"

"No! It's not a damn STD. This is why I didn't want you in here."

"What is it, then?" Dylan asked.

"A couple of weeks ago, I only had sex with the same two people for a whole week."

Dani gasped dramatically and slapped a hand over her mouth. "*Nooooo!* That's horrific!"

Dayne ignored her.

Dylan's eyebrows pinched together. "Okay? So what?"

"So what?" Dayne practically shouted. "Have you ever known me to do that?"

Dylan's eyes rolled toward the ceiling for a few seconds, as if he was searching his memory. When he looked at Dayne again, Dylan simply answered, "Not that I can recall."

"Right. A whole damn week with the same two people and now I'm broken."

"I still don't understand how you're broken," Dylan said calmly. Too calmly, like this wasn't an emergency.

"I'm struggling to be interested in anyone else."

"Give it time," his brother suggested.

"Time?" burst from Dayne. "It usually takes me less than twenty-four hours to move on. It's been...*two...damn...weeks.* I haven't had sex since they checked-out and left."

"Who are *they*, brother?" Dani asked.

"Their names don't matter."

"Apparently, they do to you," Dylan murmured.

He was right. Heath and Cara mattered to him. "I need your advice on what to do in this scenario."

"Go have sex with someone else," Dani suggested with a shrug. "Isn't that what you'd normally do?"

"*Nothing* is normal in this situation. I can't stop thinking about them. I can't even *look* at anyone else. I haven't even been up to Heaven. Not once since then."

"Okay, you were right. You're broken," Dani said. "Just go dig a grave and jump in. Your life as you know it is now over."

Dayne ignored his sister *again* and kept his eyes on Dylan. "What do I do?"

"I think you have me—a humble architect—confused with a psychologist. Totally different college degree, dude."

"I simply need advice from my brother. I'm afraid I'm turning into you."

Dylan frowned. "What does that mean?"

"You're locked in a committed relationship and no longer have your sexual freedom."

"We have sexual freedom."

"As long as you clear it with your partners first. That's not freedom. Those are chains."

Dani sighed loudly. "Oh...my...God...Dayne! You're an idiot. Dylan must've got all the brains when Mom's egg split in two."

"And I got all the brawn. In my cock."

"We already know that's not true," Dylan answered dryly.

Dani made a choking sound. "I prefer to think of you two as eunuchs, thank you very much."

"Okay, so you're broken," Dylan continued. "What do you want from me?"

"Advice."

"About?"

"How to fix it."

Dylan shook his head. "Fix what?"

"My desire for the same two people and my lack of desire for anyone but those same...two...people!"

Dylan stared across his desk at him with pursed lips. Then he threw his head back and laughed and laughed and fucking laughed some more.

Dayne sighed. "I don't find it funny."

Dani tsked. "Poor baby. He's gone and fallen just like Dylan."

"I haven't fallen. It was only one damn week."

Dani lifted a single eyebrow. "But that week changed everything, didn't it?"

"No, it—" Dayne scraped his fingers through his hair. "Shit."

"Maybe you simply clicked with...who are these people?" Dylan asked.

Dani followed up with, "The two you sat together with at dinner every night a couple of weeks ago?"

Should he admit it? "The same."

"She was very pretty and he was smoking hot. Cara and

Heath, right? I thought it was weird you shared dinner with them every night. I figured it had to do with investments or finances, or something, since they didn't join us for breakfast every morning. Now I know they are just as damaged as you since they *voluntarily* spent a whole week with you."

Dayne once again ignored his sister and focused on his twin sitting behind the desk. "So, what do I do? Force myself to move on by grabbing someone else and having sex with them?" Maybe that would push them from his mind and end this crazy obsession.

"Mom's better at giving advice than I am."

"I'm not asking Mom!"

Dani giggled next to him. "Why don't you invite them back to the resort? Spend some more time with them and see if it was a fluke."

That was actually a good idea but he wasn't telling his sister that. The only issue would be comping them rooms in the lodge. They needed paying customers to keep the resort running, especially since they were still trying to recover their investments. "If I invite them, I don't feel right charging them."

Dylan's answer surprised him. "Then don't."

"You want them taking up two rooms that could be filled with paying customers?" That couldn't be right.

"No. But they could stay with you."

Dayne grimaced.

"Did you have any doubts about them while they were here?" Dylan asked next.

"No." If he did, he wouldn't be in this predicament.

"Then it shouldn't be an issue, right? And on the chance you find out they aren't compatible with you and them staying with you gets awkward, I'm sure we can find temporary accommodations for them elsewhere."

He considered his brother's suggestion. He could invite them up for a weekend since they both lived within driving distance. Either could easily leave if things didn't work out and they found their week together had been a fluke.

No matter what, he needed to do something, *anything*, to figure out why he couldn't forget either of them. It was like an obsession. Or an addiction. He thought about them constantly.

Maybe if they came back for a weekend, he'd find something about them that would turn him off. Something, *anything* that would show that they weren't as compatible as he thought.

Another visit could be a good dose of reality.

For all three of them.

Chapter Nineteen

Cara didn't recognize the number that came up on her cell phone. She normally didn't answer calls from unknown people since they were usually scammers. For some reason, she had an unexplainable urge to answer this one. When she did, she had been prepared to hang up and block the number if her instinct was wrong.

It wasn't.

"Hello?"

"Hey," filled her ear. It was the same voice that answered her questions all those weeks ago when she originally made her reservation at the Double D Ranch.

"Are you calling for additional feedback on my stay?" she teased, since she had filled out the survey emailed to her after she returned home.

Dayne chuckled. "No. But I'll still listen if you have any."

"I figured mentioning that my stay was worth every dime spent said it all."

"Honestly, I don't read those surveys. Our Guest Services

Manager does. But that's good to know. I hope I had something to do with making your stay worthwhile."

"*Mmm hmm.* Heath, too."

"I'll assume that means you'd be open to returning for another visit." After a slight hesitation, Dayne asked, "When can you come again?"

"I have a couple of vibrators so...anytime? Or did you mean phone sex?"

"No. Though, that sounds intriguing and I might take you up on that since phone sex is right up my alley. I meant come to the ranch."

"I have work." She already took a whole week off. She doubted the library director would be quick to approve another week.

"No vacation days?"

"I've accumulated plenty since I haven't used many for years, but it will leave the library short-handed."

"That's their problem, not yours. You earned those days."

"I did, but it's not fair to my coworkers."

"It's not fair to me that you're not here."

She clicked her tongue. "*Aww.* Poor baby. You live on a ranch resort. There are plenty of others available. Have you forgotten that?"

"Of course not." He paused. "Maybe I don't want anyone else."

Wow. What? "Not even Heath?"

"Heath isn't here."

Of course not. He left the resort at the same time she did. After the three of them said their goodbyes. "Does he have plans to return?"

"He said he would."

"When?"

"This weekend."

"Well then, he can keep you company." Did she want to be with them? Sure. She actually missed seeing their faces—as well as other parts—every day. To be expected, the three of them had grown close during their stay a couple of weeks ago.

But, truthfully, she figured Dayne would simply move on afterward like he normally did after hooking up with guests. Him reaching out to her, and even Heath, surprised her. She hadn't expected Dayne to miss them, too.

"Sure he could. I invited him to stay with me. In my wing. In the farmhouse. I'm extending that invitation to you."

"To come stay with you?" Did her voice squeak?

"Unless you want to share my sister's room."

She rolled her eyes despite him not being able to see her. "Funny."

"Not really. I'd prefer not to watch you eating out my sister."

Cara just about choked on her own spit. She cleared her throat. "While two women having sex doesn't gross me out, the thought of you watching your sister doing it does."

He chuckled. "Same here. I was only messing with you."

"I know."

"So?"

"So...you're asking me to come for a weekend and stay with you?"

"Yes."

At least she wouldn't have to ask for leave. Despite it being an almost-three-hour drive one way, the long hours in the car wasn't the only reason making her hesitate. "Can I think about it?"

"No."

She laughed softly. "You might not be a Dom but I've noticed you can be demanding."

"Absolutely. When I want something, I go after it. I want you."

"Again, you have plenty of—"

"You want me to fuck others?"

Truthfully, no, she didn't, but they owed each other nothing. "You'll be fucking Heath or vice versa, correct?"

"That's different."

"It's not," she countered.

"We both had sex with Heath. Would you rather me bring in a new third?"

"Why must you have three?"

"I've had more," Dayne answered.

"I'm sure."

"Cara, it's not about having a threesome. It's about who'd be involved in that dynamic."

"Dayne, while you're making me feel wanted, I'm simply a shiny new toy for you. I'm sure I'll lose that shininess soon."

He groaned. "You wound me."

"Is that not true?"

"We won't know until we get tired of each other."

"Have you gotten tired of others?" She already knew the answer since he didn't hide the fact he rarely had sex with the same person—or persons—more than once. Why would he want the same dish over and over when he owned a smorgasbord?

"Absolutely."

"Have you ever been monogamous?"

"Yes, when I was young and dumb."

"And now you're older and smarter?"

Amusement colored his voice when he said, "Smarter than back then. I want to spend more time with you, Cara. Heath does, too."

"Is it because I'm a blank slate to mold however you'd like me?"

"No. I like seeing this world through your fresh eyes. I'm asking that you don't close them."

"I can't simply pick up and go there whenever you ask, Dayne. Not only do I have a job, I have a dog." One she loved very much and had missed while she'd been away. "I can't leave her at home alone."

Her sister had been kind enough to watch Buttons for her, but Amelia had her hands full already with three children under the age of eight, along with two large dogs and a cat. Not to mention, her man-baby husband who rarely lifted a finger with the kids or around the house.

"What kind?"

What did that matter? "A Boston Terrier."

"Bring it."

"Her. Her name is Buttons."

Silence filled her ear for a moment. "Is she house trained?"

"Yes."

"Will she chase our livestock? Eat our chickens?"

"I don't know. I never take her off leash."

"Then we'll keep her on leash until we know those answers."

Boy, was he persistent!

"I didn't think guests were allowed to bring their pets." If she stayed with him, though, she wouldn't technically be a guest. Of the resort, anyway. She'd be a personal guest of one of the owners.

"Unless it's a certified service dog, they're not. Lucky enough, you have connections and you won't be staying where the guests do. Bring her."

"Dayne..."

"I'm serious. As long as she isn't shitting on the floors or chasing the livestock, no one will care she's here."

Cara doubted that. Buttons could be sassy. "Are you sure?"

"As sure as I want you here."

She was *sooo* tempted. The three of them had quickly created a bond. She'd like to see if she had imagined it. With what he was proposing, it wouldn't cost her a dime to go this time, except for the gas to get there. How could she say no? "Okay."

"Okay what?"

"I'll come and bring Buttons, but not this weekend. It's too short notice. However, even if I'm able to swing taking off the Friday on the weekend I come, I wouldn't get there until the late afternoon. If I can't, then it'll be sometime in the evening."

"Cara, it's only a three-hour drive. Technically, you could be here by breakfast if you left early enough."

She laughed. "I'd think you've gone without sex for years by the way you're acting."

"It feels like years."

"You really haven't had sex with anyone else since we left?" That was impossible.

"No."

"Dayne..."

"I figured you might not want me fucking others."

What? "Dayne, you owe me nothing. *Us* nothing."

"Not even respect?"

"You abstained out of respect?" *Bullshit.*

"Look, it's no secret that I love sex. I've had plenty of it with a vast amount of people since opening the resort, not counting my prior partners, but..." The phone went silent.

"But?" she prodded.

"But the truth is, none of the rest compared."

He was really laying it on thick. "Are you saying I'm a natural when it comes to sex?" That was laughable.

"You are. You wanted to run that first night, but you didn't. You stayed and gave the resort, and me, a chance. You expanded your knowledge and experience because you were willing to try new things and keep an open mind."

"I don't get it. If this is only about sex, then you could have plenty of it without us. You don't need to have me or Heath in your personal space."

Dayne didn't respond for the longest time, and when he finally did, he said, "This isn't only about sex."

"Explain."

"I've been struggling with this, but the truth is, I want to explore the connection the three of us had."

So, he felt it, too.

"I want to know if it's real and find out how deep it goes."

She didn't expect any of this to come from Dayne. "What does Heath think?"

"I don't know. I didn't ask. I sent him an invite for this weekend via text. He accepted. Maybe I'm wrong about this connection but I won't know—*we* won't know—unless we spend more time together."

"I definitely didn't expect any of this from you," she whispered. Not when she thought she'd never hear from him again.

"I didn't expect this from myself, either. Like I said, I'm struggling with this whole thing, but I also can't ignore it. My life hasn't been the same since you two left."

Wow. That was some confession. Especially from a man who considered the resort as his personal playground.

"Are you asking us to return so you can work on getting us out of your system?"

"Not at all. An invitation wouldn't be needed for that. Having sex with others would do that job."

"But you can't."

"No. I can't stop thinking about you and Heath, Cara."

"I can't stop thinking about you and Heath, either," she admitted softly. "Fine. I'll let you know when I can come. Hopefully, before the end of the month."

———

WITH ONE HAND on his hip, Heath used the T-shirt hanging around his neck to wipe away the sweat beading on his forehead.

He was definitely getting more into running on trails rather than on the treadmill in his building's gym. The terrain might be rougher but the run itself was easier.

The scenery also made it a bit easier, too. Not of the mountains or the pastures, but of Dayne's ass and legs. And possibly his bare chest and back, too.

After driving to the resort last evening, he had spent the rest of the night holed up in Dayne's bedroom breaking a sweat in a different way.

He had been disappointed to find out that Cara couldn't join them this weekend. Dayne said she'd be back two weekends from now.

To Heath, that was far too long.

He had been surprised to find, once he left after their week together, how much he missed both her and Dayne. It was like the both of them had burrowed deep into his chest and planted themselves there. Even though he doubted that was their intention.

He was shocked when Dayne reached out and invited him to stay in his personal residence. Heath figured he was the only one who felt their strong connection. And then he thought he had imagined it.

Apparently, he was wrong.

The resort was Dayne's sexual oyster. Everything was available to him. He could find anything he wanted at any time with anyone willing to participate. So again, this invitation was so damn unexpected.

Of course, he couldn't say no. He, like Dayne, wanted to see if the emotional attachment between the three of them was real, and not simply about sexual desires.

Even if it was, the sex between them *had* been great. And great sex had been the original goal. That and good company.

In the past couple of weeks, he had thought about Cara and Dayne often. Actually, too often. It had been a while since he'd obsessed over any lover. Crazy enough, here he was now obsessing over two.

By the time they walked into the farmhouse, they had both cooled down enough and the early morning run had worked up their appetites. On the way back, Dayne kept teasing him with how good his sister's breakfasts were.

His stomach had growled right before he asked, "You sure she won't mind a stranger sitting down at the kitchen table with you?"

"You're not a stranger," Dayne answered. "At least to me."

"You normally invite your sexual conquests to share a meal with your family?"

Dayne only answered with a shrug. Between that and how his siblings didn't even blink when they walked into the kitchen together, Heath had his answer.

It was clear that he was definitely not Dayne's first lover to join them for a morning meal.

One of the women raked her eyes down his bare chest

and paused briefly at the crotch area of his running shorts before turning back to the stove with a sigh.

He quickly yanked his damp T-shirt over his head and down his torso.

"Heath, the one who just eye-fucked you is my baby sister, Danica."

Glancing over her shoulder with raised eyebrows, Dayne's sister responded, "Well, this is new. Since when do you actually tell us their names?"

Damn. His sister was hot as hell. But then, so was his twin, since he was a mirror image of Dayne. The slight difference between the two were their haircuts and Dylan had some very short facial hair. Then, as for the other two with Dylan...

A quick glance at Dayne showed that his lover was watching him closely while fighting a grin.

Busted.

"She's in charge of all the food for the resort," Dayne finished.

Danica turned to face where they all stood by the large rustic kitchen table. "By the way, I didn't eye—"

"Save it, sis," Dayne cut her off, sounding amused.

"Well, I was surprised. It's usually a harem of wom—"

"Save it!" Dayne shouted, again, cutting her off.

Heath wasn't the only one smothering a chuckle in the room. "Pleasure to meet you, Danica. I have to say, for an all-inclusive resort, your food is top notch. I hope you don't mind me joining your family this morning for breakfast."

"We're used to it," came from Dayne's twin.

"That's my brother Dylan. The second D in Double D."

Heath glanced over at Danica. "But there's three of you."

"That's what *I* said," Dani griped.

Dayne shook his head impatiently. "Anyway, that's Ford and Erin, Dylan's balls and chain."

"Ha ha, as funny as ever," Dylan scoffed.

"Nice to meet you all. I don't mean to intrude."

Ford finished pulling out creamer and milk from the fridge and placed them on the table. "Believe me, you're not. Like Dylan said, this is a common occurrence." He frowned. "Though, he hasn't had a constant parade of...*guests* joining us lately." His lips twitched. Once Ford's hands were free, he jutted one out and Heath shook it. "I'm the resort's Facilities Manager. Erin here is the Guest Services Manager."

He shook a smiling Erin's hand next. "Pleasure."

"Same," she responded. "Have a seat. I'll grab another place setting." She glanced at Dayne. "Unless someone else will be joining us?"

"No. Only Heath this weekend."

Dylan raised an eyebrow. "And the other one we discussed?"

"She couldn't make it. Hopefully soon."

Dayne discussed him and Cara with his brother? He tucked that interesting tidbit away to ask about later. In private.

"Is that your G90 out front?" Ford asked next.

"Yes," Heath answered.

"Sweet car."

"It is, and it gets me here from Hoboken in record time."

Dani carried a plate of sausages over to the table and set it in the center. "Hoboken, huh?"

"I was lucky to find a resort within driving distance."

Erin arranged the extra place setting on the table. "You mean this type of resort." She flipped a hand toward the chair, indicating he should sit.

He did. "Of course."

"I'm glad you found it worthwhile," she continued. "We do our best to make it an experience that guests would like to repeat."

Danica snickered as she brought a platter of Belgian waffles over the table. "You might want to chalk this returning guest up to something other than my food and the amenities, Erin."

"I'll take credit," Dayne boasted, pulling out the chair next to Heath and settling in it.

"Thanks for helping, brother," Danica said smartly.

"You're welcome!"

"We'll clean up," Heath assured Dayne's sister. "You weren't expecting an extra mouth to feed this morning."

"Untrue. Like I said, when the door opens from Dayne's wing, we usually expect a hoard of hungry, horny guests following him out like the Penis Pied Piper. Coming out alone or with only one person is not the norm."

"Thank you for that," Dayne said.

"Own it," Danica replied back.

"He's been quite open about his past encounters," Heath assured her.

"Really," Dylan murmured.

"I'm also not stupid. Or jealous," Heath continued. "I understand why he'd take advantage of owning this resort."

"So understanding," Danica muttered under her breath.

Dayne clapped his hands together sharply. "Okay! Let's eat! And not talk with our mouths full, shall we?"

Everyone at the table, except Dayne and Heath, snorted at his irritation.

"I cannot wait until your house is done and I only have to deal with Dani."

"Who said we won't stop in every morning for breakfast? You think we'd miss this great food and even better sibling bonding time?"

Chapter Twenty

DAYNE NOTICED Heath's eyes flick between the door through which Dylan had disappeared and him.

"What I wouldn't do to be sandwiched between you two."

They were now blissfully alone in the kitchen and on clean-up duty, since Heath promised Dani they'd take care of it.

He assured Heath, "That'll never happen." Once Dayne rinsed a dirty dish or utensil, he handed it to Heath to place in the dishwasher.

"Of course not, but at least let me have this fantasy for a few seconds, will you?"

Simply thinking about sharing a lover with his twin churned Dayne's stomach. He shook his head. "What about Cara?"

"She's welcome to join us."

Dayne snorted. "I prefer not to have sex with my brother in the vicinity, thank you very much."

"Understandable. It would probably be like peering in a mirror."

"Only this 'reflection' wouldn't have the tattoo and dick piercing." He handed Heath the last plate. "Do you have siblings?"

"Three." Heath grimaced. "All sisters."

Dayne dried his hands off and offered the towel to Heath next, then turned and leaned back against the counter. "Ouch. One's enough for me. Where do you fit in?"

"They're all older than me and are now spread out around the country. All are also married with kids."

It was Dayne's turn to grimace.

"They drank the Kool-Aid."

"What flavor?"

"The one that makes people think you can't be happy unless you're in a traditional marriage and popping out mini-mes."

"I wonder how many of them are truly happy," Dayne murmured.

His parents had seemed very happy in their traditional marriage. For some reason that hadn't rubbed off on their children. At least for Dylan and him. Their mother still might be holding out hope for Danica.

Not that their mother cared about tradition. She only wanted her children to be happy, no matter who it was with. Or how many. She hardly blinked an eye when she found out about Dylan being in a polyamorous relationship.

"My sisters? None. However, they hide it well. But then, I was once in their shoes, too. Only, I didn't have kids so it was easier to extract myself from a situation gone ugly."

"I actually meant anyone in that situation. Not only your sisters," Dayne clarified.

"My guess? Few. It's like you see on social media. Everyone puts on a fake front, pretending their lives are so damn perfect. The perfect marriage. The perfect children. The *perfect* life." Heath fake gagged.

"Yeah, like we don't see the truth behind the wooden smiles and dead eyes. Not to mention, being forced to share a profile with their spouse."

"Their eyes scream, 'Help me!'"

Dayne laughed.

Heath hung the kitchen towel up to dry, then stepped toe-to-toe with Dayne, grabbing his hips and pulling him closer until they were pressed together. "We didn't fuck on the trail this morning."

Dayne cupped the back of Heath's head and stared into his heated dark-brown eyes. "I was tempted. We can make up for it. Since it's the weekend, I don't have any official duties to attend to except to say hello to guests when I see them. Maybe we can make use of my big shower since we both need one."

Heath leaned in and *mmm*'d against Dayne's lips. "I like the sound of that. Hot water. Hot man. Accidentally dropping the soap..."

Before they could lock lips, a pounding on the front door interrupted them. "I *don't* like the sound of *that*." Dayne sighed and skirted around Heath to answer the door.

On the other side stood their Head of Security, Cameron. Of course, he wore his resort-issued security uniform of a red polo shirt and black pants that fit his physique perfectly. The torso-hugging short-sleeved shirt had the Double D logo embroidered over his right breast and his job title on the left.

All the red shirts provided to Cam's team had large block lettering across the back stating they were "security."

His employee was as hot as Heath. Dark eyes, dark hair, beard. His left arm was almost fully tatted. During his interview, Cam mentioned he'd wanted a full sleeve his whole adult life but couldn't get it until he retired from the Pennsylvania State Police. Apparently, they had rules about tattoos.

"Sorry to barge in. We have a minor incident." His brow furrowed. "Is Dylan around?"

What, was he chopped liver? "He's in his wing. What's going on?"

"A guest brought a pet with her."

This was an *incident?* "Not a service animal?"

"No. It's a little dog. She insists she isn't a guest, though. When the guard sitting at the gate checked with the front desk, he found that she doesn't have a reservation. So, he won't let her in until we confirm who she is."

Good call. "Did you try calling Dylan? You know we have these modern forms of communication called cell phones."

"I tried a couple times. I even texted. He didn't answer. Which is why I'm standing here."

Dayne's eyes sliced over to Dylan's door off the kitchen. His brother probably had the same idea as he did about some after breakfast fun.

Suddenly, he felt heat at his back and knew Heath stood behind him. Dayne didn't miss the fact that Cam was eyeing up Dayne's lover.

Back off. He's mine.

Ours.

Whatever.

Wait a minute...

A "she" with a dog and not a registered guest? "Is the woman blonde, by any chance?"

"Yes." Cameron scowled. "How did you know?"

Dayne sighed again. "Because I invited her. She's *my* guest. Only, I wasn't expecting her to show up this weekend."

"Cara?" Heath asked.

Dayne glanced over his shoulder at him. "Has to be." He turned back to Cam. "Is the dog a Boston Terrier?"

Cam shrugged. "Not sure. It's small, has four legs, a tail, and barks. A lot. What's her name?"

"Buttons."

Cam's dark eyebrows launched to his hairline. "The woman's name is *Buttons*?"

"It's Cara Leone," Heath corrected before Dayne could.

Cam pulled a handheld radio off his belt and contacted the security guard at the gate. Once he got a response, he asked, "You checked her ID, right?"

That should be automatic. No one was allowed past the gate unless they were a registered guest or had an invitation.

"Affirmative," the gate guard answered.

"Is her name Cara Leone?" Cam asked his team member.

"Affirmative," came the answer.

"That's her," Dayne told him.

"She's approved. Let her in and tell her to come directly to the boss's house."

"I would've warned you," Dayne started, "but she said she couldn't make it this weekend."

"Should we put her on the pre-approval list the same as you did with him?" Cam jerked his chin toward Heath.

"That would be for the best."

"You got it. Sorry to bother you, Dayne."

"Nothing to apologize for. You're doing what we pay you to do."

Cam shot him a two finger salute and headed back to one of the ATVs that his security team used to patrol the property.

Dayne was pretty damn sure he wasn't the only one checking out Cam's fine ass as he walked away.

"Damn," Heath whispered. "Who was that?"

"Head of our security."

"I can read, Dayne. I mean who. Was. That?"

After closing the door, Dayne turned and grabbed Heath's crotch over his silky running shorts. He squeezed gently. "I'm not asking him to join us. Especially now that Cara's here. Even if she wasn't, I don't do employees."

Heath grinned. "I could understand that might get sticky."

"I wouldn't want shit to get awkward and lose him as an employee. Cam's a huge asset to our team since he's a retired trooper. He also lives in one of the cabins on the property. That could make it even more uncomfortable if things went south."

"I was only thinking about one night."

"It only takes one night for shit to go sideways."

Heath sighed and suggested, "We could watch him fuck Cara."

"You'd have to ask for her consent first. And then him, of course."

A gleam filled Heath's brown eyes. "Think he'd be into it? Is he committed to anyone?"

"Down, boy, down! Yes, he's single. He's also divorced. One reason he didn't mind moving onto the property. Fewer expenses for him, more money for child support."

"I hear that. If I had kids with my ex, I wouldn't mind paying child support. I do mind those massive alimony payments so she can buy the latest designer bags and shoes."

"*Oof.*"

"Yeah. If she was struggling to make ends meet, I wouldn't mind helping out until she could get on her feet.

But those manicured toenails are wedged into Louboutins, so knowing that makes paying alimony even more painful."

Dayne patted his chest. "As soon as Cara gets here, we'll help take that pain away."

"I wonder why she came this weekend when she told you she couldn't make it..."

"I don't know," Dayne answered. "But I'm not complaining. My bed and shower are big enough for the three of us."

Heath chuckled. "That they are."

———

Cara somehow managed to extract herself from the tangle of hairy, muscular limbs without waking either man.

"Her men" was now how she thought of them. Two months ago, she showed up at the resort unannounced. She had known Heath was spending the weekend with Dayne and she didn't think she could get away. But come Saturday morning, the thought of the two of them having "fun" without her made her pack an overnight bag, pack up Buttons, and drive the three hours north.

She didn't regret it.

Well, Dayne and Heath made sure she didn't regret it.

Now, both Heath and Cara were Dayne's personal guests just about every other weekend.

Buttons was getting used to all the livestock. And the barn cats. And the chickens. Luckily, besides thinking she could intimidate a cow—she couldn't—she hadn't caused any injuries or fatalities. She didn't want her dog to get banned from the resort. If so, she wouldn't be able to visit as often as she did.

Both she and Heath fell into a pattern of making sure they were on the property at the same time. Would she mind if Heath came more often to spend time with Dayne? No. Heath said the same about her.

But it didn't feel right if one of their triad was missing.

Their relationship was comfortable. It was also steaming hot. The sex amazing and plentiful.

Sometimes she appreciated being alone during the week. It gave her a chance to rest, despite the fact that she had to work.

Not only did Dayne and his siblings not mind her bringing Buttons along, Dani had fallen in love with Cara's Boston Terrier. In fact, unless Dani was working in the commercial kitchen in The Mane Lodge, she tended to steal Buttons. Of course, Buttons didn't mind.

Traitor.

Cara had never been into dressing up her pets, but practically every time she returned to the ranch, Dani had purchased a new outfit for Buttons. It was getting out of hand since Buttons's wardrobe seemed to be bigger than her own.

Before she could finish climbing off the bed, a hand clamped down on her arm and tugged her back. She collapsed on top of Heath.

"Where you going?" he asked sleepily, despite the fact his cock was certainly awake.

She turned around and slid down until she was settled between his thick thighs. "I was going to check on Buttons and help Dani with breakfast. It's not fair that she cooks for us *and* cooks for the whole resort."

"She doesn't cook for the whole resort." Dayne's voice was rough from sleep. "She *directs* the cooks."

"She also creates the delicious menus. And makes sure the food is top quality. That's a lot of work. Don't discount what she does, Dayne," she admonished him.

Heath gently swept her messy bedhead hair out of her

face, then his fingertips trailed softly along her jawline. "Buttons is fine. Dani wouldn't let anything bad happen to her."

"Of course not, but she's not Dani's responsibility."

"She sure is," Dayne said. "The second my sister sneaks into *my* wing and absconds with *your* dog, Buttons becomes her responsibility."

Cara disagreed. Yes, Dani fell in love with Buttons, and yes, Cara completely trusted her to keep her dog safe, but still...

Heath grabbed her chin and forced her to meet his eyes. "Stop letting your thoughts spin. Instead, concentrate on us."

"But breakfast—"

"Can wait," Dayne finished for her, rolling away from them and getting to his feet. "I forgot to give you something last night."

"You gave me plenty last night," she countered with a grin. Her eyes took a long stroll down Dayne's exquisite naked body. She couldn't get enough of it. Nor of Heath's.

She was so damn glad she didn't have to choose between them. The two worked together seamlessly to make her come every time they had sex. They always made her the priority and each other secondary.

At least when the three of them were in the same room, bed, shower, or wherever. She knew that sometimes the two had sex without her when they went running out on the trails.

They didn't hide it from her and she didn't mind one bit.

Dayne returned her grin, but his looked a bit more wicked. "I bought something for you." He pursed his lips as he considered them on the bed. "Well, it's more for me and Heath."

Heath's eyebrows shot up his head. "What is it?"

Without answering, Dayne headed over to the wall of

cabinets and closets, opened one, and pulled out a gift bag. When he returned to the bed, he perched on the edge close to Heath and her. He held it out. "Open it."

She rolled off Heath and sat up. After taking the bag, Cara glanced in it, but it was full of purple tissue paper. She pulled it out and unwrapped whatever it was.

Whatever it was was very light.

It turned out to be a negligee. Not a regular negligee, of course. This was far more naughty than a silky outfit to wear to bed. She'd never worn anything like this before. Since there wasn't much to it, he could've skipped the gift bag and put it in a small pouch instead.

She held up the black teddy. While it had straps for her shoulders, it would not cover her breasts at all, leaving them completely exposed. The crotch area was open, too, for easy access. She turned it around to see it was a thong. Her breasts wouldn't be her only body parts on full display.

She agreed it was certainly sexy. Before coming to this resort and meeting Heath and Dayne, she never would've considered wearing anything even *close* to this.

"While I prefer you naked, sometimes it's fun to switch it up."

"I approve of that outfit," Heath said huskily while slowly stroking his hard cock from root to tip.

"I figured you would," Dayne told him, pulling Cara's attention from Heath's erection back to him. "You can wear it the next time we have a pajama party in the event hall."

Heat flooded her cheeks. "I..." She swallowed in an attempt to relax her tight throat. "I can't wear that at a party."

"Sure you can. That will cover you more than what a lot of guests will be wearing."

"Dayne, my breasts will be completely bouncing free. My crotch exposed..."

"Put it on and let's see how it fits. We'll be the judge whether or not you should wear it during an event."

"Sweetheart, you know no one will blink an eye if you show up in that," Heath assured her. "Dayne's right. That outfit isn't risqué at all on this resort."

"Put it on," Dayne insisted.

She gave him a pointed look. "That sounded like a demand and not a request."

Dayne shrugged. "Because it is."

"And if I say no?"

"You can always say no. I promise, it will be loads more fun if you say yes."

"For you two."

"We promise to make it fun for you, too."

She pulled in a deep breath as she considered it.

Every weekend they got together, the men nudged her further and further, testing her limits. They constantly showed her that she didn't need to be afraid of her sexuality and desires. That she needed to lean in and always be willing to try something new. They also assured her that her body was worthy of being shown off. Not only to them, but the world.

Did she like everything they suggested? No. But most of the time, she found that she did.

She swore they were beginning to know her better than she knew herself. They were both very observant and always gave her grace if she was uncomfortable.

But it was one thing to wear this in front of her lovers; quite another to wear it in front of the resort guests. A crowd at that.

Maybe one day she'd be brave enough, but she wasn't ready for that just yet.

Look at her, thinking about the future. The unknown.

She had no idea where their relationship, if they could call it that, would go. Or how long it would last. But one thing was for sure, she would enjoy it, and them, for as long as she could.

She was going to make every minute count.

Chapter Twenty-One

"Put it on, sweetheart," Heath urged. "I need to see it on you."

When the three of them were together, they normally slept naked. Because of that, and since there wasn't much to the teddy, it didn't take long for her to pull on the outfit.

And what an outfit it was.

It framed her breasts perfectly and gave them a peek-a-boo view of her crotch.

Good thing they didn't need to remove it for them to have sex, otherwise, she wouldn't be wearing it long.

Cara was sexy as hell without the black teddy. But with it...it was like framing a work of art. It didn't take away from the beauty, it enhanced it.

Appearing uncomfortable, she tugged at the black fabric in an attempt to adjust it. Most likely, she had never worn anything similar before.

No surprise.

Heath followed Dayne when he got to his feet.

"It's not going to cover any more than it already does,

baby. That's the point," Dayne pointed out as she continued to fuss.

Her hands fluttered in the air. "Why does this make me feel more exposed than if I was simply naked?"

Heath grinned. "You *were* naked only a few seconds ago."

"If you feel too exposed, you could wear pasties over your nipples and a miniskirt over it for the pajama party," Dayne suggested. "It would still give us easy access to you without flashing your goodies at everyone else."

"Is there a pajama party this weekend?" Cara asked.

"Tonight."

"What will you two be wearing?"

"How about we make a deal? If you wear that, you can decide what we wear," Dayne offered.

"Anything?"

Dayne nodded. "Anything you desire. We aim to please."

"You certainly do," she murmured, running her fingers over the smooth black fabric at her stomach and already looking a little more comfortable.

Heath was pleased how quickly she adapted to new things once she got over her initial discomfort.

Both Dayne and Heath began to circle her as if stalking prey. Their fingers and lips brushed over her flushed, heated skin. Heath tweaked a nipple while Dayne slid a finger between her folds to test her slickness.

Heath then stepped behind her and reached around to twist both nipples. At the same time, Dayne dropped to his knees at her feet, parted her pussy lips and flicked his tongue over her clit, pulling a gasp and a shudder from Cara.

Since she enjoyed her hair being pulled, Heath roughly grabbed a handful, yanked it up, and sank his teeth into the back of her neck, making her groan softly. Then he nibbled along her shoulders. Goosebumps rose all over her body from their attention.

It was a relief to know months later she was still highly reactive to their touch and attention. That they could still turn her on. Make her wet. Give her multiple orgasms. Drive her out of her mind to the point she was begging for their cocks.

The interest between their triad hadn't waned even a little.

Since he saw no end for them any time soon, it would be great if they could finally convince Cara to try double penetration. It was something both Dayne and he wanted to do regularly with her, if she was willing.

In the past couple of months, they had been carefully working her toward that goal. While one was fucking her ass or pussy, the other was using a dildo to work her other hole. The more ass play they did with her, the more she enjoyed it. Of course, taking it slow, along with proper preparation, had been the key.

Since Heath and Dayne were well schooled in anal sex, they knew what was needed to make it more comfortable and enjoyable for her. But two cocks penetrating her at the same time could be a bit much. They would need to stay observant and constantly check in with her to make sure it didn't turn into a disaster.

This morning, the thought of them both fucking Cara at the same time made his already hard cock swell even more.

"Does it make you feel sexy?" Heath murmured against her bare shoulder.

She threw her head back against Heath's shoulder as Dayne continued to eat her cunt like he had skipped a few meals. "It does now."

"Good," he whispered, his breath dancing across her skin.

Heath's gaze dropped to Dayne's cock hanging hard and heavy. Their shared lover used one hand to give him access to her clit and the other to stroke his own erection.

Releasing Cara's nipples, Heath cupped her breasts instead and began to knead them. "What do you want us to do to you, sweetheart? What's your desire?" he whispered into her ear. "Tell us. Tell us what you want. How you want us to make you come."

"You already know how to make me come." Her voice shook as Dayne continued to lap at her pussy.

"We can both fuck you."

"*Yesssss,*" she moaned.

"At the same time," he added to make sure she understood his meaning.

Dayne lifted his head at the same time Cara did.

"This morning?" she asked.

"Why not? You know we've been working toward that goal. Don't you want both of us inside you at the same time?"

When Dayne rose to his feet, he stayed close and exchanged his tongue in her pussy for his fingers. Sandwiching Cara between them, he took her mouth in a thorough kiss. He continued to finger fuck her while moving on to share an intense kiss with Heath next.

Heath tasted her arousal on his lips and tongue. So damn delicious.

"I'm not sure," Cara said once Dayne broke off the kiss with him.

"You can always use your safe word if it gets to be too much. We want it to be a good experience for you. If it's not, then it won't be for us either," Dayne assured her.

She cupped Dayne's face at the same time reaching back to cup Heath's. "I appreciate that about you two. You always consider me first."

"Well,"—Dayne grinned—"without the filling, there can be no sandwich."

Cara softly laughed. "I'm not always the filling. Sometimes I'm the bottom bun and one of you is in the middle."

She was right. Plenty of times, Dayne had fucked Cara while Heath fucked him at the same time. Or vice versa. However, it wasn't the same. Two cocks penetrating at the same time would definitely be a different experience.

"Say yes," Heath whispered into her ear. "Let's give it a shot and you can always tell us to stop."

"No risk, no reward, right?" Dayne asked her.

"You constantly push my boundaries," she murmured.

Was that a complaint or a compliment?

Heath quickly released her and joined Dayne so he could see her face. "That's what you wanted."

"I didn't say it was a bad thing. It's simply a fact. I actually appreciate that you do. As you already know, my previous sex life sucked and that's how I ended up here. You two have completely turned that around for me. And for that, I thank you."

Heath's sex life had never sucked, even with his ex-wife, so he couldn't imagine it. Despite that, being in a threesome had actually enhanced it. Especially with these two as partners.

Not once had they dealt with any kind of jealousy. The three of them aligned perfectly and without much effort. Funny enough, this relationship was much smoother than the ones he'd had with only a single person.

Not to mention, having three people involved gave them endless possibilities during sex. One night, Cara had even donned a strap-on and fucked Dayne as he sucked Heath's cock. Heath was surprised to find how much seeing that turned him on.

But no one was pegging anyone this morning.

"Are you ready to try taking both of us at once?" Dayne asked.

It was hard to ignore the string of precum dangling from the tip of Dayne's cock. With Heath's mouth watering at the sight, he thumbed it off Dayne and plugged his thumb between his lips to suck it clean.

Dayne's hazel eyes flared as he followed that movement.

He tasted as good as Cara.

Once he was done, Heath said, "We'll use lots of lube and go as slow as you need, sweetheart."

She pulled in a deep breath. "You two are really determined to do this."

"If you don't like it, we won't try again," Heath promised. That would be a damn shame, but they would respect her decision.

"Okay," she agreed.

"Safe word?" Dayne prodded.

Cara rolled her eyes. "Cabbage."

Dayne took her hand and led her back to the bed while Heath went to the toy cabinet and found some silicone lube instead of a water-based one. He hoped that would make anal sex a bit easier for her.

He also grabbed a couple of vibrators to keep nearby, just in case.

Now the only problem was, they hadn't yet decided who would plunder which hole. They *could* play rock-paper-scissors again like he and Dayne did the first time they fucked out in the woods.

"Do you have a preference?" he asked Dayne.

"I want her ass."

No surprise.

Cara raised a single eyebrow. "Who is smaller?"

Heath chuckled. "Good point. I guess that means you get what you want, Dayne."

Dayne huffed, "There isn't much difference between us."

"Of course you'd say that," Heath teased before glancing over at Cara. "You make the decision, then. Who do you want where?"

Her head tipped to the side as she considered that question. Finally, she answered, "Dayne isn't as girthy as you, so..."

Heath snorted, then gave Dayne a toothy smile. "See? Told you."

Cara sighed. "Why is dick size always a competition? It shouldn't be since it's not the size that counts but how you use it."

In Heath's opinion, size was debatable. He'd been with very small men who were very skilled and extremely large men who were horrible. He preferred the perfect combination. Like Dayne.

"And we're both pros, right?" Dayne winked at her.

"I don't have any complaints."

"*Umm.* You did after I fucked your ass last time," Heath reminded her.

"I was sore afterwards, that's why."

"And you weren't as sore after Dayne fucked you there, right? That's proof—"

"Of nothing," Dayne finished for him. He sighed. "Fine. I'll live with my tiny dick as long as I get to claim her ass."

The resort owner certainly did not have a small dick. But it was all in good fun to put the cocky man in his place. While Dayne wasn't as cocky now as he had been months ago when they all first met, the man still had his moments.

Heath gave Dayne the tube of lube and a condom, keeping the other for himself. The three of them needed to sit down soon and have a discussion about ditching the condoms. Cara was already on birth control pills and they had all been tested and cleared for STDs. Plus, none of them have had sex outside of their threesome. They could always don condoms if they invited anyone else to play with them for a night.

He made a mental note to have a discussion about this before the end of the weekend and they all parted ways.

After rolling on the condom and spreading the lube generously over his latex-covered cock in preparation, Dayne ordered Cara, "Get on the bed and on your hands and knees."

As soon as Cara climbed on the bed and moved into position, Dayne tugged the thong portion of her teddy to the side, exposing her tightly puckered hole. Heath slowly stroked himself as Dayne liberally spread the lube on the outside before working some inside. Afterward, he plunged his fingers in and out of her, working it even deeper and making her groan in pleasure.

"Do you like that?" Dayne's question sounded a bit tense. Since it had taken so long to get her to this point, he was probably as impatient as Heath.

"It feels so good."

Dayne drove his fingers harder and deeper, giving her a preview of what was to come. Heath's eyelids slid shut as he imagined his cock replacing Dayne's digits.

"Remember how full you feel when we fuck you there? It's going to be much more intense when we fill both holes," Dayne warned. "We might stretch you to the point where you worry, but give it a chance. Let your body adjust to us. Remember to push out when I push in and try not to tense. It'll only make it more difficult for all of us."

Cara glanced over her shoulder at him. "You've done this before?"

"I have," Dayne answered.

Her green eyes landed on Heath next. "You?"

Heath nodded. "I have. However, not many women are willing to attempt it. I love the fact you'll try almost anything once. You at least give it a chance before saying no."

That willingness was a huge turn-on for him.

She rose up on her knees. "How are we doing this?"

"I'm going to lie on my back, you're going to climb onto my cock, and I'm going to stretch you out a little before Heath joins us. Is that okay with you?"

"Yes."

Not that anyone asked... "I'm okay with that, too."

Dayne shot him a grin. "I figured as much."

"She should face away from you. I think it'll make it easier on her. Especially for her first time."

Dayne nodded. "Good idea."

After Dayne climbed back onto the bed, he reclined and propped some pillows under his head.

Heath offered Cara his hand to help her into place. Still on her knees, she faced the foot of the bed and lined herself up over Dayne's cock. He held it in place while she slowly lowered herself, taking his length little by little.

Heath began to stroke himself again while watching Dayne's cock slowly disappear into her ass.

Now he regretted letting Dayne have that spot instead of him.

Next time.

If there was one.

They had to guarantee there would be.

She kept wiggling her hips to drive him deeper and once

Dayne was fully seated, she stilled for a moment, closed her eyes, and simply breathed.

After Heath realized he also was attracted to men, anal sex became a regular thing for him, whether he was on the giving or receiving end. However, watching Cara brought back some of the memories from all the way back to the beginning. So, he understood her initial hesitation to them fucking her there.

Dayne grabbed her hips and gently urged her to move. "You're in control, baby. Go as slow or as fast as you want. We need this to be comfortable for you before Heath joins us."

With her bottom lip clamped between her teeth and a flush running up her neck and into her cheeks, she nodded.

"Try to relax as much as possible. If you need more lube, tell us. It's close by for that reason." Heath instructed, "Once you think you're ready, say the word."

Soon, hopefully. He'd rather be involved than only an observer. Especially when his cock was now so damn hard from anticipation that it ached.

Dayne reached around and played with her clit as she rode him slowly and tentatively.

Heath watched her face carefully, waiting for her expression to soften. He watched the fingers dug into Dayne's thighs for her grip to loosen. He watched her clenched jaw for it to relax.

When the point came she seemed to be comfortable enough, he asked, "Are you ready?"

Cara met his eyes, then dropped her gaze to his cock, where his hand was nothing but a blur with how fast he was jerking it. She needed to give him the go ahead soon so he didn't explode prior to joining them.

What a wasted opportunity that would be.

"I..." She closed her eyes again for a moment and when she opened them, she said, "I think I'm ready."

That was his cue.

He climbed onto the bed, instructing Dayne to hold her legs up and open, to give him easy access to her pussy. Her plump folds were shiny already. A good sign.

Once he straddled Dayne's legs, he held himself back for a moment.

Now that Dayne was holding her legs in position, Cara no longer had control of her movements. She was basically pinned against him.

Heath fought the urge to plunge into her immediately and instead decided to get her worked up even more first.

He slapped her pussy with short, sharp strikes he knew had to sting. She said nothing to stop him and instead cried out with each one.

Dayne blew out a loud breath. "Every time you do that, she squeezes me tight."

"Is it too much?" Heath asked him.

"Not for me. Cara?" Dayne asked next.

"No, it's so good. Please do it some more."

Even though his cock was screaming for relief, he dug deep for the patience to continue. But this time, he tongued her pussy between the slaps. But the second he saw her getting so aroused she was dripping onto Dayne's balls, he... was...done.

He did not want to come before even getting to the goal line.

Rising up on his knees, he shuffled forward. Then using his cock, he slapped her pussy hard twice before lining himself up and drawing the swollen crown through her folds, spreading her arousal.

Both Dayne and Cara remained still as Heath began to work himself inside. It was not easy. "She's so damn tight."

The farther he went and the deeper he filled her, the more he could feel Dayne's cock. Only a thin wall separated them.

"Are you okay?" he asked between gritted teeth.

"Yes. Oh my God," she moaned.

"I can feel your cock against mine," Heath told Dayne. He was losing his fucking mind. He had obsessed about this moment since that first week and it was finally here.

They were both inside Cara. Both inside the woman they shared.

At the same time.

Chapter Twenty-Two

Once again, Heath wished they were already past wearing condoms. He would love to leave his load inside her at the same time Dayne did.

He'd love to see their cum sliding out of both holes. He never cared about that with any of his previous partners, but for some reason with Cara—and even Dayne—that urge was strong.

Now was not the time to bring it up with them, was it?

Once he began thrusting, he wouldn't be able to form a solid thought, so if he was going to propose it, now *would* be the time.

He met Cara's hooded eyes. "I want to come inside you."

"You always—"

"Without a condom," he finished.

Her eyes widened slightly.

Dayne whispered, "Holy shit. I'm onboard with that, too. But it's up to you, Cara."

Heath pleaded their case. "You're on birth control. We've all been cleared of any STDs. But Dayne's right, it's up to you. Only say yes if you're completely comfortable with the idea."

"We've been exclusive for months now," Dayne reminded her. "We've been with no one else but each other."

Whenever Dayne admitted that out loud, it was always a relief to hear. Especially since the man previously admitted he used the resort as his personal playground. It was hard to believe he gave that up for both him and Cara.

But he had.

It was easier for Heath and Cara to be exclusive to the triad since it took more of an effort to find a potential partner, unlike Dayne who was surrounded by them daily.

"If you remove the condoms, we'll have to start all over again," she answered.

It took a second for it to sink in that she meant the anal sex and not their relationship.

"It'll be easier the second time." Dayne was just as eager to ditch the condoms.

She hesitated for only a few seconds before nodding. "Okay."

Heath quickly pulled out and ripped off the condom, tossing it over his shoulder and not caring where it landed. Dayne dropped her legs and Heath grabbed her hands, lifting her enough for the resort owner to pull himself free and remove his condom. Heath didn't follow the trajectory of it, but he was damn sure it also ended up on the floor in his enthusiasm.

Clean up in aisle five.

"We'll need more lube," Dayne announced, reaching for it and spreading a generous amount on his now-bare erection. He worked more inside Cara before tossing the tube aside.

Gripping the root, he held his cock in place and gave Heath the signal to help Cara mount him. As soon as she was once again seated on his cock, he pulled her legs back and held them wide open, giving Heath full access.

Heath quickly got back into place and drove his cock home.

Home.

He realized at that moment, that was the feeling he got in his chest whenever he sank deep into Cara or Dayne. Even the second he arrived on the resort and saw the other two-thirds of their triad.

Holy shit.

"*Fuuuuuck.*" Dayne's groaned curse pulled Heath from his rattling discovery.

Dayne only made slight movements when Heath began to thrust. The tight heat of her pussy combined with the friction created between the two cocks filling her was almost too much for him to bear.

"Jesus," Dayne ground out. "I'm hardly moving and I'm struggling not to come."

"Put yourself in my place," Heath somehow managed to say.

Instead of offering to switch, Dayne began to do what he did best: talk dirty.

He was so good at it that during the week, when Heath wasn't at the ranch resort, and they regularly jerked off together during video chats. The filthy words and suggestions that Dayne so skillfully spewed would fill his ears and fuel his imagination.

Dayne also had those types of phone and video chats with Cara. It was the next best thing when they couldn't be together in person.

But right now, Heath had to block out his barrage of filthy scenarios or he'd lose it too quickly. Hopefully, his dirty talk, along with their actions, would make Cara climax sooner than later.

Heath only paused long enough to snag one of the vibrators he'd thrown on the mattress earlier and switch it on. Placing the buzzing toy directly against her clit, it pulled a gasp from her, while Dayne pinned her tighter against him so her hips wouldn't dance around, possibly dislodging them both.

Their teamwork was seamless.

To help push her over the edge, he began plucking her nipples with his lips and fingers. At first, he was gentle, then she begged him to do it harder and rougher. It got to the point he was scraping his teeth over the very hard tips and sinking them into her soft flesh.

Her unbridled wail filled the space around them at the same time her body bowed, fighting against Dayne's hold. With her eyes rolled back, she bucked against them. "Please... please...*Yessss*, like that...Give me more. Fuck me harder. Please...Please...*Please!*"

Heath gritted his teeth and did his best to give her what she wanted. Dayne's constant stream of erotic talk ceased, as did his thrusts, when Heath rammed his cock inside her over and over.

Dayne blew out a ragged breath before releasing a growled, "Christ."

"Come, sweetheart," Heath encouraged, ignoring how much the bite marks he left behind on her breasts created a fire in his gut. Ignoring the intense clenching of her core around his throbbing cock. Ignoring the fact Dayne's knuckles had turned white while holding onto Cara and his willpower.

Heath didn't need to feel the way Cara's inner walls rippled around him when she came. Or the way she exploded, soaking his cock. Her loud wail was enough evidence.

He drove up and into her once more, then waited for the waves of her orgasm to pass as well as the threat of his own. Once they subsided, he tossed the vibrator aside and began to fuck her again. Slower this time, for his own self-preservation.

"I have to move now," Dayne warned.

They found a rhythm that worked and made it easier for all three. Heath pushed forward every time Dayne pulled back slightly. Dayne thrusted as deep as possible whenever Heath retreated enough to give him more room.

They worked like a well-oiled machine. A cohesive unit.

A team.

Lovers. Partners...

Was it becoming more?

Did he want more?

Did they?

Shit.

"I can't hold out anymore," Heath warned Dayne, who responded through clenched teeth, "You and me both."

Cara wasn't helping either of them when she insisted, "Fill me up. Both of you. Come inside me. Make me yours."

Didn't she know she was theirs already? That she belonged to them inside and out?

Heath would do anything to keep her happy and satisfied. To keep a smile on her face. To hear her tinkling laughter when he or Dayne said something funny, ridiculous, or even dumb.

He'd do anything to keep her coming back for more. To keep her returning to them. And only them. He was damn sure Dayne would agree.

The cocky player was gone. The dedicated lover had taken his place.

Cara wasn't the only one in this equation that Heath didn't want to lose.

What he *did* lose was his load when, with a grunt, he filled her cunt at the same time Dayne filled her ass.

His hips continued to twitch as his balls emptied deep inside her.

They remained where they were and took a moment to recover, to catch their breaths, to think about what just happened.

The only woman Heath hadn't worn a condom with previously was his ex. And as for his male partners...he hoped Dayne would be open to being the first.

To him, coming inside them was the same as claiming them, as marking both of them as his.

After he slipped from Cara, Heath urged Dayne, "Continue to hold her there." He wanted to keep the cum inside her as long as possible.

When Dayne requested a towel so he could pull out and not leave a mess behind on the bed, Heath headed to the bathroom to get one. On his way back, he grabbed the inflatable wedge they sometimes used during sex. Once Dayne pulled free of Cara, they placed the triangular pillow under her hips, lifting them.

Heath leaned in closer and drew a finger through her folds to check out his handiwork, then he did the same where Dayne had made his deposit.

Cara lifted her head. "Are you inspecting me down there?"

Heath lifted his own. "Why not? Do you know how hot that is, not only knowing, but seeing our cum inside you?"

Now on his way to the bathroom to clean up, Dayne threw over his shoulder, "Wait until we both fill her pussy."

Heath climbed back into bed and claimed the spot to her right. "Are you comfortable like that?"

"I can't stay like this all day, you know," she said.

"I know. But bear with it for a few minutes?"

"Anything for you," she whispered and cupped his cheek.

The contrast of this woman sometimes caught him off guard; super sweet one moment and very, very dirty the next. She showed the world the part of her where she was a straight-laced librarian; she shared with him and Dayne the part where she was far from that.

Dayne returned to the bed. "Will you do anything for me, too?"

"Of course."

Heath pressed a kiss to her lips. "You've come so far, sweetheart. So damn far. I'm so proud of you for trying almost everything we suggest."

She gave him a soft smile. "That's because you make sure I'm ready before you suggest it. Thank you for keeping your patience with me as I explore and learn."

"You're worth it."

Dayne settled to her left and tucked an arm under his head, using it as a pillow. "I second that."

Cara yawned. "I can't say I'd like to do this every day, but I would definitely do this again."

More proof her confidence in the bedroom had grown exponentially.

With a smirk, Dayne leaned over to press his mouth to hers next, murmuring against her lips. "I'm sure you already know, we'll be up for it whenever you are."

———

WHILE THE SEX with Dayne and Heath was always heart-pounding, sweat-inducing, and orgasmic, Cara also appreciated the quiet times they shared together. Like tonight.

She sighed with contentment as she stared into the flickering flames of the bonfire set up next to the lake. The sky was clear, the stars bright and the weather cool enough to need a blanket despite the heat emitting from the fire.

Dayne had resort staff set up the firepit, the chairs, two chilled bottles of wine, along with a boxed dinner from the lodge's kitchen and everything needed to make s'mores for dessert. Her mouth watered when she learned about the s'mores since she hadn't had them in years.

Most of the time, they ate dinner in the lodge together, surrounded by dozens of others, and breakfast was shared with his siblings and their significant others at the farmhouse. So, tonight was a real treat since it was only the three of them enjoying a glass of local wine, great food, and light conversation.

Despite her stomach being full from the dinner expertly prepared by Danica's cooks, Cara accepted a metal skewer from Dayne. He'd already jammed an oversized marshmallow on the end.

Cara glanced to her left and took in Heath's strong profile. His Adirondack chair was butted up against hers and Buttons snuggled in his lap. He stared into the fire with his lips slightly curled at the ends. In one hand, he held his roasting stick over the fire and used the other to mindlessly stroke her dog's ears and back.

Buttons was in Heaven whenever she came to the farm. Her Boston Terrier loved all the attention, not only from "Aunt" Dani, but Dayne and Heath as well as all of the resort employees and guests.

Dayne, holding his own long metal stick, set the container

of graham crackers and chocolate nearby before settling into his seat to Cara's right with a groan. He stretched out his long legs. "Man, I haven't made s'more since I was a kid. We'll have to do this more often."

More often.

There seemed to be no end in sight for the three of them. But right now, they were living weekend to weekend without discussing the future.

Of course, they hadn't set out to forge a permanent relationship. Despite it starting out solely about sex, somewhere along the way, it had grown into something deeper. But, again, none of them brought it up. They allowed this connection to simmer below the surface.

In truth, she had no idea what Dayne and Heath thought about their triad. Did they simply want to continue on as it was until it petered out? What if it never dwindled? What if their bond only grew stronger?

Of course, being burned in the past made her cautious about entering into another serious relationship and she had a feeling that Heath felt the same way due to his ugly divorce.

And as for Dayne...

She had no idea where his thoughts lie. While he was an open book, most of his pages were blank.

Since they lived separate lives during the week, maybe the current state of their relationship was the perfect scenario for both men.

She would love to spend more time with them, so it wasn't as perfect for her. During the week, she not only looked forward to their shared weekends, but her heart didn't feel whole.

One night, while she laid in bed at home with Buttons curled against her side, she realized why.

She had fallen in love with both of them.

After Glenn, she hoped to be able to love and trust again, but never in her wildest dreams did she think her love would be shared between two men. But here she was, enjoying a peaceful night sandwiched between the men she loved.

Maybe she could spur some conversation to see if either, or both, had any thoughts on their future. Though, at this point, she'd keep her feelings to herself since she didn't want to pressure either of them into saying anything they don't mean.

She rotated her marshmallow to brown it evenly. "What a perfect night. If a year ago, you had told me I'd be sitting in front of a fire at a sex resort roasting marshmallows, I would've thought you had booked a one-way ticket on the crazy train."

"I'd have to agree with that," Heath said on a chuckle. "Came for the sex, stayed for the s'mores."

That's it? He stayed for the s'mores?

Dayne snorted. "Well, you know how we go above and beyond for our guests."

"But we're no longer guests," Cara reminded him, hoping that would be a good opening.

"You're my personal guests."

"Is that all we are?" Cara asked Dayne.

"Of course not." He extended the hand not holding the stick between them.

When Cara clasped it, he gave it a slight squeeze before interlocking their fingers.

It was awkward assembling her s'more with one hand, but she didn't want to let Dayne go to do so.

She tried again. "I have to thank you both for everything you've done for me in the last few months. For showing me I can trust men again and helping me come out of my sexual shell. Even treating me like a queen by spoiling me." Her eyes flicked to Heath's lap. "And, of course, accepting Buttons."

"You don't have to keep thanking us, sweetheart." Heath squeezed her blanket-covered knee. "Doing so was our pleasure. Literally."

Dayne smirked. "Lots and lots of pleasure."

"Neither of you had to invest so much time in me," she continued. "You did it willingly and, Dayne, you gave up the guests available at your disposal to concentrate on us."

"It wasn't a sacrifice. I wouldn't have done it if I didn't want to. Plus, I love seeing you flourish. I'd say that's the best revenge after what happened between you, your rotten friend, and your ex."

"Maybe my former friend did me a favor by sleeping with him. I might have stayed, despite the shitty sex, if Glenn hadn't cheated. I can't deny the betrayal was painful at first but, sitting here tonight, I can now say I'm grateful. She's now stuck with that shitty sex and"—she squeezed Dayne's hand while pointing a smile at Heath—"I'm not."

Truthfully, she'd never had a man cherish and respect her as much as Dayne and Heath do.

She dangled the carrot next. "Even so, I'm going to be a lot more careful if and when I choose to ever settle down again."

"Same," Heath grumbled. "I said it before and I'm going to say it again: I never want to go through another divorce. I've spent too much time and energy trying to recover from all of the financial and emotional damage. Though, I have to admit, I'm finally getting there with the help of you two. I also can't ignore the fact she finally got married again last month and I no longer have that insane alimony check as a monthly reminder."

"I'm sure that's a relief." Dayne released her hand so he

could tuck his burnt marshmallow between two graham crackers and a piece of a chocolate bar. After taking a big bite, he moaned as he chewed. "Damn, that's good. Almost as good as your pussy, Cara."

"I'm not sure what to do with that compliment." Despite teasing him, she was disappointed neither man tried to take a bite of that carrot. "Would you ever marry again, Heath?"

It took him a few seconds to respond. "I don't know."

"What about having children?"

When he turned to face her, the firelight reflecting off his face deepened the shadows of his furrowed brow. "Since I'm forty-five, it would be something I'd have to consider soon. I wouldn't want to be the oldest father at my kid's graduation. Plus, who wants to be changing diapers and running after toddlers in their fifties?"

"Plenty of men do it," Dayne said.

"I'd never say never. I'm just relieved I didn't have any with my ex. That might have made our divorce an even bigger disaster and force me to be tied to her for years." He shuddered dramatically.

"But if you did, you would have loved them no matter what," Cara said.

"Of course."

She waited for him to expand on that, but instead, he went back to eating his s'more. "Dayne?"

"What?"

"What about you?"

"Yes, I could eat another s'more," he answered.

She clicked her tongue. "I'm asking about marriage and children."

"Oh." He sighed. "I don't know. I kind of like how my life is now."

"Nothing could improve it?"

"Oh, plenty could improve it, but I'm not sure marriage and children would fit that bill."

"So, you never want to settle down?"

He stared at her. "Why are you asking?"

"I'm only curious. You said you've had relationships in the past, but nothing serious. I understand why Heath and I would be gun shy about it, but what's stopping you?"

"Nothing is stopping me except personal choice. Marriage and children aren't for everyone. But like Heath, I'd never say never."

Then he stopped talking and concentrated on lighting his next marshmallow on fire.

She mentally sighed.

Maybe now wasn't the right time to talk about their future and what it meant for the three of them. While she didn't want to keep pushing them and ruin the evening, if this relationship kept continuing on its current path, it would need to be addressed at some point.

Chapter Twenty-Three

Dayne wasn't happy. He had wanted to sit down with both Cara and Heath and talk to them. Actually, more like propose an idea.

Unfortunately, Cara couldn't come to the resort this weekend because her sister was throwing their cousin a baby shower. Not only was Cara attending, but she needed to help with the party.

That meant this was the first weekend since both Heath and her began staying with him on the ranch that it would only be the two men.

It didn't take long before they had moved from every other weekend to spending every weekend with Dayne. In fact, he couldn't imagine spending one without Heath. Or Cara.

But without her here, they felt off. Incomplete.

Their threesome had fallen into an easy rhythm. Every weekend they learned something new about each other. Every weekend they pushed their sexcapades a little further.

Not once had the sex been boring.

Not once had it been unsatisfying.

Not once had it been forgettable.

Not once had Dayne thought about hooking up with anyone else during the days and nights Heath or Cara weren't around.

Not even once.

He was definitely broken.

Or, it could be as Dylan suggested. Instead of Dayne being broken, maybe his two lovers made him complete.

A few weeks ago, his brother had approached him as he stood out in front of the farmhouse, once again watching Heath's Genesis G90 and Cara's Subaru disappear down the paved lane.

"Look at that, brother. You claimed those two broke you, but what if they actually make you whole?"

Dayne ground his teeth at Dylan's unrestrained laughter as he walked away.

Bastard.

But, *damn*, his brother might be right.

For once.

In the past few months, his twin had obviously been watching their triad closely—especially since they all ate breakfast in the shared kitchen—but he hadn't said much about his observations. At least in front of Cara and Heath.

When Dayne and Dylan were alone, though, his brother had dropped slight hints. Made vague comments. Shot him smug looks.

Finally, last Sunday evening, as he once again watched them leave, Dylan slapped him on the back and bluntly asked, "When are they moving in?"

That question made his lungs seize and his heart tumble violently. Whatever expression was on his face—most likely horror or shock—made Dylan laugh *again* and walk away shaking his head.

Moving in?

Were they even at that point? Did he want to cohabitate with them? Would it destroy the easy relationship they had now?

Dayne stood frozen in place waiting for the invisible choke collar around his neck to tighten.

It didn't.

The longer he stood contemplating what Dylan asked, the easier it was to breathe. His pulse slowed. Any sense of impending doom dissipated. A sense of peace came over him.

It became obviously clear what he had to do next. Only, Cara kind of screwed up his plan when she couldn't join them this weekend. In the meantime, he could see what Heath thought about his proposal and if he was onboard, then maybe they could both work on convincing Cara.

But, *shit*, once he mentioned his proposition to Heath, he wouldn't be able to take it back. It would be out of his internal thoughts and into the world.

His feelings would be known. He'd also be vulnerable.

After hearing Heath's answers to Cara's questions about marriage and children a few weeks ago, maybe the man would laugh his ass off and say no. Then that would be the end of that. They would simply continue on like they have been until one or more of them tired of their weekend trysts and they decided to go their separate ways.

Or...

He studied the hard lines and curves of Heath's broad, bare back. He was lying on his side, facing away from Dayne, with the top sheet loosely draped over his hips and covering his long legs. Dayne rolled into him and brushed his lips along the nape of his neck.

With a soft moan, Heath flopped onto his back. His morning wood tented the sheet and tempted Dayne, but he needed to get through this first.

"Ready to go again?" Heath's voice was rough with sleep.

"Again? The last time was last night."

"Yeah, like at two a.m. It's"—he lifted his head to glance at the digital clock on the nightstand—"six. That was only four hours ago." With a groan, he dropped his head back onto the pillow.

"Four hours is a lifetime ago."

Heath scoffed, "I know I'm irresistible…"

"About that." Dayne hauled himself across Heath's warm, lickable chest so they could be face-to-face.

Heath cocked an eyebrow. "About what? How irresistible I am?"

"I have an idea."

"Of how irresistible I am? Of course you do."

Dayne sucked on his teeth. "No. I have an idea I want to bring up."

Heath's other eyebrow rose to join the first one. "Should I be worried? Please don't ask me to dress up like a clown and—"

"That's not it." And never would be. Having sex with someone dressed as a clown would give him the creeps. He probably wouldn't even be able to get hard.

"Hold on. If it's *your* idea, why do *you* look worried?"

"Because it would mean a big change." That was putting it mildly. It would be *life* changing.

Those same eyebrows now pinched together. "I don't understand."

"Because I haven't had a chance to explain yet!"

Heath pinned his lips together but the wrinkles at the

corner of his eyes deepened, giving his amusement away. "Well then, explain."

Dayne sighed. "Maybe now I don't want to."

"Holy shit. Are you going to pout? Let me get rid of that for you." Heath curled his hand around the back of Dayne's head and pulled him down until their mouths touched.

After a long, thorough, breath-stealing kiss, Heath was no longer the only one in that bed with a hard-on.

Damn it, he needed to stay on track.

"Tell me what you want to talk about," Heath whispered. "Otherwise, I'm going to fuck you because my cock is desperate to be in your ass. It's my turn."

Dayne sucked in a bolstering breath. He needed to hurry and get it out before this whole conversation went sideways. Or he ended up on his hands and knees getting fucked doggy-style. "Okay, but don't freak out."

Heath propped himself up on an elbow and frowned. "You're the one freaked out, not me. Did you have sex with someone outside of our threesome?"

"No, that's the problem..."

The creases in Heath's forehead deepened. "I'd say it's a problem because we all agreed—"

"No, I didn't fuck anyone else! The problem is that I have no desire to do so."

Heath's expression twisted. "How is that a problem?"

"Because I want you to move here...move in...with me. Here...on the ranch..." *Damn it! Stop rambling!*

He hoped to hell he didn't regret opening this Pandora's Box. He didn't want to lose Heath or Cara and maybe his suggestion would come off as pushy.

Heath only stared at him, unblinking, for far too long.

Dayne's heart was no longer beating in his chest but was now in his ears.

Was he having a panic attack? A heart attack? Why won't Heath respond?

His "Well?" came out louder than he planned.

Shit.

"Well…" Heath repeated carefully. "On the chance I was looking to move, I'd be searching for beachfront property, not one in the mountains. However, moving here…on *your* property, in *your* home…I don't want to be beholden to someone else, Dayne. I like my freedom and what I do for a living gives me that. I might lose some of it by moving here."

That pounding heart dropped into his stomach. Did he just screw the pooch? If so, he needed to fix it. "Think how much money you'd save by living here instead. With me. With us."

Heath's head jerked. "So, you've run this idea by Cara already?"

"No, not yet. I planned on bringing it up to you both this weekend, but…"

"Right. She couldn't make it." Heath sighed, dropped his head back onto the pillow and stared up at the ceiling. "You were right about this being a big change. I wasn't expecting this from you."

"You're not interested."

"I didn't say that. But there are a lot of factors to consider first."

At least it wasn't a flat out no.

"You can work from anywhere," Dayne reminded him.

"True. But you know who can't?"

That right there would be a major obstacle. One he wasn't sure how to overcome.

"Of course I want her here with us," Dayne started, "but…"

"But she has a life that she can't just pick up and leave."

"Not unless we can figure out a way."

"She's a librarian, Dayne. I'm sure there's no need for one in Fisher Falls."

Well, at least Heath sounded as disappointed as Dayne felt. "No. The public library is too small here and doesn't have much of a budget."

Heath pursed his lips. "Schools have librarians."

"Sure, if there are any openings. Public libraries in State College might be a possibility, but that's about an hour drive and come winter..." Dayne trailed off.

He wouldn't want Cara commuting to State College. Of course, more opportunities existed there than in Fisher Falls, but not at the risk of her getting into a crash.

"Yeah. Ice, snow, freezing rain. I wouldn't want her driving in treacherous conditions, either." Heath scraped fingers through his hair. "Okay then, how could this work? Besides asking her to continue to come up every weekend? Come winter, that drive could be worse than her commuting to State College. Something else to consider: would us living together without her possibly make her feel like a third wheel? That could fracture what we've built together."

Dayne agreed. "That two and a half hour drive will get old quick if she continues to drive up every weekend. And if it's a bad winter..." Her driving back and forth wasn't what he wanted anyway. "This is why I asked you to move out here. I know your drive is even longer."

Heath slid up from his reclined position to sit back against the heavy-duty headboard. His brown eyes bore into Dayne. "That's the only reason? You're concerned about my long drive?"

"Your long haul wasn't a factor. Getting rid of it is simply a benefit."

"What was a factor?"

Shit. Dayne squeezed his eyes shut. Of course Heath would want the reasoning behind his suggestion.

"Why do you want this?" Heath pressed.

"Why not?"

Heath shook his head. "No. Our long drives are no skin off your nose. It affects us, not you."

"Okay, how about the fact I want you two here more than only on the weekends?"

"I think we all want that, but that doesn't mean we should live together. You don't ask someone to move in with you unless you need to split household expenses, which, in your case, I know isn't necessary. Another reason would be because you can't trust your partners and want to keep tabs on them. I can think of another reason, too..."

While Heath really wanted Dayne to confess to the real reason, he wasn't sure if he could let the truth pass his lips.

Heath released another long sigh. "Look, as you know, I've been through one ugly divorce already. Cara suffered through a rough relationship. While you've only skated along, plugging your dick into available holes here and there. You never locked yourself down in a serious relationship before and now you propose this. That means you consider our relationship serious and more than sex. Am I right?"

"You don't?"

Heath tilted his head and studied his sheet-covered lap for a second. "Of course I do. I wouldn't continue to do that drive if I didn't."

"Then, there you go."

Heath huffed. "No, Dayne, you're avoiding the real reason."

Being called out was irritating. "If you think you know what that real reason is, then say it."

"Why can't you?"

Dayne dropped his head and rubbed his forehead. When he lifted it again, he whispered, "Because I've never felt anything like this before and I'm not sure what this is."

"Break it down, then. You don't need us for companionship or sex since"—he swept out a hand—"you have a resort full of people here who can provide that for you. You don't need me or Cara—"

"I do need you!" Dayne groaned at his own outburst. *For fuck's sake.*

Heath grabbed his hand and interlocked their fingers. "You're getting closer."

"Closer to what?"

"To the true reason."

"If you know it, just say it!" Dayne tried to pull his hand free but Heath held on even tighter.

"Fine. I'll admit how I feel since you can't. The drive is worth it for me since I've fallen in love with you. With Cara. I don't want to be with anyone else. I don't want to wake up and not have you two next to me. But this *is* a big step and I want to make sure all of us are ready for it—especially you—because I never want to go through what I did during my divorce again."

"I wouldn't have asked if I wasn't."

"Dayne, you look like you're about to puke."

His stomach *was* kind of churning.

"Do you *really* want this? You want both of us to move onto the ranch? Not only onto the property but move in *with* you? I need you to be sure before I'll even consider it."

"Yes," Dayne answered. "The weekends aren't enough for me, either. When you two aren't here, I struggle to concentrate on work. I think about you constantly. It's never been like that for me. Never."

Heath held his gaze when he asked, "Do you miss one of us more than the other?"

"No. I don't feel complete unless I'm with both of you."

Heath blew out a breath and shook his head.

"Why are you doing that?"

When Heath didn't answer right away, Dayne counted his heartbeats as he waited.

Heath finally admitted, "Like you, I wasn't looking for anything serious." He tossed his head back and ground his hand against the back of his neck. When he met Dayne's eyes again, he finished with, "But I guess it found me."

"That's how I see it, too. But I'm seeing this resort differently now. Just because we'd be exclusive doesn't mean our sex lives would become stale and boring. As long as we all agree, more guests could continue to join us. We could still use the playrooms. Instead of this place only being my personal playground, it would become one for all of us."

"Our relationship would be a democracy."

"Of course."

"If I say yes, I want to be clear: I'll keep my place in Hoboken and rent it out. I'm not sure I'm ready to give it up yet. Especially if we don't know if Cara wants to live here, too."

"If..." Dayne shook his head, then continued with more confidence than he felt, "No, not if. *Once* you say yes, I'll need your help to convince her."

Chapter Twenty-Four

"How about this? We give it a trial run first. If we fail, at least I'll still have my penthouse to go home to."

Dayne wasn't sure he liked the idea of Heath having an easy escape. What if they were having problems and instead of working them out, he returned to Hoboken because it was easier?

However, he also didn't want Heath to feel trapped. He wanted the three of them to share their lives together. Willingly.

"We won't fail." Dayne was determined for that to be true.

Heath shot him a skeptical look. "Relationships are difficult enough with two people, but three?"

"It's working out for my brother. Of course, every relationship can be bumpy. We have to be willing to work at it." And not just haul ass if and when things got rough.

Heath narrowed his eyes on Dayne. "Who *are* you?"

He finally let himself relax enough to chuckle. "Believe me, I'm wondering that myself." So were his siblings.

"I can't believe you want to give up your freedom."

"Freedom feels worthless if you aren't with the people you love."

"Love," Heath repeated in a murmur.

Shit. He needed to own it. Admit it. Skirting around his feelings wasn't fair to himself. Or Heath. Or Cara. They deserved to know. "Yes, *love*. Otherwise, I'd be fine with leaving things as they are."

Heath pressed the back of his hand against Dayne's forehead. "Nope. No fever."

Dayne shoved his hand away as an idea popped into his noggin. "If you or Cara need more privacy, or even a break, you could always use Dylan's wing. Once they move into their new house, that'll give us extra space. We could also put your office over there. It'll give you peace and privacy to work."

"Have you run that idea past your siblings?"

No, he hadn't since he just thought of it. "I will." If taking over Dylan's wing didn't work, they could always build their own house on the property, just like his brother, Erin, and Ford were doing. And if they did that, they could potentially close off both wings from the main house and rent them out like they did the lake cabins.

More income was always good.

"So, you love us, huh? It's more than hot sex?" Heath asked.

"You're going to make me say it?"

Heath grinned. "Of course. Did I not admit that I fell in love with both you and Cara? And guess what? I didn't break out in a cold sweat."

"Have you told Cara?"

"No, not yet. But I will," Heath answered. "Will you tell her?"

"Yes."

"Will you tell me?"

"Can I show you instead?"

"You can *after* you actually say the words. To me. Directly." He gave Dayne a toothy smile.

"Damn it," Dayne grumbled, pretending to be annoyed.

Heath chuckled. "I'm confident you can do it."

Dayne glanced at Heath's lap to see his erection was gone.

He tried again. "Can I give you head instead?"

"You're capable of doing both." Heath tugged on Dayne's bottom lip with his thumb. "Now, how about making good use of that mouth."

Dayne yanked the sheet back and uncovered Heath's now-soft cock. That was an easy fix.

Heath grabbed his chin and held it until their gazes met. His brown eyes sparkled with amusement. "Repeat after me: I love you."

Like moving in together, saying you loved someone, once out into the world, couldn't be taken back.

"You love me."

"Yes, I do, but you know what you were supposed to say."

Dayne leaned in until they were almost nose-to-nose and enunciated each word slowly, "I. Love. You. There. Are you hap—"

Heath grabbed Dayne's face and slammed their mouths together, driving his tongue deep and exploring every nook and cranny.

Their tongues warred for a moment before the kiss softened and became less intense. When they parted, both were breathing heavily and Heath's cock was once again a steel pipe.

Heath dropped his voice an octave when he ordered, "Now...suck my dick."

Doing so would not be a hardship. Besides loving Heath, Dayne loved sucking his cock as much as he loved eating Cara's pussy.

Heath parted his legs and patted the space between them. Once Dayne moved into place, he collared the root of Heath's cock with two fingers and squeezed tight. As soon as the veins bulged and his length darkened, he encircled the swollen crown with his mouth.

Heath's groan filled his ears. His fingers traced Dayne's stretched lips and stroked his throat as he swallowed the man's whole length. He took Heath so deeply, the tip butted against the back of his mouth.

The taste and scent of this man—his lover and hopefully life partner—had become so familiar to Dayne that in a blind taste test he'd be able to recognize Heath easily. Most likely he could do the same with Cara.

Lifting his head, his tongue drew along the thick ridge on the underside of Heath's shaft. Then his tongue and mouth explored the velvety smooth skin encasing it, while his fingers gently kneaded the warm, soft sack hanging heavily between muscular thighs.

When he sucked at the crown as hard as he could, Heath's hips jerked and a loud groan escaped him.

"The only downside to you sucking my cock is your mouth's full and you can't talk dirty to me. That's becoming one of my favorite things." He suddenly blew out a loud breath. "God, your mouth...you're about to make me come."

Dayne pulled free only long enough to warn, "Once you do, I'm going to fuck you."

Heath's pulsing cock was a sign that he was about to explode, but Dayne ignored it and continued sucking him deep, licking the length and scraping his teeth over the head. The sooner Heath came, the sooner Dayne could get his own relief by fucking him.

Good morning to me!

When Heath's hips slammed forward—Dayne swore he almost knocked one of his tonsils free—cum spilled down his throat. After licking him clean, Dayne raised his head and was pleased to see the man's lax features paired with heavy eyelids. "Now, I think I want you to—"

A loud pounding on his door stopped him abruptly. *What the fuck?* He glanced over at the clock. It wasn't even seven yet and too early for anyone to be bugging him at his residence.

It had to be important.

"I better get that while you get the lube. Make sure to be on your hands and knees when I get back. I want that ass tipped up in the air and ready for my cock." He shook his own hard length before snagging his boxer briefs from where he'd thrown them last night and quickly yanked them up his legs.

"Umm, Dayne?" came from the bed before he could rush out of the room.

He paused in the doorway and raised his eyebrows at Heath in question.

"Are you sure you want to answer the door like that?" Heath jerked his chin toward Dayne's very obvious erection.

"Did you forget where I live? And where you'll soon be living? Anyway, whoever's interrupting us deserves not only an eyeful, but an earful."

Heath grinned. "You're right. Hard-ons are a normal thing to see around here. Carry on."

Dayne strode through the large living space and toward the front door. Once unlocked, he swung it open. Only to be met with a familiar face. "You? Again?" He added a big exaggerated sigh.

"Sorry to disturb you this early." Cam's eyes dropped to the bulge in Dayne's boxer briefs. Of course, Dayne didn't bother to hide it and smirked instead.

When Cam quickly jerked his gaze back up to Dayne's face, his nostrils were flared. He rubbed his palms down the sides of his black uniform pants in what appeared to be a nervous gesture.

But that wasn't what piqued his attention. It was the fact that Cam was fighting to keep his eyes above Dayne's shoulders.

Well, well, well. Dayne had no idea about their Head of Security. He wondered if anyone knew the man's tastes or if he was hiding it from everyone.

Maybe even himself. "Are you here to join us?"

The blood drained from Cam's chiseled face and a, "What? No!" burst from him. He cleared his throat and repeated, "No," more quietly.

The former State Trooper couldn't be blushing, could he? "Then, why are you here and not standing on Dylan's doorstep instead?"

"I...I have a family emergency and need to head to Maryland."

"You could've left a voice message or sent a text."

"I didn't want to leave without letting you know. You're the one who signs my paychecks."

That was true. And the former cop certainly liked to dot all his I's and cross all his T's. Cam obviously had a typical type-A personality.

"You're fine. Go. You're a great employee and we trust you. Go take care of what you need to take care of. Just keep us updated when you can."

With a relieved nod, Cam thanked him and spun on his heel.

Dayne once again couldn't resist studying the man's muscular ass as he took long strides to the pickup truck parked next to Heath's sports car. Someone else would get a lot of pleasure out of that ass, but it wouldn't be Dayne.

He had the ass he wanted waiting for him in his bed. It just so happened to be attached to someone he loved.

The trajectory of his life had certainly taken a crazy turn. But now was not the time to analyze that change.

As soon as he closed the door, he rushed back into his bedroom, announcing, "Now, how about we video call Cara and have her watch?"

Heath was waiting for him the way Dayne wanted. In the center of the bed, on his hands and knees, with a towel and a tube of lube abandoned next to him but close enough to grab if needed. "I like the sound of that. Is everything okay?"

"When you're in my bed? Perfect." As he set up his iPad, he said, "Let's keep my idea of living together under wraps for now. I don't want to mention it until Cara's here with us in person."

"Good call. We can ask her next weekend when we're all together."

"That will also give us a week to come up with a possible solution for her job." Dayne sure hoped they could come up with one. Otherwise, his plan might fall apart.

"I think if we do, convincing her to live with us might be much easier."

"I'm counting on that." He was worried that if they couldn't make it work for Cara, Heath might change his mind.

Once Cara's sleepy face filled the tablet's screen and they

told her about their desire for her to watch, Heath ordered, "Now, fuck me like you mean it."

Dayne stroked his cock as he approached the end of the bed and let his eyes roam over his glistening target. "You don't have to tell *me* twice."

———

"Where's Heath?" Cara asked Dayne as he hauled her over-stuffed overnight bag into his wing of the farmhouse.

Buttons darted around his feet, barking excitedly at seeing Dayne again. Her brindle and white Boston Terrier jumped enthusiastically into the car whenever she realized she was coming to the resort. Her dog certainly didn't hate all the attention showered her way. However, the barn cats weren't so thrilled with her visits, but they were slowly learning to co-exist.

Dayne dropped her bag in the corner of his bedroom and turned. "He's waiting for us."

"Where?"

"Patience." He grabbed her hand and interlocked their fingers, giving her arm a tug. "You'll see him shortly."

She wasn't sure if she had any patience left. Not after having to skip last weekend to attend that damn baby shower. During the party, she managed to plaster a smile on her face, but her thoughts hadn't been in the same room. They had been up here on the ranch.

They woke her up last Saturday morning to share via video what the two of them were doing without her. She wasn't jealous, of course, but more like envious of what she was missing out on: spending time with her men.

Though none of them had said it out loud yet, every week it became more obvious that a deep connection and strong bond had formed. Because of that, her heart ached every time she left the ranch to drive home on Sunday evenings and she missed them every day when she was back in Carlisle. She swore Buttons did, too.

Of course, they called during the week, texted and video chatted with each other, but it wasn't the same as being here in person. However, last weekend that video call was one for the books.

Watching Dayne first fuck Heath, then Heath do the same to Dayne, had taken a big chunk of time out of her morning, but it had been worth running behind. Especially since she also got involved while watching and listening. She tried not to distract them, but she couldn't help but participate in her own way.

While it had been fun, and even satisfying, she had wished she could climb through her computer screen. Since winter was almost upon them, she was afraid her time up on the ranch would be limited even further due to foul weather. That might mean more video sex and less in-person intimacy.

That possibility—and most likely, reality—was depressing.

He led her through his wing and into the main portion of the farmhouse where Dani was splayed out on the couch watching TV. Immediately, Buttons jumped up and joined her with her little butt wiggling and her tongue darting out in an attempt to lick Dayne's sister's face.

"Do me a favor and keep an eye on her, sis?" Dayne asked.

Dani scooped Buttons up into her arms and finally allowed tongue-to-cheek contact. *Gross.* Cara loved her dog, but she also was aware of where that tongue had a habit of going. Unfortunately, those places certainly weren't sanitary.

Dani laughed at the dog's lapping tongue. "Of course. If

it was up to me, I'd never give her back. Isn't that right, my *liddle widdle* love bug?" she cooed, using a baby voice.

Dayne drew his thumbnail across his forehead while shaking his head. "You're ridiculous."

Dani glared at him and made a shooing motion. "Go away now." She turned her wide, pleading eyes to Cara. "Can she sleep with me tonight?"

"Sure." Despite how oversized his custom bed was, with three adults—two of them being large men—taking up so much real estate, there wasn't a ton of space for an extra body. Not even one as small as Buttons.

Dayne tugged on her hand again. "Let's go."

"If she becomes a problem, just—"

Dayne pulled her outside before Cara could even finish. "She'll be fine."

"Dani or Buttons?"

"Both. C'mon. Heath is waiting."

She expected Dayne to escort her over to The Mane Event Hall and upstairs to Heaven.

But that was not where he took her.

Chapter Twenty-Five

THEY WALKED hand-in-hand around the sprawling lodge and down toward the huge lake.

The moon's reflection on the eerily-still surface of the water created a huge white ball. Cara glanced up and, as always, was amazed that out here, unlike in Carlisle, no light pollution marred the cloudless sky. The stars appeared as twinkling diamonds.

Absolutely stunning.

Just like the man now leading her down the slight embankment to the lake.

Just like the man waiting for them, sitting on the ground near the crackling flames in one of the lake's fire pits.

No, not directly on the ground. On a large blanket.

Next to Heath sat a bottle of wine and three stemless metal cups. As they got closer, between the bright moon and the fiery glow coming from the fire pit, she spotted a spread laid out consisting of fruit, cheese, and crackers.

They were having a picnic? At night?

It hit her then. Unlike when they had shared dinner at

the lake a few weeks ago, this was the exact spot where she and Dayne encountered Heath for the first time. She didn't know it at the time, but it was the start of something great.

However, the nights were becoming too cold to be sitting outside since winter was right around the corner. Reminding her again, bad weather would make it a lot more difficult for her to continue to drive from Carlisle to Fisher Falls every weekend.

She was so different now than the first time she stepped onto this property. She was more open-minded, more well-rounded, and so much more sexually fulfilled.

It didn't take long for her to feel as at home here as in Carlisle. Maybe even more so at Double D, since she was never alone. If she wasn't with Dayne or Heath, plenty of activities could keep her occupied and someone was always around to talk to, whether it was a guest, employee, or one of Dayne's siblings.

Dayne and Heath helped her settle on the blanket before Dayne joined them both on the ground.

Heath's rumbled, "I missed you," paired with a quick lip touch swelled her heart.

"I missed you, too." More than they knew.

"Two weeks felt like a lifetime," Heath admitted next.

It was crazy but true. "Agreed. Thank you for that titillating entertainment you two provided last weekend."

Heath's lips curled up at the corners. "Knowing you were watching—"

"And participating," Dayne added, grabbing the wine and working free the cork partially jammed into the bottle.

"Made it even better," Heath finished, handing him the first glass to fill.

As soon as it was, Dayne offered it to Cara. "Don't drink yet. We should make a toast."

Hmm. "What are we toasting?"

Dayne avoided her question as he filled the other two glasses, giving one to Heath and keeping the other for himself. He lifted his cup in the air. "To six months together."

"Has it really been half a year?" Cara whispered, also lifting her wine. Time had flown.

Heath lifted his cup, too. "Crazy, right?"

At once, they tapped their glasses together before taking a sip. The Cabernet Sauvignon was from a local vineyard and was one of her favorites.

What was going on here?

This picnic by the lake that included both her favorite wine and favorite men couldn't be because they'd been seeing each other for six months. There had to be more to it than that. She couldn't imagine someone like Dayne celebrating six months of exclusivity.

"So..." Dayne started after he downed what seemed like half his wine.

Her eyes sliced between the two men. The fire reflected off their faces, creating pockets of shadows so she couldn't read their eyes or expressions.

Her stomach twisted. "So..."

"We have to tell you something," Dayne announced next instead of simply saying what needed to be said.

Why was he dragging out whatever it was?

She pressed the backs of her knuckles to her mouth and held her breath.

"I'm moving onto the ranch."

For a few seconds, what Heath said didn't sink into her brain. When it did, her mouth dropped open and she glanced between the two. "What does that mean exactly?"

"He's moving into the farmhouse." Dayne then added, "With me."

Wow. That was unexpected. Especially when there hadn't even been hints of this previously. "When?"

"As soon as I can sort some things out," Heath answered. "As you know, I can work from anywhere."

"I hate when he's gone so I asked him to move in." Dayne shrugged like it was no big deal.

But it *was* a big deal. That also meant the men viewed their relationship as more than just sex. At least between the two of them.

Them excluding her bruised both her heart and ego a little. Had they bonded with each other more than with her? Had she been too much work for them? Would they eventually cut her out all together and find someone more their speed?

Of course, she hadn't come to the ranch with the expectations to fall in love with any man, much less two, but... "That's...great." She was struggling to be more enthusiastic about their news.

Apparently, Dayne wasn't done with his announcements. "I also hate when you're gone." He lifted her hand from her lap and pressed his lips to the back of it.

Hold on here.

He continued. "We want you to join us. It wouldn't be the same without you. *We* wouldn't be the same. You're an important part of this relationship."

They wanted her to do *what*? "You mean you want me to move in with you, too?"

A minute ago she was sad when they didn't include her. Now that they were, her anxiety spiked. While this was something she wanted, she had no idea how to make a move like that happen.

She couldn't just pick up and leave Carlisle. She owned a house and had a job. Add in the fact that a job like hers wasn't easy to find and it became next to impossible. She had worked too hard and too long to earn her master's degree to simply walk away from her career.

She was torn. While this was what she hoped for, she couldn't simply give up everything. What if things went wrong? How would she support herself? She didn't want to be financially dependent on Dayne or Heath. She didn't want to be a "kept" woman where she had no independence.

And while she was sure positions were available on the resort, she was doing what she loved: helping people find their next favorite read, do research, or utilize all the resources provided for free in a public library.

Mucking stalls or sanitizing playrooms was not for her.

The bottom line was, wanting to live with her men and actually doing it were two different things.

"I can't simply quit the job I love. That's just crazy."

With a tilt of his head, Heath swept a lock of her hair over her shoulder. "But we're crazy about you."

Cara shook her head. "While that's all well and good, that doesn't pay my bills."

"What bills would you have if you sold your place in Carlisle and came to live with us here?" Dayne lifted one finger. "You would have no mortgage." He lifted a second. "No utilities." Then a third. "Hell, you'd even eat for free. Your expenses would be slashed."

Sure they would, but at what cost to her self-reliance? "It's not as simple as you're making it out to be, Dayne. How about my self-sufficiency? How about the whole reason I earned my master's degree? Should I simply throw it all away? It's not like Clearfield County has a huge library system. It doesn't."

Dayne's eyebrows pinned together. "How do you know?"

"Because I already checked out of curiosity." While she

assumed they weren't thinking about a future together, she had been.

"Then, your reluctance has nothing to do with me or Heath?"

"Not at all. Believe me when I say, I miss you two when I'm not here. I think about us all the time. I look forward to our weekends together. But you expect me to give up my home and the job I love for us to be together full-time. What if I do then we realize it's not working? Then what? I'd be in a jam. I could end up unemployed and potentially homeless." That was a scary thought.

"She's right, Dayne. She deserves to feel secure in her life."

Dayne responded with, "I wish I could offer you a job here at the resort. What I could offer you would be *nothing* like the career you're so passionate about and we do understand what an accomplishment it was to earn that degree."

Cara rubbed her forehead. "I want to be here with you two, I do. Believe me. There's nothing my heart wants more. But my head is telling me to be reasonable and responsible."

"Sweetheart, we're good with whatever you decide," Heath assured her. "We don't want this to be the reason we lose you, because that's the last thing we want. But before you make your decision, I want to mention that I'm keeping my place in Hoboken. For now, at least. I might rent it out. That's always an option for you, too. You could keep your house in Carlisle and find a tenant. This way you have that security net."

"At least until you're ready to let it go. Or it couldn't hurt to keep it as an asset. You probably have equity in it already and that investment will continue to grow." Apparently, Dayne had put on his official Chief Financial Officer's hat.

"That could work, but what about my income?" That was a huge obstacle she couldn't ignore.

Heath blew out a breath. "This week we tried to come up with a solution for that but without your input we struggled."

Interesting. "What *did* you come up with?" She was pleased to hear they wanted her with them badly enough that they made an effort to find a way.

"We thought about the obvious first. Between Penn State University and Centre County, there's a larger library system in State College, but neither Dayne nor I are thrilled you'd have to drive that distance during winter."

"They would need openings, too," she reminded them. "Those are few and far between."

Heath sighed. "Right. We even checked for librarian openings in the surrounding school districts."

"And you found nothing." She didn't want to admit that one night she had checked, too. Just in case.

"Another option we considered was you starting a small bookstore here in Fisher Falls," Dayne added.

"I can't imagine that decision would be financially sound." Especially with the town's population being so small. She eyed up Dayne since he was the numbers guy.

"It wouldn't," he admitted reluctantly.

"So, not really an option but good if I was looking for a hobby," she surmised.

"Yes. However, after that, I began sending out inquiries to some of my former clients. I figured it couldn't hurt to throw a wider net."

Heath nudged her shoulder with his. "I put out some feelers, too."

Before she could respond, Dayne announced, "Yesterday, I got an email from the library director at Stockford, an accredited online university. She said they might be looking for a virtual librarian for their academic library. Since all their classes are held online, they don't have a physical location. You would never have to drive anywhere to do your job. It's not a sure thing, but at least it's a lead. If you're interested, I can pass along the director's information."

Holy crap.

A *virtual* librarian? Why hadn't she looked into that before now? There had to be more positions similar to that since online education was growing every year. It was the wave of the future. "I definitely want her information."

"Good. I was hoping you'd say that. If you land a position like that, your problem—*our* problem—would be solved. If you keep your house, what else would it take for you to shack up with us?" Dayne wiggled his eyebrows.

"I could think of one," Heath answered. "There's something else we haven't discussed yet that's as important, if not *the* most important."

Cara's eyebrows raised. "What's that?"

"How we truly feel about you."

Her heart did a somersault. After six months she had a good idea, but not one of them had revealed their true feelings yet. At least not to her.

"Last weekend, we admitted we loved each other," Heath started, then grinned. "I think Dayne had a panic attack doing so, but he survived."

Dayne flapped a dismissive hand around and huffed, "No, I didn't."

She was sure Heath was telling the truth and Dayne wasn't. Cara pinned her lips together to keep from laughing since this was supposed to be a serious moment. "That's great." She meant it, too.

"We also love you, sweetheart. Truly and completely with our hearts and souls. That's what fueled the desire to live together and to find a way for you to be with us. We love you and we want you here, too. You're a big part of us and our lives wouldn't be the same without you."

Her mouth opened. She needed to tell them she felt the same. But first... "Are you only telling me this now so I'll agree to move up here?"

"No," Heath answered. "We're telling you because we want you to know what's deep within our hearts."

"Of course we're telling you now to help influence your decision!" Dayne spouted. He then shrugged. "But it *is* true. We're not lying about loving you. We both do and we can't live without you." He glanced over at Heath. "Or each other."

"It's fine if you don't feel the same way yet. We have no doubt that, in time—"

She cut Heath off. "I *do* love you, Heath." She didn't wait for his reaction before turning to Dayne. "And I love you, too, Dayne. Missing my time with you last weekend only proved it to me once more. I need to be a part of your lives. I want to be with both of you. I do want to live with you and create a life, even a family with you, if that's what we decide. No matter what, my life would be empty without both of you."

"You have Buttons." Dayne smirked.

Cara rolled her eyes. "True. She's a great companion and I love her to death but it's not the same. You are my lovers. My partners. My supporters."

Maybe even the future fathers to her children. Of course, they'd have to revisit that discussion another day. Or moonlit night.

"I wouldn't want to be with anyone else," Dayne said next.

Heath pressed the back of his hand against Dayne's forehead. "Still no fever."

She had no idea what that was about but she could guess.

"Is this all a dream and I'm still in my bed back in Carlisle?" she whispered.

"It's real." Heath leaned in and brushed his lips over hers. "Did you feel that kiss?"

She smiled. "Of course, but who said my dreams aren't full of your kisses? Dayne's, too."

"Look at that, she dreams about us." Apparently, Dayne's cockiness decided to make an appearance tonight.

"Well, it's only fair since we dream about her."

"Just to make sure I'm not asleep, kiss me again, Heath."

He immediately took her mouth, driving his tongue deep and leaving her breathless. As soon as he backed off, Dayne took his place, sharing a kiss that made her heat up and wish they were in his wing of the farmhouse.

Naked.

With a closet full of toys nearby.

Boy, had her life changed. Over six months ago she would only read about these types of stories.

Now she was living it.

As soon as Dayne broke the kiss, the three of them pressed their foreheads together and whispered *I love yous.*

Hearing those words filled her heart. She really, really needed to make the move to the resort work. It might not be immediately, but she'd do everything in her power to make it happen sooner than later. She didn't want to spend more time apart than necessary.

When they finally separated and sat back, Dayne said, "Like I told Heath, if you find you're not comfortable living in the farmhouse, we could always take the same route Dylan is and build our own house. We could have my brother draw up what we'd want and Ford could help build it. But if we want to stay in the farmhouse, I told Heath we could set up an office for him in Dylan's wing once they vacate it. If you find a remote position, we could do the same for you."

"No matter what, we'll figure it out," Heath assured her.

Dayne nodded in agreement. "We'll figure it out one way or another."

Their determination shot a thrill through Cara. She blew out a breath and whispered, "Are we really doing this?"

Dayne grinned. "We are, if you say yes."

Cara closed her eyes and listened carefully to what her gut was shouting. "Then, I say yes!"

Once they finished off the wine and ate all the food, Cara laid her head in Heath's lap while he laid his head in Dayne's. For over an hour, they clasped hands and stared up at the vast night sky. No words were necessary.

But Dayne's came back to her from all those months ago: *The only limits will be of your own making.*

The sky was now her only limit.

Not only were they celebrating the last six months together, but now they could celebrate their future.

Together.

Forever.

———

Keep an eye out for book 3 of the Double D Ranch Series (Cam's book): Unrestrained. Coming soon!

———

Sign up for Jeanne's newsletter to learn about her upcoming releases, sales and more! https:// www.authorjeannestjames.com/

What could be better than waking up next to a hot guy? Waking up sandwiched between two of them.

Quinn Preston, a financial analyst, is not happy when her friends dare her to pick up a handsome stranger at a wedding reception. What better reason to give up men when her previous long-term relationship had not only been lackluster in the bedroom but he had cheated?

Logan Reed, a successful business owner, can't believe that he's attracted to the woman in the ugly, Pepto-Bismol pink bridesmaid dress. And to boot, she's more than tipsy. After turning down her invitation for a one-night stand, he finds her in the parking lot too impaired to drive. He rescues her and takes her home. His home.

The next morning Quinn's conservative life turns on its ear when Logan introduces her to pleasures she never even considered before. And to make things more complicated, Logan already has a lover.

Tyson White, ex-pro football player, is completely in love with Logan. He has mixed emotions when Logan brings home Quinn. But the dares keep coming...

Turn the page to read the first chapter of Double Dare (Dare Menage Series, Book 1)

Double Dare

Dare Menage Series, Book 1

Logan Reed jammed a finger into the neck of his white oxford and pulled. He needed some fucking air.

What the hell was he doing here anyway?

As he surveyed the church, a bead of sweat popped out on his forehead. His breathing had become shallow and quick. He was going to hyperventilate right there and pass out, making a fool of himself in front of everyone.

With a start, he realized one of the ushers was speaking to him. "What?"

"Bride or groom?"

Bride or groom? Did he look like a bride?

All he wanted to do was strip off his stiff shirt, strangling tie, smothering jacket; throw on a soft, worn pair of jeans and one of his comfortable shirts; sink into his couch; toss his feet on his coffee table; and chug a nice frosty beer.

Now that was a fantasy!

But here he was, standing in a monkey suit in a church, about to be struck down by lightning at any second. He blew out a long breath to settle his thumping heart.

Logan stared at the confused usher. Unfortunately, he understood the feeling. "Neither."

"Are you okay?"

Logan had vowed to himself to never do this again. Never be in a church again.

He reminded himself he was only there to observe. He didn't have to participate. But it didn't help. Anyone with as many sins as Logan should've been barred from religious houses. That should've been a law. But it wasn't.

For fuck's sake, he had to get a grip. This was a wedding, not a crucifixion.

He had promised his sister he would be here. And even though Logan was a sinner, he never broke a promise. Never.

The usher cleared his throat.

"Dude—"

Logan pinned the suddenly flushed, sweating kid, whose suit looked two sizes too big, with a glare. "Dude?"

He watched the teen's Adam's apple bob up and down a couple of times before he felt a *whoosh* of air against him, and someone grabbed his elbow. Hard.

"Logan! How nice of you to get here on time." The female voice was singsong and syrupy sweet. And it held a lot more meaning in the tone than in the words.

Logan turned to face his sister. He had to look down because she was nearly a foot shorter than him. "Hey, Shorty. Good timing."

The petite brunette gave him a tight smile. "I see that." She turned to the usher. "We're with the bride," she said sweetly. "We'll just seat ourselves. Thank you."

The usher looked relieved, and Logan almost felt bad. Almost.

The grip on his elbow tightened, and without warning,

his sister dragged him down the aisle and over into one of the pews on the left.

"*Sit down,*" Paige said through gritted teeth, even though her face held the biggest smile.

He sat.

She smoothed her dress and tucked it ladylike as she settled into the pew beside him.

"Jesus Christ, Shorty. What the hell is your problem?"

Logan watched her plastered smile falter.

"Logan, you're in a church, for God's sake. It's not the best place to take the Lord's name in vain. And if you keep doing that, I might have to move to another pew so when lightning strikes you dead, I'm in a safe spot." She smoothed her done-up do and gave a pacifying smile across the aisle to the older couple staring at them, mouths agape.

"Hey, I didn't want to be here in the first place."

"I ask you for one favor—"

"One? Hmm. You must have a short memory."

"Okay, okay. Knock it off. Believe me, I appreciate your coming."

"And the thanks I get is a bruised elbow?"

"Sorry, I thought you were going to make that guy piss his pants."

"Well, shit, he called me *dude.*"

"Oh yeah, that's so much worse than you calling me *Shorty.*"

"I thought you liked it—" Paige elbowed him in the gut before he could say anything besides "ooof."

The wedding march started, and the double doors opened to reveal the bride.

His sister owed him big-time.

———

Quinn Preston almost choked on her Alabama Slammer when her friend elbowed her in the ribs. "Ooof."

She saved her drink before it could spill all over her ugly bridesmaid dress. Yeah, that would have been a shame: to ruin such a nice, frumpy, pukey pink taffeta dress. One the bride had said she would be able to wear in the future. Like to a cocktail party. Or maybe her own funeral. *Yeah, right. No one in their right mind would want to get caught dead in this thing.*

Ruining the dress wouldn't have been a loss, but losing her drink would have. She was drinking Slammers for a reason—to get good and drunk.

Lana nudged her again. "You see that?" She nodded her head toward the back of the room.

"What?" Quinn really didn't care what Lana was excited about. She just wanted to get this day over with. She was tired of watching the happy couple. She was tired of pasting on a plastic smile for the photographer. And she was really tired of listening to the sappy congratulations. All things she might never have—the wedding, the husband, the bridal bliss. Something her parents never failed to remind her. Especially now that she was in her early thirties. And single. Again.

"Not what. Who."

"Huh?" She sucked on the dainty little straw the bartender had put in her drink. Hardly anything would come out of it. Maybe it was designed just for stirring. She pulled it out and threw it onto the bar. She really needed one of those giant straws that came in those fancy frozen drinks.

"Him. Over there." Lana grabbed Quinn by the shoulders and turned her around to face whatever had caught her friend's attention.

"Oh, him." She took a deep draw of the punch-like drink,

only there wasn't a bit of punch in it. Not the fruit kind anyway.

"Yeah, him." Lana dragged out *him* like she was sucking on a maraschino cherry and enjoying the sweetness on her tongue.

Quinn didn't even take a good look. Men were on her shit list at the moment. She didn't care how hot they were. The potent drink in her hands was all the company she needed. She smiled into her glass; it was the best date she'd had in a while.

Another pink taffeta blur whirled up to them, out of breath.

"Jeez Louise. Did you see that hunk of man meat?" Paula, another victim of the wedding fashion nightmare, was flushed and had a bead of sweat running down her chipmunk-like cheeks. "Do you think he's single?"

Quinn raised one shoulder in a half shrug and turned back to the bar. It was bad enough when the three of them had to stand next to each other at the altar, then throughout the grueling pictures, followed by having to sit beside each other at the head table. All in that awful pink froth. But now that it was all over, and they had done their duty for their friend Gina, there was no reason they all had to stand there looking like someone threw up Pepto-Bismol.

She leaned into the bar and asked the semi-cute bartender the time. When he answered that it was six, she gritted her teeth. They had only been at the reception for an hour. It was way too early to bail.

Damn.

With a sigh, she turned back to her friends. They were still ogling the male eye candy across the room.

Paula's sigh drifted over her. "I wonder if he likes women with a little meat on their bones."

A little meat? She opened her mouth to correct Paula, but shut it quickly. Her friend didn't need to be on the receiving end of her miserable mood.

"Quinn, I bet he'd make you forget Peanut."

Quinn winced and took another long draw from her drink. She loved the flavor and the tanginess on her tongue. And she was trying to forget Peanut. She hated the nickname her friends had called her ex-boyfriend, Peter. Once they had actually called him Peanut in front of his face—by accident, of course. *Right.* It had taken her a while to brush that one under the rug. He had never liked her friends after that.

On the other hand, her friends had never liked Peter from the beginning. Unlike her parents, who loved the bastard. Probably more than they loved her.

"Yeah, Quinn, he could probably fuck your brains out, and you'd never remember that douche again."

Quinn frowned at Paula. She noticed her friend's string of pearls hiding in the skin around her neck. Quinn's hands automatically went to her neck to finger a similar necklace—a part of the stupid wedding costume. *Ugh.* She hated pearls!

She hated taffeta. She hated pink. She hated frilly dresses.

She took a long swig from her glass.

And she hated Peter. The asshole.

His gift to her last Valentine's Day wasn't an engagement ring. Oh no, after five long, wasted years of dating the shit, he couldn't have gotten her a ring. Nope. Instead he sent her a text message.

That was it.

A stupid little text message. Two simple lines.

This isn't working anymore. I've found someone new.

She deserved more than that. Something better. After all those years of loyalty, standing by his side, being the "good, proper" girlfriend. As Peter had expected. As her parents had expected. The girlfriend any decent man would want on his arm. Right?

Not even a sorry. Not even an explanation. Nothing.

And the next day, FedEx had delivered a box with all the things she had left over at his apartment during the last half decade.

Quinn emptied her glass and turned back to the bar, blocking out her friends' chattering over that man.

She needed another man like she needed a hole in the head.

She slid her glass over the bar top, and before she could ask for another, a deep voice washed over her.

"Put her next drink on me."

Dumb ass. The drinks are on the house. She turned to ream out whoever it was, and stopped. Her mouth opened, but nothing escaped.

"You look like a fish out of water with your mouth hanging open like that." When he smiled, the lines around his eyes crinkled. He was tan, an outdoorsy tan, not a manmade one. And he had beautiful green eyes. Shit. She had never seen such beautiful eyes on a man. His nose was a little crooked, like it had been broken, and it made him even more beautiful. No. Not beautiful. He was... He was...

Quinn closed her mouth and swallowed hard. He was so *unperfect*, he was perfect. His hair was a dark brown with natural highlights, more proof he liked being outdoors. It was long and pulled back into a neat ponytail.

She hated long hair on men. But it was right on him.

He had a beard that wasn't a beard. It was like a longer five-o'clock shadow.

She hated facial hair.

He had a strong, corded neck that disappeared into a stiff

dress shirt. The collar had been already released and one more button undone below that. The knot of his tie was loose and hung crookedly from around his neck.

The sleeves of his crispy white shirt were rolled up to his elbows, and his forearms were tan covered in dark hair. His hands...

Oh. Damn.

His hands were large. Working hands. Not soft and pampered, but calloused, thick and strong.

Capable. Capable of doing all kinds of things.

Quinn's nipples hardened under the scratchy taffeta.

His hands could do all kinds of dirty, nasty things.

Things Peter had never wanted to do...

Quinn ripped her gaze from him and spun back around to the bar, bracing herself against it for a second to catch her breath. She grabbed her fresh drink and took a gulp.

"Whoa. Slow down there."

Pressing the cold drink against her forehead, she attempted to cool herself off.

She needed to go change her panties, she was so freaking wet.

She could feel his heat next to her; his body was like a furnace. She wanted to plant her hands on his chest and feel how hot he really was. Her fingers convulsed around her glass.

"Are you okay?" The deep timbre of his voice sent a shot of lightning through her body, landing right in her core.

Quinn could only nod her answer.

Palming her bare shoulder, he turned her to face him. He stared down into her eyes, his lips widening into a smile.

His lips. *Oh man.* Those lips probably could do all sorts of things to her, with her. Lips that were made for more than kissing...

"*Yes.*"

Holy shit. That was the kind of yes she blurted when she was in the midst of an orgasm. At least from what she could remember. It had been so long since she'd come... with a partner, anyway.

Heat crawled up her neck as she stepped back, breaking the contact.

"I... I'm fine." She cleared her throat. "Thank you for the drink." She took another sip before raising the glass to him in thanks.

"It was nothing." When he laughed, her knees almost buckled. "Enjoy it."

He stepped away and then paused. But it looked as though he thought better of whatever he was contemplating, and he continued on his way.

Quinn leaned back against the bar and let out a shaky breath.

She was suddenly flanked on either side by her friends. She had been so distracted, she hadn't even realized that they disappeared.

"Quinn—"

"Quinn!"

"Oh. My. God!"

"I told you he was hot!"

"Oh! I wish I weren't married already."

"I wish he liked chubby chicks."

Quinn couldn't take any more. She raised her palms in surrender. "Stop. Enough."

"But, Quinn—"

"But nothing," Quinn answered Paula.

"You're just going to let him walk away?"

"Paula, he isn't going anywhere. Unfortunately, I'm not

going anywhere. We have to be here for two more hours, at least."

Lana said, "Are you going to let Peter ruin the rest of your life? All men aren't assholes like him."

Quinn snorted and took another sip of her Slammer.

"Why don't you at least dance with him?"

"No."

"Why not?" Lana asked.

Why not? Because if she did, she might come right on the dance floor. Because she might end up in a puddle of her own juices. The picture in her head shocked her: it was of her lying in a heap in the middle of the dance floor in the throes of an orgasm. Surrounded by all the wedding guests...

This drink was stronger than she thought.

"Because no one is dancing yet."

"Sure they are. Look."

Quinn glanced over at the area cleared for dancing, and sure enough, a crowd of people were out there shaking their groove thing. Quinn had been too busy trying to get her drink on to notice.

From the looks of the participants on the dance floor, a few of them had been partaking in the open bar also. Even the bride and her new husband were bouncing and shim-mying in the crowd.

At least *they* were a happy couple.

Quinn took another drink.

Lana frowned at her. "Are you just going to drink tonight, or are you going to do something about your situation?"

"Situation? What situation?"

"Getting laid."

Quinn checked over her shoulder to see if the bartender was listening. He was. He had a big grin plastered on his face. *Great.*

The father of the bride came up and asked for a gin and tonic. While he was waiting, he turned to them. "Hi, girls. Enjoying yourselves? You look great in those dresses. My wife picked them out."

Oh joy. Quinn would have to remember to smack—she meant thank—her. She couldn't wait to rip the scratchy, ugly piece of shit off.

All three women gave him a smile but bit their tongues. Eventually he wandered away, and Lana and Paula jumped right back to harassing her. Good thing they were her friends.

"C'mon. It's not going to hurt to have a one-night stand. Look at him."

"I already saw him." Holy crap, she knew they meant well, but they were getting on her last nerve.

"Yeah, and we saw how you were drooling, too."

She had not drooled. Her hand automatically went up to her mouth.

Paula said, "He probably isn't interested in you anyway."

"Yeah, you couldn't get someone like that. You attract losers like Peter," Lana said.

If they thought their reverse psychology was going to work, well, it wasn't.

"Looks like he's with Paige Reed, anyway."

Quinn's gaze shot over to the corner of the ballroom where the tall man stood next to the petite, dark-haired beauty. Paige Reed. *Figures.*

"I thought Paige was dating Connor Morgan," Quinn mumbled.

She must have mumbled loud enough, because Lana answered her. "She is. Connor had to fly back to Australia for something to do with his job."

"So why is she with him?" Quinn asked. Why was she so curious all of a sudden? Why did she care?

She didn't. She nursed her drink. After one and a half Alabama Slammers, she was starting to feel pretty tipsy. She wasn't used to drinking. And when she did drink, she usually had wine, not hard liquor, and especially not such a hard-hitting mix of liquors.

Paula leaned into the both of them and said in an exaggerated whisper, "Maybe he's an escort," like it was a scandal, and then laughed.

Maybe he *was* an escort.

He was probably worth every penny, too.

His back was to them now, but that just gave Quinn the opportunity to study how broad those shoulders were in his dress shirt. When he moved, the fabric bunched and pulled with his muscles.

Lana gasped, jerking Quinn out of her thoughts. "He's not an escort! That's Logan Reed, Paige's brother. I haven't seen him since we were kids. Holy shit, did he grow up."

"I'll say." Paula agreed. "Quinn, I dare you to go ask him to dance."

"Not interested."

Lana joined in. "Yeah, I dare you too. Don't be a wuss."

If she were a wuss, she wouldn't have come out in public in this pink atrocity. And the matching shoes were killing her feet. The last thing she needed was to be dancing. She'd be crippled.

"That's a double dare, you know, with the two of us daring you."

Oh, boy, a double dare. She would definitely do it now—not. "You're crazy."

"No, you are, if you pass up this opportunity."

"How do you know he's available?" Quinn asked them.

"You don't know until you ask him," Lana said. "But if I

remember correctly, his wife left him a while ago. There had been some rumors..."

There had been some rumors about her and Peter too, but rumors were just that: rumors. She didn't take any stock in them.

Paula suddenly shouted, "Truth or dare?" making Quinn jump. It was like they were teenagers all over again.

Lana quickly said, "Truth." And bounced on her toes like she was fifteen.

Jesus, would someone please put a bullet in my head? Quinn needed to be put out of her misery.

Paula asked Lana, "Do you shave or wax?"

"Shave. Okay, Quinn, your turn. Truth or dare?"

Quinn was not playing this juvenile game. It was stupid; she was not going to fall into what was clearly a trap.

"Truth."

"How bad was Peter in bed?" Lana asked.

Damn. She wasn't going to answer that one. Even as drunk as she was. She didn't want to relive their vanilla, boring sex life. And she definitely didn't want to admit it or talk about it.

There was only one thing left for her to do.

Get the rest of the story here: https:// books2read.com/Double-Dare

If You Enjoyed This Book

Thank you for reading Unbridled. If you enjoyed this polyamory romance, please consider leaving a review at your favorite retailer and/or Goodreads to let other readers know. Reviews are always appreciated and just a few words can help an independent author like me tremendously!

Want to read a sample of my work? Download a sampler book here: BookHip.com/MTQQKK

Also by Jeanne St. James

Find my complete reading order here:

https://www.jeannestjames.com/reading-order

Buy direct from the author here: https:// jeannestjamesauthor.com

Standalone Books:

Made Maleen: A Modern Twist on a Fairy Tale

Damaged

Rip Cord: The Complete Trilogy

Everything About You (A Second Chance Gay Romance)

Reigniting Chase (An M/M Standalone)

Brothers in Blue Series

A four-book series based around three brothers who are small-town cops and former Marines

The Dare Ménage Series

A six-book MMF, interracial ménage series

The Obsessed Novellas

A collection of five standalone BDSM novellas

Down & Dirty: Dirty Angels MC®

A ten-book motorcycle club series

Guts & Glory: In the Shadows Security

A six-book former special forces series

(A spin-off of the Dirty Angels MC)

<u>Blood & Bones: Blood Fury MC®</u>

A twelve-book motorcycle club series

<u>Motorcycle Club Crossovers:</u>

<u>Crossing the Line: A DAMC/Blue Avengers MC Crossover</u>

<u>Magnum: A Dark Knights MC/Dirty Angels MC Crossover</u>

Crash: A Dirty Angels MC/Blood Fury MC Crossover

Romeo: A Dark Knights MC/Blood Fury MC Crossover

Beyond the Badge: Blue Avengers MC™

A six-book law enforcement/motorcycle club series

<u>Double D Ranch</u>

A six-book MMF ménage series

<u>COMING SOON!</u>

Property of Stone (Kings of Anarchy MC: Pennsylvania)

Dirty Angels MC®: The Next Generation

WRITING AS J.J. MASTERS:

The Royal Alpha Series

A five-book gay mpreg shifter series

About the Author

JEANNE ST. JAMES is a USA Today, Amazon and international bestselling romance author who loves writing about strong women and alpha males. She was only thirteen when she first started writing and her first published piece was an erotic short story in Playgirl magazine. She then went on to publish her first romance novel in 2009. She is now an author of almost 70 contemporary romances. She writes M/F, M/M, and M/M/F ménages, including interracial romance. She also writes M/M paranormal romance under the name: J.J. Masters.

Want to read a sample of her work? Download a sampler book here: BookHip.com/MTQQKK

Buy ebooks and audiobooks directly from the author here: https://jeannestjamesauthor.com

www.jeannestjames.com

Newsletter: https://www.authorjeannestjames.com/
Jeanne's Down & Dirty Book Crew: https://www.facebook.com/groups/JeannesReviewCrew/